MW01614791

Rupert Smith is a writer and journalist, and lives in London. He is the co-author of *Man Enough to be a Woman*, the acclaimed biography of Jayne County, also published by Serpent's Tail

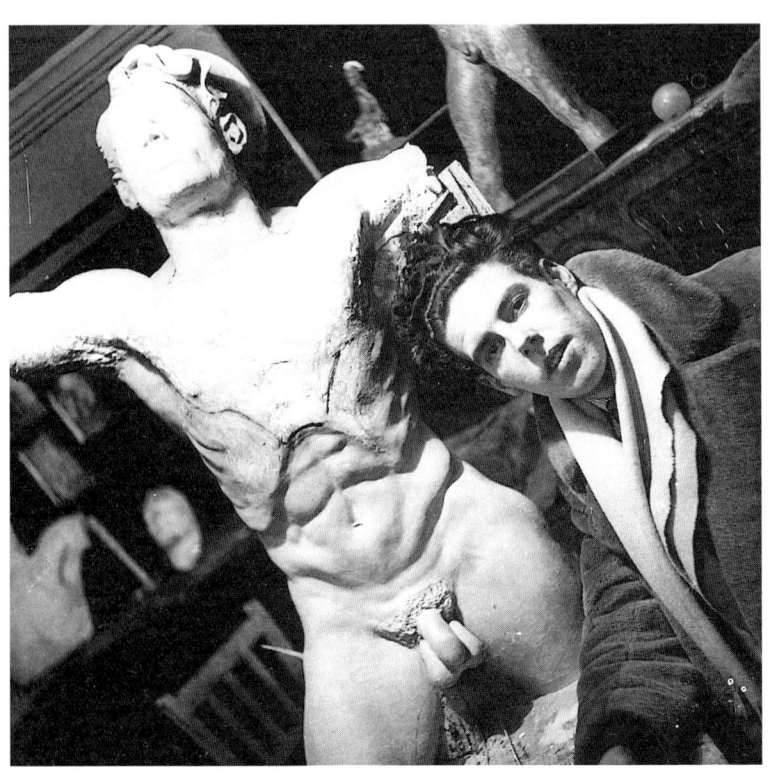

Physique

The Life of John S Barrington

Rupert Smith

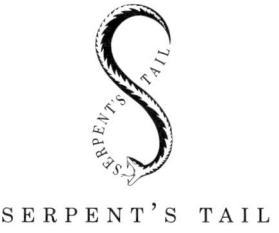

SERPENT'S TAIL

Library of Congress Catalog Card Number: 96-067910

A complete catalogue record for this book is available from the
British Library on request

The right of Rupert Smith to be identified as the author of this work has
been asserted by him in accordance with the Copyright, Design and
Patents Act 1988

Copyright © 1997 Rupert Smith

First published in 1997 by Serpent's Tail,
4 Blackstock Mews, London N4, and
180 Varick Street, 10th floor, New York, NY 10014
website: www.serpentstail.com

Text and cover designed by Roy Trevelion
Printed in Great Britain by Butler and Tanner Ltd, Somerset

Contents

Acknowledgements

With thanks to David Dulak, Teri Towe, RC Larking, Mike Arlen, Roy Trevelion and Laurence O'Toole.

Introduction

I first heard of John S Barrington in the mid 70s when I bought, or possibly stole, one of his magazines from a local newsagent. It was one of the many titles that he turned out at that time, *Man to Man Quorum* or *Hy! Gay World* – they were all much the same, hastily assembled, poorly designed with cracked letraset, full of spelling mistakes. But the pictures were something else. These were real men, not the over-groomed, over-tanned models that posed in *Playgirl* or the musclemen of the bodybuilding mags. They looked like the sort you might meet, the gym teacher you fantasised about, the swimming champion at the local pool, your best friend's older brother. They looked real.

After that, I got hold of Barrington magazines whenever I could. And they were always the same: page after page of models, interspersed with insane editorial, bogus advice columns and tacky adverts. They were shoddy, sordid, infuriating and compelling.

Years later in London, I was researching an article on 70s gay magazines. Browsing through the stacks in the British Library, I came across dozens of Barrington titles, full of faces familiar from ten years ago. Some of them dated back to the 60s, even the 50s. I was aware from the regular adverts in *Gay Times* that he was still around, and phoned him with a view to an interview. He was suspicious but flattered, and agreed to spare me an hour at his gallery – which was also his home – in south-west London. At our first meeting John treated me to the full grand manner, the aristocratic accents, the name-dropping of Coward, Shaw, Agate. He insulted me ('Of course, these names mean nothing to you, dear boy') and then, satisfied that I had recognised enough of his references, began a monologue of anecdotes, opinions and outrageous lies. He presented me with two of his books, showed me a tantalising selection of his favourite photographs and sent me on my way. As I was leaving, he told me three vital pieces of information, delivered casually as he relished the astonished reaction. First, that he was happily married, had been for 30 years, had two daughters and one grandchild. Second, that he had leukaemia and expected to die within the year. Third, that he was looking for a Boswell, someone to help him write his autobiography.

The article on gay pornography appeared in *Square Peg* magazine, followed by a feature on John himself, a much-condensed version of our first conversation with a little publishing history and a selection of vintage photographs. John was pleased with the results and invited me back to outline his ideas for our collaboration. In return for a weekly retainer, I would wade through his reams of notes and diaries, typing up pertinent sections, and conduct a series of interviews with him based on that material. I would then write it up as a narrative.

The collaboration worked happily for a few months. But John began to elaborate. The book, he decided, was a psychological detective story, a search for an elusive character 'JSB' as told by his bemused alter ego to a third party. It would comprise diary entries, letters, interviews, essays and poetry. It would jump around in time, now starting with his marriage, now starting with his death, now starting with whichever emotional trauma was uppermost in his mind. After a year, John had changed his mind so often about the structure of the book that we had already reached version six without being any nearer a final structure, let alone attracting a publisher.

Finally, after two years of close collaboration, I pulled out. John had now decided that *Inside My Skull*, as he wanted to call it, would be a *roman à clef* cum psychologist's report. The drafts that he was producing were incomprehensible and rambling. At the time of his death in 1991, he was overhauling his autobiography once again. In our last conversation a few days before he died, he asked me to 'try and do something with this fucking book', and requested that all the material pertaining to his autobiography should be handed over to me.

The story of John S Barrington is not a catalogue of success. He never made it in films, literature or theatre, although he hammered on the door long and hard enough. He was famous only to a small, enthusiastic coterie who collected his photography. He was not a great man, but he had a great story to tell. Although his life was littered with failures, each of which he bitterly resented, he bounced back and went on to the next project, the next insane money-making scheme. From the age of 15 to his death, he carried on outrageously, brazenly picking up young men in the streets, hatching plots, causing havoc in his personal life. At a time when most people are thinking about settling down to a quiet retirement, John was launching himself into the video pornography market. On the day that he collected his free travel pass as an Old Age Pensioner, he celebrated by screwing his 22-year-old boyfriend and 'auditioning' a new model he had met on the walk to the post office.

John loved the effect that his behaviour had on people. He cherished his uniqueness, his eccentricity. He could walk into a restaurant and order the staff around like visiting royalty, all the while wearing a second-hand suit with the Oxfam label (£6.95) still sticking out of the breast pocket. Above all he prided himself on his personal life. He took the raw materials around him – a 35-year marriage, a stream of friends and lovers – and turned them into an X-rated soap opera with which he entertained himself and his audience. John was an artist in the medium of his own life, a Pygmalion constantly creating, and falling in love with, a new Galatea. He made himself desperately unhappy over the years with all this upheaval, but could never give it up. For all the pain, it was just too much fun.

* * *

The man that emerges in this story is not always loveable. He lies, cheats his friends when it pleases him, and creates chaos in the lives of those close to him. But the memory I retain of John is of a generous, witty and sometimes brilliant man, whose behaviour at 70 could still shock a man less than half his age. He was a great lunch companion, talking too loud, abusing the waiters, handing out cards to any young man who tickled his fancy, grilling you on every subject from your choice of meal to the finer details of your sex life. Friendship with John was like tumbling down the rabbit's hole to Wonderland, where normal rules don't apply.

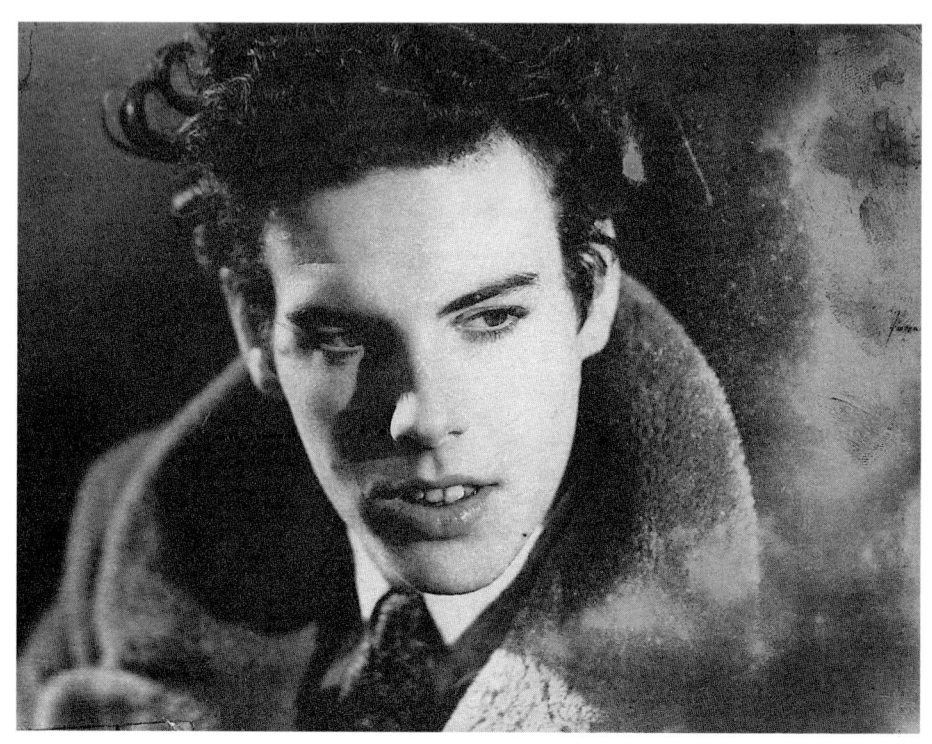

John in 1941, photographed by Angus McBean

Book One: Single

1920-1955

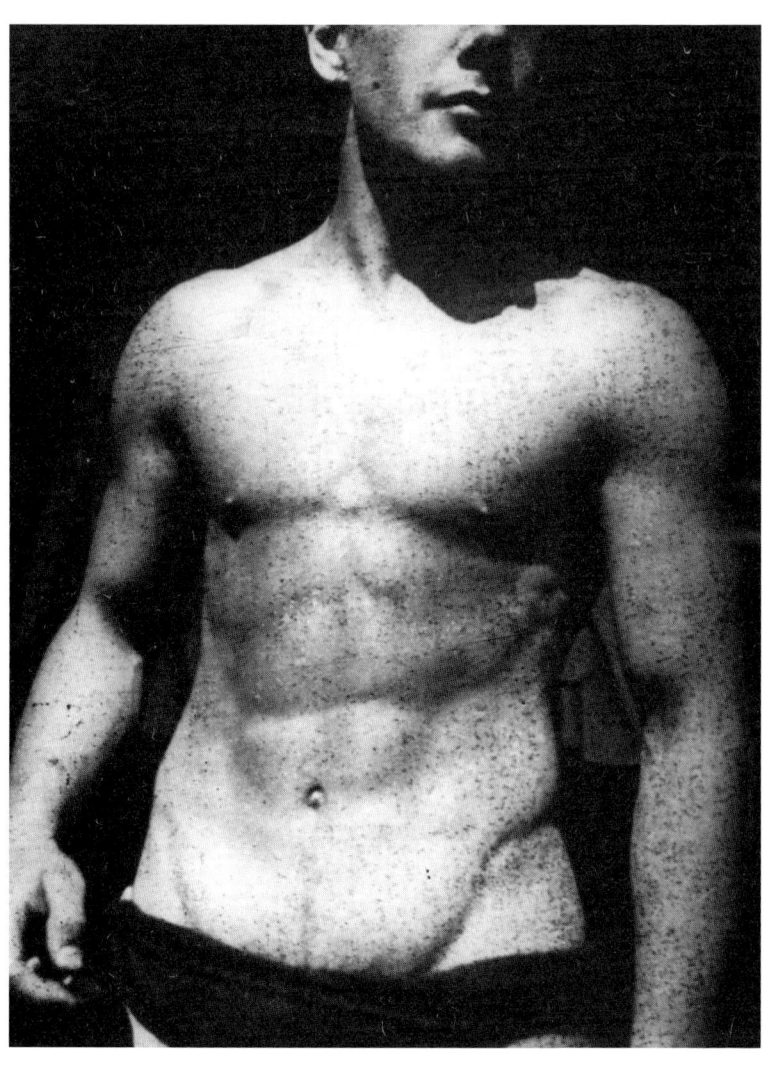

David on Hampstead Heath, summer 1938

Chapter One
The Aristocrat

John Barrington found his vocation one sunny afternoon at the men's pool on Hampstead Heath. It was during the long, slow summer of 1938, when Londoners took to the parks to sunbathe, swim and discuss the day's news, and for the 17-year-old art student there were many attractions. Armed with a sketchbook and his first camera, he could study at leisure his favourite subject – the male form. The bathers at the men's pool came in all shapes and sizes, from the elderly philosophers who speculated on the possibility of another war to the athletic young men who improved their suntans and their diving. One day in August, John persuaded one of the pool beauties to pose for him as he carefully set up his camera, a 2¼ x 2¼ inch folding bellows model. Those shots of a wet, grinning boy basking in the Hampstead sun were his first male nude photographs.

Soon afterwards, John found his first star model, a 16-year-old cabinet maker named David Dulak, whom he had befriended on the streets of Tufnell Park where they both lived. David posed for photographs at the pool the day after they met, unaware that his new friend was anything other than an eccentric student with a keen amateur interest in photography.

To David and his friends John was already a local figure of

fun, an effeminate dandy who would rush through the streets in one bizarre outfit after another.

He would fly along like a phantom, always at high speed, always wearing a long camel-hair coat, or if it was warm long corduroy trousers, open sandals and great flamboyant ties made out of wool, his hair very long for those days. And always a camera slung round his neck. He'd charge down the street carrying a huge portfolio with 'Vogue' or 'Mode' written on the side in silver paint, on his way to St Martin's School of Art where he was studying. John strutted around with this aristocratic demeanour. We always called him 'The Aristocrat' before we knew his real name. We used to rib him – 'Oh John,

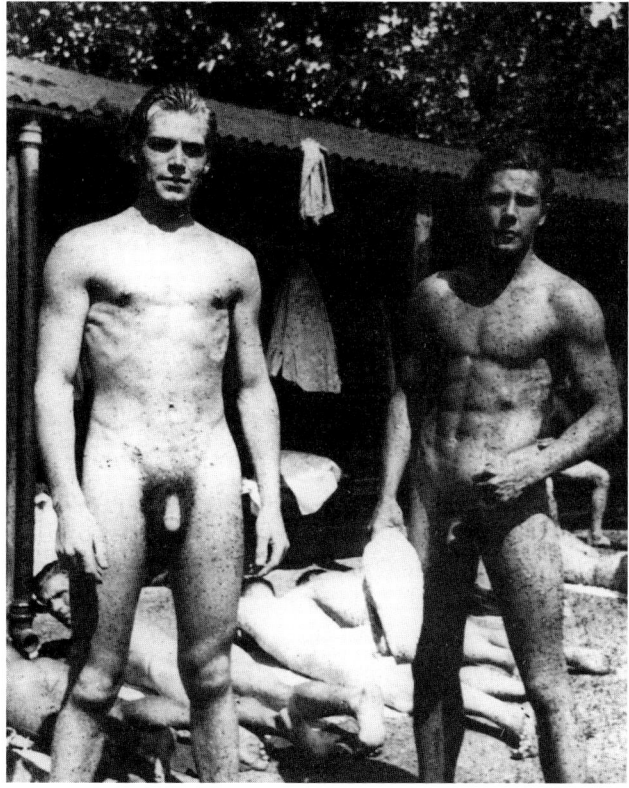

Vic, David and naked sunbathers at the men's pool, Highgate Ponds

you're so fucking aristocratic, it's ridiculous.' He'd just shrug
and say, 'Absolutely, dear boy!'

One night David and his friend Vic were hanging around on
a street corner when they saw the Aristocrat approaching at
his usual rapid pace. They fell into step with him, asked him
who he was and what he did, and were treated to a monologue about John's art school studies, his adventures in the
West End, his visits to the film studios at Denham and
Pinewood. They fell under his spell and agreed to meet him
at the men's pool the next day, where they posed naked in
the sunshine for their new friend's camera.

* * *

Who was this character who could charm the boys off the
streets, out of their clothes and in front of his camera? 'I am
the Viscount Engljähring von Engljähringer,' he wrote on the
flyleaf of his 1935 diary, bound up in a fantasy of aristocracy
that had been encouraged by his mother. The truth was less
grand and far more complicated than that. John was the ille-
gitimate son of a cultivated and very proper middle-class girl
who had fallen out with her family to marry an Austrian
playboy. Grace Pigott was a colonel's daughter from Kent,
raised with the expectation of a materially comfortable existence and a respectable marriage. But in 1912 she had met
the handsome young Austrian Franz Engljähringer, the
guest of a local grandee who set matronly minds racing with
his tales of a title and great expectations back home. The
match was encouraged until 1913, when growing anti-
German feeling made Franz persona non grata. Grace's
father ordered her to break off the engagement; she refused
and left home never to return.

Franz was interned in 1914 and Grace was left to fend for
herself. She befriended a young dancer named Dolly, a vet-
eran of the *Folies Bergère* who was now working in touring
shows for the impresario Albert de Courville. Dolly introduced Grace to the company as a singer, and for the rest of

the war she worked her way around the music halls and theatres of Great Britain. It was a long way from the genteel life to which she had been bred, but she learned quickly to adapt and prosper.

When the war ended, Grace and Franz were reunited. She returned to Kent to marry him, but straight after the wedding travelled north again to fulfil her touring commitments. 1920 saw her working in Liverpool while Franz found work at the Savoy Hotel in London. By March, Grace knew she was pregnant – and that the baby was not Franz's. She turned to Dolly for help, and at the end of October she was admitted to a small maternity hospital in London where, on 2 November 1920, she gave birth to a son, John. A few days later she joined Franz in Deal, where he had inherited a large estate, the Willows, from his former patron. John was left in London with his godmother Dolly until he was two years old.

The shadow of this scandal marked John's childhood with an air of secrecy and denial. Instead of telling him the truth

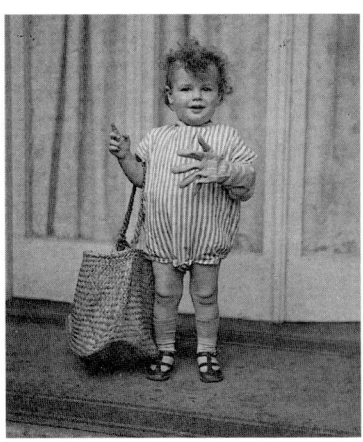 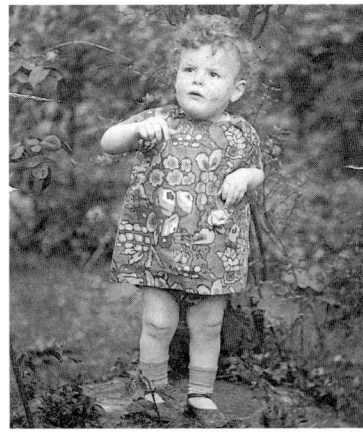

John aged two in the grounds of the Willows, Kent

about his parentage, Grace encouraged John to believe that he was an aristocrat by birth, and, as Franz's firstborn, the heir to titles and vast tracts of pine forest back in the fatherland. His early life only reinforced that impression. The Willows was an impressive set-up, with a butler and a nanny for John and his new brother Michael, extensive gardens and a friendly neighbour with a Bentley whose chauffeur drove them all over the district. John's first memories were of a rambling orchard with a dangerous, ivy-clad well and miles of Kent countryside all around.

The high life didn't last. Bad management had left the Willows estate in bad shape, and by 1924 the money had run out. Franz took his young family back to Austria to claim his inheritance, but found the Engljähringer fortune ravaged by inflation and his brothers unwilling to share what little they had with an English wife and children. So the family settled in London and began a decade of scrimping and saving and making do, moving from one cheap flat to another, as Franz earned what he could from tips at the Savoy and Grace took a job as a wardrobe mistress in the Windmill Theatre.

John and Michael were sent to the local elementary school, where Michael, fond of football and fighting, was immediately accepted. John stuck out like a sore thumb; at the age of 12 he was already affecting the speech of a Victorian tragedian, and was branded an arty cissy who

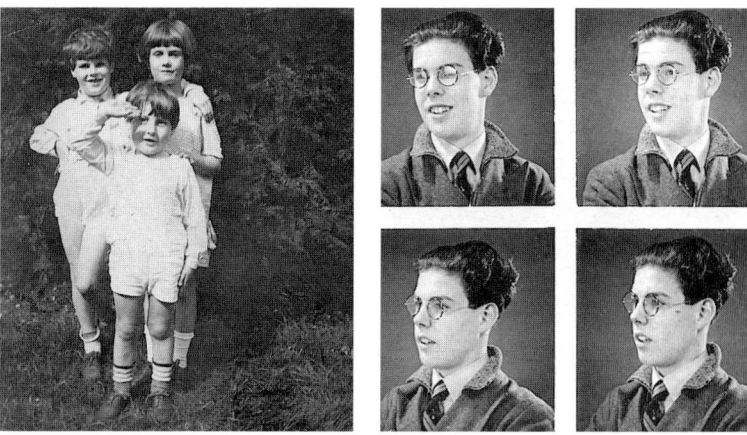

Left: brother Michael gives a military salute while John poses as a bathing beauty. Right: John aged 15

wouldn't fight to defend himself. He was moved to a grammar school, but lasted one term. Finally he was placed at the Acland School in Tufnell Park, a 'central' school for difficult students, where he was happy, if not academically successful. He read voraciously ('By 15 I had polished off the Bible and Shakespeare, some Plato, some Pepys, a little Boswell, a lot of Gibbon and Chaucer') but never did his homework. He excelled at art, but preferred covering the art room walls with sensational, Bosch-inspired murals to executing the still lives that his teachers demanded. He was encouraged by his English master, Mr Green, who took John and his mother to the theatre and on shopping expeditions to the huge, flare-lit Caledonian Road cattle market, where he would buy props for his toy theatre and Grace would pick up a fan or a pair of gloves for pennies. But John was far more interested in his big new discovery – boys.

He fell in love for the first time at 14, with an older student, an athlete and local Romeo, Jim Trotter. Trotter was good-looking and popular, but lacked John's easy manners and conversational charm – useful in the seduction of the local girls. Together they made a formidable team, John chatting up the girls and making dates for tea and walks across the Heath, Trotter initiating sexual activity. 'Had Vera in porch with Trotter' reads one early diary entry, although what the 'had' consisted of John could not remember. More private pleasures were enjoyed in his attic den at the new family home in Dartmouth Park, a large Edwardian mansion block that marked an upturn in the family's fortunes. Up in the attic John and Trotter would play with the toy theatre, eat the sandwiches that Grace prepared for them, and indulge in mutual masturbation on the floor.

In 1937, his parents and teachers were beginning to show some concern about the boy's future, and started quizzing him as to his ambitions. John seems to have been rather above it all: he wanted to be involved in show business, in literature, in art in some way. He had started visiting film studios with a neighbour, posing as cub reporters and getting access to press conferences with the stars. When Mr Green suggested he might try for a place at St Martin's School of Art, John put up no objections. In the spring, during his last few weeks at school, he diligently prepared a portfolio of sketches for theatrical costume and set designs, which were submitted to St Martin's. After a ten-minute interview at County Hall, he was awarded a grant and a place at the school situated in the centre of the West End, its windows overlooking Leicester Square. His reaction was cool.

> Saw Trotter. Told him news about art school. He thinks I'm a different person, or soon will be, when I spend all day being posh in the West End, all arty. Maybe.

And Trotter was right. When John started at St Martin's, he quickly formed a new, arty persona to suit his surroundings.

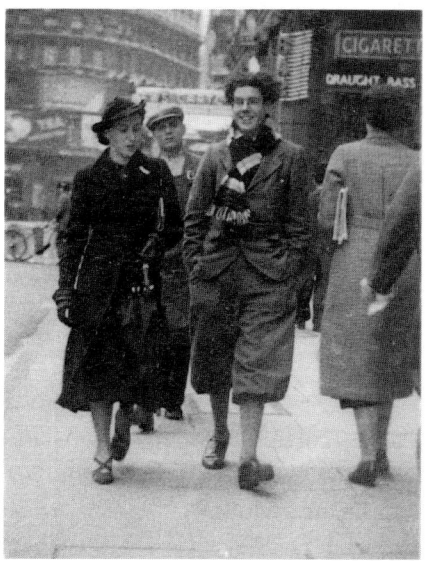

Discovering the West End in plus fours and a school muffler

Photographs of John up to the age of 16 show an unexceptional young man dressed in the sweaters and baggy trousers of the period; after his introduction to the West End his hair became longer, curling down to his shoulders by the following year. Chamois gloves, cravats, walking canes and a rimless eyeglass all appeared over the next two years. Big coats slung over the shoulders of a slight figure, jewelled tie-pins and cufflinks (mostly shoplifted), even plus fours with wool socks and brogues. With the new image came a new name – John Shreeve Barrington, after two of Grace's brothers who had died in the First World War. Little wonder he was noticed on the streets of north London as he strode through on his way to the West End.

John Shreeve Barrington took to the West End like a duck to water, and launched an energetic campaign to establish his new persona at the heart of its intellectual and artistic circles. In his first term at St Martin's, he started visiting some of the more famous London watering holes – the French House in Dean Street and the Fitzroy on Charlotte Street were soon favourites. Here he engaged in debates and drank, polished his aphorisms and made friends, particularly with the more daring art school students who would accompany him on his jaunts. Around some of them he even worked up a little romance. Despite his fumblings in the attic with Jim Trotter and a few other school friends, John was also interested in finding himself a nice girlfriend whom he could take home and introduce to Grace. The first one was Joan, who came to tea at Tufnell Park and indulged John in the comforting fantasy that they might one day marry.

With his art studies progressing nicely, John began to look around his new territory for further professional opportunities. Grace had been working as a wardrobe mistress for the entrepreneur Alfred Esdaile at the newly refurbished Prince of Wales Theatre, and agreed to show him some of her son's costume designs. John was quick to exploit the connection, became a regular backstage visitor at the Prince of Wales and even managed to get a 'JSB' design on the front of one of the theatre's programmes. His new backstage acquaintances introduced him to the other end of London's theatrical spectrum, the politically-committed left wing groups Unity Theatre and St Pancras People's Theatre. John had no illusions about his acting ability, but enjoyed the opportunity to perform: 'Two more parts at St Pancras,' he noted in his diary in March 1939, 'Mr Lovatt in *King of Nowhere* and Aesthetic Youth in *The Composite Man*. The latter should be easy!'

Full of confidence after his professional successes, John began a correspondence with the Parisian costumier Max Weldy, another associate of Esdaile, who invited him to study in the city's studios and fashion houses. He jumped at the opportunity to visit Paris for his first unsupervised foreign travel: no parents, no chaperones, no restraints. At 17, John was ready to enlarge his territory.

His original brief had been to work for three months in the costume department of the *Folies Bergère* as an assistant designer, and while he certainly spent some time there he was more interested in exploring the sexual and artistic milieu of Paris. He rented two small attic rooms at 47 rue Lamercier, just off Place Clichy, and played up his *milord anglais* manner to the hilt. He spent his days visiting the couture houses of Schiaparelli and Chanel, explored the museums and art galleries, drank in the cafés of the Left Bank and Montmartre. At the Café Flore, the Brasserie Lipp and the Dôme he saw the Parisian intelligentsia in full spate, and at the *Folies* he watched Mistinguett, Josephine Baker and Maurice Chevalier. Passing himself off as an English journalist, he visited the studios where Marcel Carné was making *Le Jour se lève* with Jean Gabin. He interviewed Jean-Pierre Aumont, Simone Simon, Simone Signoret, Louis Jouvet, Carné and Gabin – presumably in English, as his French was limited to a terrible schoolboy stumble augmented with dialect he picked up in the bars. His art studies were not abandoned either. Two or three times a week John attended life classes at the Ecole des Beaux Arts, and there learned the silverpoint technique much in evidence in his later graphic work.

This was the daytime world; by night, John headed for the brothels, bars and clubs. In gay bars like the Boeuf sur le

Toit, rich gentlemen made discreet financial arrangements
with the gigolos who worked the circuit; at the subterranean
steam baths in the rue Colisée, John could enjoy anonymous
partners at no financial outlay.

Before returning to London, John took a slow and uncomfortable third-class train journey to Cannes, where he had his
first full, uninhibited sexual experience with a male partner.

> It started on my first night there, when I met a handsome
> beach boy leaning against the statue of Lord Brougham on the
> Croisette. He took me to the Zanzi Bar – the first of many
> hundreds of visits over the years – then to share a hotel room
> by the station for four very memorable nights. Francisco was
> 18, an Italian, and he died defending Tobruk in a battle in
> which my brother also took part. He was important in that he
> was the first person to introduce me to uninhibited homosexual
> behaviour. I never understood that I was being homosexual,
> and I don't suppose that young men like Francisco did either.
> We did all the things that men usually do together, except
> that I didn't get buggered or bugger him.

It was important to John throughout his life to emphasise
the distinction between his homosexual behaviour and the
actual fact of being 'a homosexual', something he never
admitted or accepted. Even more important was that
Francisco (and practically all his subsequent male lovers)
was a normal, 'healthy' young man, indulging in gay sex for
the sheer physical pleasure, and most emphatically not a
queen, a queer, a class of person upon whom John heaped
scorn despite the fact that he was to all appearances a major
queen himself.

In July 1938 John reluctantly left Cannes and returned to
London with a suitcase full of books which would have been
confiscated had customs officers inspected his luggage. Many
of them were publications of the Obelisk Press, Minateur
and Transition: *Ulysses*, *Lady Chatterley's Lover*, Frank
Harris's *My Life and Loves*, all at that time unavailable in

Great Britain. He also bought an imitation gold bracelet for his mother from the Galeries Lafayette, and a tangerine rose lipstick for a new girlfriend. For himself, he had an address book full of useful contacts and a more decided idea of the persona he wanted to cultivate.

> Shall we say that Paris was the developer of the negative, and Cannes the fixer? From then on all the prints were the same. When I got off the boat train at Victoria in mid July 1938, I knew exactly what I wanted from life, my preferences in art, theatre, films, human beings and sexual playmates.

* * *

It was this worldly figure who first captivated David in the summer of 1938. David was flattered by John's attentions, fascinated by his connections with show business; John, for his part, was soon infatuated with the beautiful young man. The friendship grew rapidly, and David was the subject of dozens of photographs, drawings, poems and sculptures, and of reams of letters. He supplied the basis for characters in John's first attempts at novels and plays, and occupied his thoughts and emotions more than anyone else in the coming decade.

At first, John was interested in photography only as an amusing hobby, a way of recording his beautiful friends and a suitable pursuit for an art student. But soon it was taking up more and more of his time and money. Film was expensive and hard to come by, and to finance his hobby he stumbled upon the idea of selling his photographs. Leafing through a copy of *The Artist*, to which David's painter father subscribed, he saw row upon row of small ads in the back of the magazine selling nude photographs as reference for life studies. He sent off for samples to see what was on offer, and was immediately convinced that his own efforts were as good as anything else in the market. It was a few years before he put the scheme into practice – in 1938, he only had snaps of

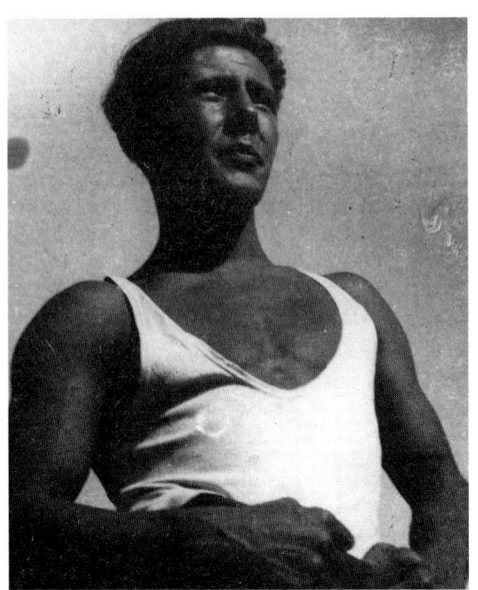 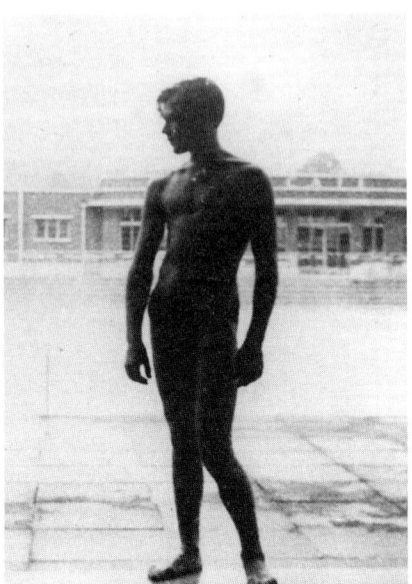

David on Hampstead Heath (left) and Vic at the Hampstead Lido, 1938

David and a few other bathers to offer, and no means of reproducing the pictures in any quantity.

Besides, John still had other ambitions to fulfil. His sights were set on a career in theatre or journalism. Ignoring the growing threat of war in Europe, he made determined inroads into the London theatrical and literary establishment, lion-hunting with considerable success. A favourite means of approach was a standard letter packed with erudite quotations which, with a few variations, was received by numerous stars of the London scene.

Any name you like to drop from that period, I was leaning against bars talking to. I was collecting people from the age of 16. I started writing letters to them: 'Dear Mr Shaw, I am 16 years of age and I've read all your books. I'm a great admirer of yours but it seems to me that there's a great deal more inside your skull than you put down on paper, and in view of the disparity of our ages you're likely to die before I do, and I feel that I could gain a lot more from you and your works if I could meet you for an hour's chat.'

By the early 40s, John had successfully used this method to meet Shaw, JB Priestley, HG Wells, Bertrand Russell and CB Cochran; the latter replied very politely in a letter addressed to 'Shreeve Barrington esq'. Backstage visits were becoming more frequent: John met John Gielgud and sketched him in the role of Disraeli on the set of *An Empire was Built* at Teddington Studios.

John began 1939 in good spirits and full of ambition. Max Weldy wanted him back in Paris and proposed a trip to San Francisco. He had also received a commission from the song-writer Michael Carr to decorate his bathroom in an under-water motif – a task he completed by the end of February, covering the walls with fish, octopus, treasure chests and crustacea. The impresario George Black intended to use one of John's sketches in a revue, and his set designs for the *News Chronicle*'s amateur dramatic contest had won the silver medal. In January he proudly took his mother to see his winning set in a performance of *The Letter Box Rattles* at the Savoy Theatre. During the spring he was working on his first screenplay, a dramatic reconstruction of the story of Hereward the Wake entitled *The Last of the English* – not a very commercial proposition in 1939 as it ended with the invasion of England by the Normans.

John's hectic exploration of the West End was interrupted in July when St Martin's closed. He withdrew to North London and spent his time with David, and within a month they escaped from the hot, uneasy city and its war-worries for a country idyll, cycling to the West Country. 'We cycled and cycled for three weeks,' recalls David.

> It was just a month before war broke out, and the weather was beautiful, the roads were quiet, and we went right the way down the south coast and ended up in a place called Blue Anchor Bay. I have one abiding memory of that long, slow

cycling holiday. We stopped by a brilliant yellow field, absolutely amazed by the colour. Then in the distance we saw a tiny red dot approaching along the road, which turned out to be an open-top MG with a very handsome couple in it. They sped past us, giving us a heartbreaking vision of privilege and luxury, almost like a Scott Fitzgerald apparition.

During this holiday, over readings of *The Symposium*, John began to fall more seriously in love with David. Neither had ever discussed sexuality seriously – it wasn't the sort of thing that young men talked about in the 30s. After the Blue Anchor Bay holiday, John began to declare his interest more openly, much to David's embarrassment.

He used to say that I was very important to him, that he was always in love with me, but he and I never had any kind of relationship with each other apart from friendship. It simply wasn't on. But you know how John would declare things in such a loud, high voice. If you went to a play, even if it was mediocre, he'd stand up at the end and clap his hands and shout and scream. He had this exhibitionist flair, which wasn't the best part of him. So when he declared his feelings for one, it could be rather awkward. It never put me off, because I knew the other side of him which was very generous and very genuine.

Back in London, John's romantic indulgences were finally overshadowed by an international crisis that even he could not ignore. As an art student and would-be anarchist-communist-socialist-Marxist, he was against war, killing, the ruling classes and the armed forces. But meanwhile, the number of ditches in the London parks grew, the piles of sandbags got higher, especially round the government buildings in Whitehall. The Cenotaph was protected, and Eros disappeared from Piccadilly Circus. Museums and art galleries began clearing out their collections to safer storage in the countryside.

On 1 September, Germany invaded Poland. Two days later, John's nude sunbathing at the men's pond was interrupted by the first air-raid warning. Of immediate importance to John was the cancellation of his eagerly-anticipated trip to San Francisco and the total disruption of two years of carefully laid plans to become a dress and set designer, actor, journalist, critic, artist, sculptor, photographer and novelist. Demoralised at first, John quickly adapted to a new world of utterly changed values and expectations.

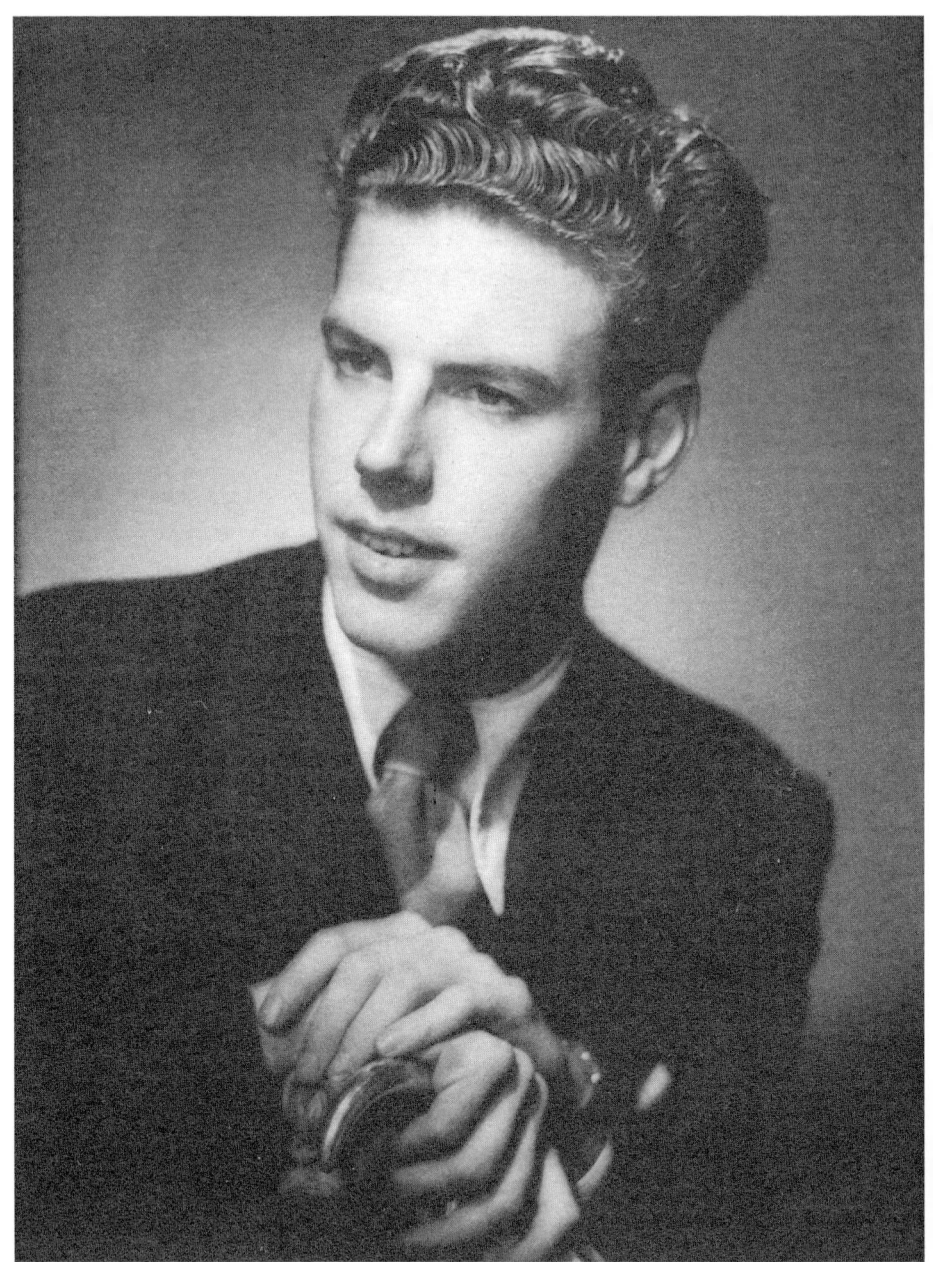

John in 1941, photographed by Angus McBean

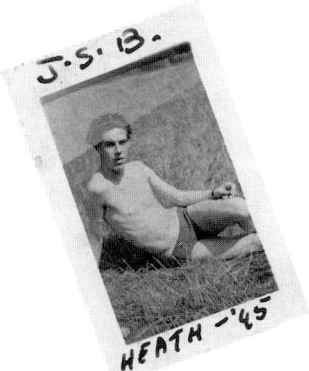

J·S· 13.

HEATH -'45

Chapter Two
The West End War

3 SEPTEMBER 1939: Wake early. Fine morning. Couldn't sleep because of last night's news. At pool by 10.45. Already crowded.

11am the sirens go! Near panic. Some of the men start to dress hurriedly. Others just run out to the pool starkers, about 50 of us, all yelling and laughing and very scared, and dive in racing to the big raft 50 yards out. Lots of noise and splashing. Then sudden silence as we listen for planes. Nonsense talk. When will the bombers arrive? Will we see our fighters in dog fights? What does ack-ack look like? How long could we stay underwater if they dropped gas? Does mustard gas float like oil on the water? How would we know when to come up? What happens if high explosive bombs hit water? And so on...

11.30am. The all clear goes. We swim back to the enclosure. No one I know feels like sunbathing. I'm quite sure that nothing on earth will make me join any service! Most of the men at the pool are looking forward to this war. All that pacifism of the last six years evaporates.

London plunged into the blackout, and John's carefully-laid plans were abandoned. Instead of a steady rise to fame and fortune, he found himself living in a crazy world where death could come at any moment, where sudden, brief moments of pleasure punctuated a life of confusion and fear. For John, the war was exciting in a special way: as London was gripped by the fear of death, sex of any and every kind was on offer from the soldiers, sailors and airmen who drifted through town, and from the girls who followed them. John stayed in London throughout the war; he barely ever left, even when the Blitz was at its worst. In fact, he enjoyed the danger of it, boasting to friends who had been evacuated from their London homes. 'You will no doubt be interested to get some first hand news of the war in London,' he wrote in 1940.

> The damage done has been really frightful. Not one square mile of the metropolis has missed damage & in places whole streets and great buildings are reduced to shambles. The mortality rate too has been serious & the most poignant phenomenon has been the nightly (or should I correct this to afternoonly – for the people claim their 'pitches' at 2.30pm) pilgrimage to the 'tubes. The poverty of the masses at 1am is appalling. There is never an inch to spare & I feel that were you to allow your fertile imagination complete licence you would still not do the scenes complete justice.
>
> Of course the West End is dead ... Damage to Oxford Street especially is frightfull. Lewis's, Hollingsworth & Co are gutted & the surrounding streets devoid of life. Traffic is diverted & raids all day keep people on the hop.
>
> The cinema has completely collapsed! 'We are going strong – carrying on' is the only announcement to be seen on the placards ... Just a few of the bigger circuits open in the afternoons. All the 2nd run out of the West End are closed. The Dominion was hit last week & the only successful pix in town is 'Amok'! ... It's a great life! But it really can't go on for the whole winter I do feel!!

When the Blitz got worse in 1941, John and David watched London burn from the top of Parliament Hill.

I can still recall those skies that night, with low clouds made crimson with the fires below, silver shafts criss-crossing from searchlights, and the continual noise of aircraft and guns. We watched a panorama more than 15 miles wide, its most conspicuous feature the flame-lit dome of St Paul's Cathedral. Walking on pavements covered with crunching glass became a momentary game. Favourite pubs and restaurants disappeared into rubble, a bus was upended and leaned against a house. I did a drawing of that.

In a few nights London seemed to have fallen to pieces, yet it hadn't. In Bloomsbury, the antique bookshops still arranged their trays of volumes on the pavements and people still browsed looking for a bargain. People strolled in the parks, lay on the grass and ate sandwiches...

While the city burned, John met his friends in cafés, his face painted with collodian to disguise the fatigue and anxiety, helped by doses of benzedrine which he bought in the form of inhalers from Boots the chemist, dipping the impregnated felt strips into his coffee. Here they exchanged the news on who had survived the night, and gossiped about their nocturnal adventures. In November 1940, John lost his first friend, a bodybuilder and occasional lover whom he had met on Hampstead Heath, decapitated during an air raid. He had the grim duty of identifying the corpse at the mortuary, 'the head set at a disgustingly inaccurate angle to the crushed remains of the once magnificent body'. Many more followed. One evening in the Café Royal, John's girlfriend Margot staggered towards his table 'looking a wreck'.

Last Monday a doodle plane hit her flat at 9am, demolished the whole block. It all collapsed on top of her and her lover André. He was in bed with her, jumped on top of her. His head smashed all over her chest. She lay under rubble, the only survivor, for sixteen hours.

Even the bars and clubs, where lights blazed behind the

heavy blackout, weren't safe. As Londoners crowded together each night seeking fun and reassurance, they knew that the next bomb could drop on them. One night there was a direct hit on the Café de Paris – the bomb dropped straight through the glass-domed roof and exploded on the dance floor, instantly killing dozens of revellers, among them the band leader 'Snake Hips' Johnson.

Braving the bombs, John celebrated his 21st birthday at the Café Royal with a party that included David, a handful of sailors and some of John's latest girlfriends. A few nights later, emerging with Margot from Jimmy's Club in Denmark Street where they had taken shelter during an air raid, they saw bombs coming straight at them down Charing Cross Road. They ducked into a telephone box to avoid the blast and started having sex; Margot perched on the shelf that held the telephone directories, which collapsed as John reached orgasm. The following week, again on Charing Cross Road, John was walking with a sailor when a bomb landed right in the centre of the street. They were blown into the doorway of a shop, where they stood kissing and trembling for a few minutes before hurrying away through Soho to Lyons Corner House.

> We diced with death every night. In Shaftesbury Avenue, 100 yards east of Cambridge Circus, a land mine blew down all the buildings near St Giles Church. The soldier I was with just rose up beside me as we walked. Thrown by the blast against a wall, he landed with very bad injuries. I was unscathed, protected by a lamp post. Getting him into casualty took a dreadful hour.

It wasn't all fun and games, though, even for John. He knew that his call-up would come, and that he was obliged to contribute to the war effort in some way. His art studies continued in sporadic fashion, but were soon eclipsed by his duties with the Air Raid Precaution Service. John had seen out the period of the 'Phoney War', that strange anticlimactic time between the declaration of war and the beginning of the Blitz, in training at the ARP headquarters in the National Central Library in Malet Place, adjacent to the University of London. Here the men did little more than read books, play cards and engage in occasional training exercises, lowering each other from the library's top-floor windows on stretchers lashed with ropes. But when the Blitz began, John and his team took turns of duty on the ARP's 24-hour-on, 24-hour-off schedule, providing first aid at bomb sites, pulling the dead and the injured from burning buildings,witnessing the horrors of war at close quarters.

Instead of spending his days off resting at home, John attended life classes at St Martin's and continued his exploration of the West End. Malet Place was an ideal base, close to Soho and Fitzrovia, an area of London given over to Bohemia. New friends and lovers could pop out of the blackout every evening. John fell in with a group of girls who lived in a flat in Greek Street where they held nightly parties that usually ended as orgies. He was a regular guest, totally bisexual in practical terms but still romantically attached to his beloved David. The parties came to an abrupt end one night when a direct hit demolished the flat and killed the girls inside it.

The Café Royal, with its long marble tables and elegant theatrical clientele, was the summit of John's West End territory during the War, but there were many other, humbler places that offered attractions of a different kind. The Coffee An', opposite St Giles Church on the corner of Denmark Street, was a café where you could get coffee – an' anything (or anyone) else you wanted. It was one of the old-fashioned London cafés where customers could order a good steak for supper or, if they were broke, last all night on one cup of coffee. For John and his friends, it became a place to finish off an evening of pub crawling. A favourite circuit was the Marquis of Granby on Charlotte Street, followed by the Fitzroy, the French Pub, the Swiss Pub and finally the Coffee An' for supper. It stayed open till one or two in the morning, and became a magnet for a cross-section of London nightlife: servicemen rubbed shoulders with writers and painters and the transvestites who came screeching out of the blackout. Among the regular denizens was the young Lucien Freud. In his 1950 novel *Out of Sickness*, John gave a fictional account of a visit with two young, impressionable friends.

To make the night complete, John decided they should have some coffee at the Coffee An'. While the searchlights quenched the stars he led them through the dark cold streets. In Charing Cross Road there were still plenty of people hurrying about, their torches stabbing at the darkness. John led them down a dark alleyway between high buildings. They had to follow its direction by watching the slit of sky, searchlight-crossed, as it appeared between the high walls. As they turned a corner, they heard voices, singing and noise. The next moment they entered the Coffee An'. As the door opened and the three pushed past the heavy curtain that acted as a light trap, they found themselves surrounded by a fantastic crowd of people all talking and shouting at once. The place was full of strange folk, half hidden in thick cigarette smoke. The floor could not be glimpsed at all, so great was the crush, and the ceiling, only a few feet above their heads, was a canopy of steam that occasionally parted to reveal grotesque drawings leering down obscenely at them. The walls of the café were also crudely painted and covered in patches by hundreds of soiled photographs of boxers, wrestlers and half-naked physical culturists ... The tables had chipped and cracked glass tops, stained with spilled coffee. The chairs, once stable, were rickety from the last fight ... It cost them a great deal of brute effort to get inside and then manoeuvre towards the bright flash of misty silver of the huge coffee urn. It was on an invisible bar, round which two hundred people of all ages seethed and eddied.

The smoky atmosphere was ghastly. Everyone was asking everyone else to stand them a coffee, give them a cigarette, sell them clothing coupons, put them up, go home with them;

financial, romantic, illegal or just plain silly suggestions filled the air ... John explained that the Coffee An' was world-famous as a rendezvous for all the strange underworld folk. Peers and queers and black market racketeers; theatricals, film folk; artists, poets, musicians, authors, dancers; wrestlers, weight-lifters, Continental gamblers; ARP workers, young men up from the country; merchant navy, military, naval and air force men and officers; chess players, members of the famous 'circle'; barristers, executives, ambassadors; Princes, Kings, 'trade', 'rent' and a thousand 'Queens'; all these were reputed to have visited this fantastic tiny democratic café – a meeting place for the four sexes.

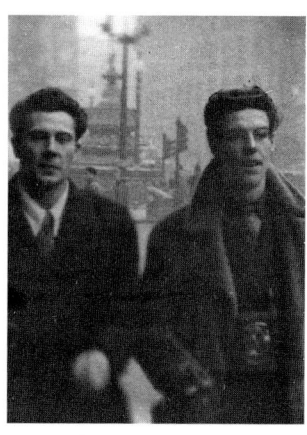

Braving the Blitz: David and John in Piccadilly Circus, 1941

The 'grotesque drawings' were the author's own handiwork. During an early visit he had impressed the proprietor with his credentials as an interior decorator and left with a commission to cover the café ceiling with a mural depicting Dante's *Inferno*. During his days off, for a fee of sandwiches and coffee, John lay on his back on an improvised scaffold painting the ceiling with nude, writhing figures, 'à la Michaelangelo in the Sistine Chapel' he noted immodestly. The ceiling was not repainted until 1945. This was not John's only decorating job in the War: the Boeuf sur le Toit, the Music Box and even the Hammersmith Palais all got the Barrington treatment.

The Café Royal and the Coffee An' were the sort of places where boys went to meet girls. But London also had its share of gay clubs, which John was exploring with a new group of friends. Until mid 1940, he had met very few gay people. There were a lot of queer folk around the West End, most of them flamboyant older queens whom John found revolting, if amusing; he certainly identified with none of them. Then one night, during the height of the Blitz, after taking a girlfriend to see Garbo in *Ninotchka*, he accepted an invitation to the Vic-Wells costume ball where he 'danced till dawn'. The Vic-Wells balls were havens of sexual tolerance, very theatrical, full of drag queens; and that night John was pursued by a young man with 'liquid eyes, brown centred and blue rimmed, soft dark hair, slim, very good looking, very charming and softly spoken'.

> We met first on the dance floor, then again at the bar, finally in the gents. He pulled me into a cubicle, kissed me and said we must meet again. He was an actor, he said, in films. I gave him a card and we parted.

The young man from the Vic-Wells ball made contact, introduced himself as Roy Peter Wilson and arranged to take John to see the Gielgud production of *The Beggar's Opera*. Roy was sophisticated for 19, welcomed at all the 'secret' gay clubs in town, and an experienced lover of men. He was financially independent, earning a living from bit parts, and had his own flat in Albany Street, by Regent's Park.

Roy became John's first homosexual affair, and one of the few gay men with whom he ever became sexually involved (he recorded in his diary his first experience of anal intercourse, in the active role). In retrospect, the affair with Roy may have put him off gay men for life; he came to fulfil all John's worst fears of 'hysterical queer behaviour' and became unhinged during and after the War, in and out of psychiatric hospitals. But in the early spring of 1940, Roy was someone John looked up to, the first person who offered a serious challenge to his image of himself as the sophisticate-about-town. Soon Roy had met all of John's friends, who accepted him as one of their own. He was even introduced to John's mother Grace, who thought him better bred than most of her son's circle ('They get on like a house on fire,' records the diary. 'I can't get a word in edgeways!')

Their sexual relationship cooled quickly, but not before Roy had introduced John to London's queer clubs. The places they visited were not openly gay in any modern sense, but many of them were used for the purposes of 'trade'. Pubs in Soho, Chelsea and Bloomsbury catered for soldiers, sailors, airmen and the men who wanted to meet them. Some were down-to-earth pick-up joints that would not seem unfamiliar today. But there was another side of the London gay scene that has not survived: the elegant, chi-chi members-only clubs, catering to a 'theatrical' clientele. As Quentin Crisp ruefully recorded in *The Naked Civil Servant*, blatant 'pansies' were not welcomed here, but for those who were willing to play the game and pass as straight as soon as they walked out of the doors, there were several places where gay men could let their hair down. One of these, the Boeuf sur le Toit on Panton Street (named after the famous Parisian Club), was described by John in another episode from *Out of Sickness*, under the name of El Toro.

> They climbed some dingy stairs and entered El Toro ... In the tiny hall a white-coated attendant produced a vellum-bound book, in which John signed his friends' names as his guests. The 'solemn formalities' completed, they went into the two large pink rooms. Everything was pink except the red and white curtains and the white grand piano; even the flowers in the amber vases were pink carnations. Pink mirrors on the walls reflected tasseled cushions, the pink 'period' candle lights on bare pink walls and the pink faces of the exclusively male but not exactly athletic patrons. In one of the rooms there was a big pink bar and the club was like a great pink drawing room, very sophisticated, quiet and clean.
>
> The place was not very crowded. The men who watched the newcomers in the pink mirrors were all extremely well-dressed and polite mannered. Those who were sitting kept

watching Dick out of the corners of their eyes. Gradually it became quieter and quieter. The pianist crooned in a soft voice 'You – stepped out of a dream', while he accompanied

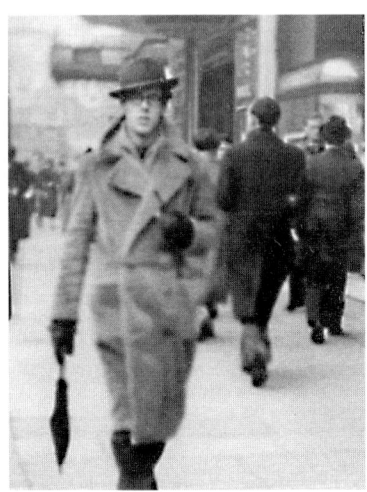

himself with an occasional minor chord ... A red-faced man, who looked too well scrubbed, limped over and asked John in a sugary voice who his charming young friend was. He patted Dick's arms and shoulders, insisted on buying them drinks, and expressed the hope that Dick would become a member. As he was secretary of the club, he said he would be only too delighted to propose him for membership – which was a very great favour.

John on the prowl in his favourite 'teddy bear' coat

This is John writing some years after the event, deliberately distancing himself from the El Toro queers and their soft, effeminate ways. Dick (a portrait of David) is in danger from these predatory creatures, and John contrasts his own healthy bisexuality with their soft, pink homosexuality. At the time, though, John enjoyed the gay clubs with their sexually charged atmosphere that spilled out on to the darkened streets. It was at this time that he started enjoying 'trade' – a term he learnt from Roy and his friends to describe the servicemen and other hustlers who frequented the clubs and streets.

Soho and Bloomsbury and Chelsea were gay and 'ever so' artistic. Uninhibited, open queerness was acceptable so long as one didn't go 'too far'. What 'too far' meant was never clear to me; it certainly didn't include propositioning attractive bobbies on the beat. London was becoming decadent, said some. It was certainly very gay. There were so many clubs: the Boeuf sur le Toit in Panton Street, The A&B in Wardour Street, The Starlight opposite, Jimmy's in Denmark Street, Lady Molly Howard's in Newport Street, the Burlington, the Rockingham and half a dozen piano-music-filled establishments discreetly catering to members and their forces guests. From June 1940 there were a lot of Free French, Free Polish, Free Belgian, Dutch, Norwegian and Swedish young men in uniform, at loose in the West End. A certain section of Londoners had never had it so good. The authorities turned a blind eye; the police, especially, had other things to do.

* * *

Rushing from high-class cafés to low dives, mixing with aristocrats, randy soldiers and ageing queens, working 24-hour shifts among London's dead, John's persona began to emerge more forcibly. His wardrobe became more effeminate, his hair long and brushed up in a bizarre, brilliantined shock. He made an inventory of his wardrobe in his diary:

Jackets: 1, Blue, Navy. 1, Blue, pale. 1 Green, bright. 1, Brown, old. Trousers: 1, blue, dark cord. 1, Green, cord. 1, Brown, cord. 1, Grey, cheap. 1, Blue, cheap. 1 pr Shorts, Brown cord. Suits: 1, Dress, dinner. 1, Blue, cocktail. 1, Blue, plus-fours. Coats: 1, Overcoat, Navy. 1, Light raincoat. Shirts: 1, check-tartan. 1, Rust. 1, navy blue. 2, Cricket, white. 1, Ivory silk. 1, Yellow silk. 2 Dress shirts. 1, Grey, silk. 2, White & brown. Scarves: 2, White silk, dress. 1, Acland school muffler. 1, Tootal blue silk. 1, Tootal maroon silk. 3, silk, blue, blue-check, grey. 3, woollen. Gloves: 1, Kid dress. 1, cotton dress. 1, Chamois dress. 3prs leather lined. Jerseys & Jumpers: 6. Hats: 2. Shoes: 11 pairs. Sox: 12 prs. Ties: 30, bows and ordinary, all silk. 20 white collars. 24 handkerchiefs, all monogrammed. 4 prs pyjamas, silk. Underclothes. Tie-pins: 1, diamond, ruby, sapphire. 1, diamond & opal. 1, diamond and pearl drop. 1, emerald and pearl. 1, turquoise dagger. 1, lapis lazuli. 1, topaz. Rings: 1, diamond and enamel, 1727. 1, diamond solitaire, 1800. 1, zircon solitaire, 1939. 1, diamond, sapphire and aquamarine. Cuff links: 1, enamal. 1, dress, pearl & mother-of-pearl. 1, red & white gold. Uniform: 1, ARP, dark blue, helmet & gasmask. Walking canes: 1, malacca and silver. 1, malacca. 2, bullock's pissils, twisted. 1, bullock's pissil, plain. 1, ebony. 1, black umbrella, ebony handle.

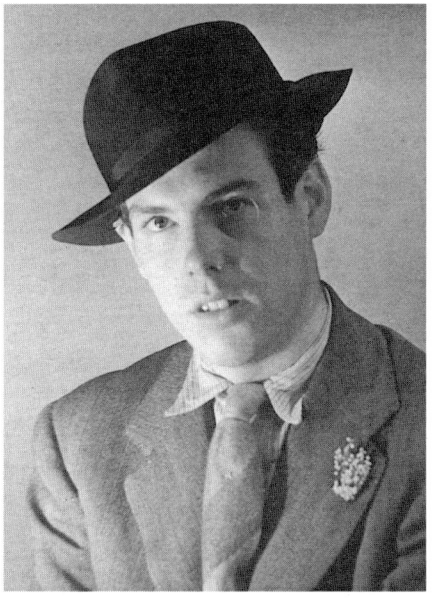

Above: a peacock in stolen feathers.
Opposite: McBean's 'double portrait' of
John, 1941

Most of this finery had been stolen; John had given himself over wholeheartedly to shoplifting.

The overall effect was enough to attract the attentions of Angus McBean, then establishing himself as the most cre-

ative photographer in the West End. They met one night in
the Café Royal, and the evening ended with John accepting
an invitation to Bath, where McBean had a house and studio. He spent two or three nights there, enjoying a holiday
from the bombs, while McBean took a series of studies of the
21-year-old John that capture perfectly his flamboyant,
effete appearance.

> I was photographed, 'had' and returned to London. Apart from
> his beard and skinny body, I liked Angus and was enraptured
> by his talent. He discovered, as you can see in some of the

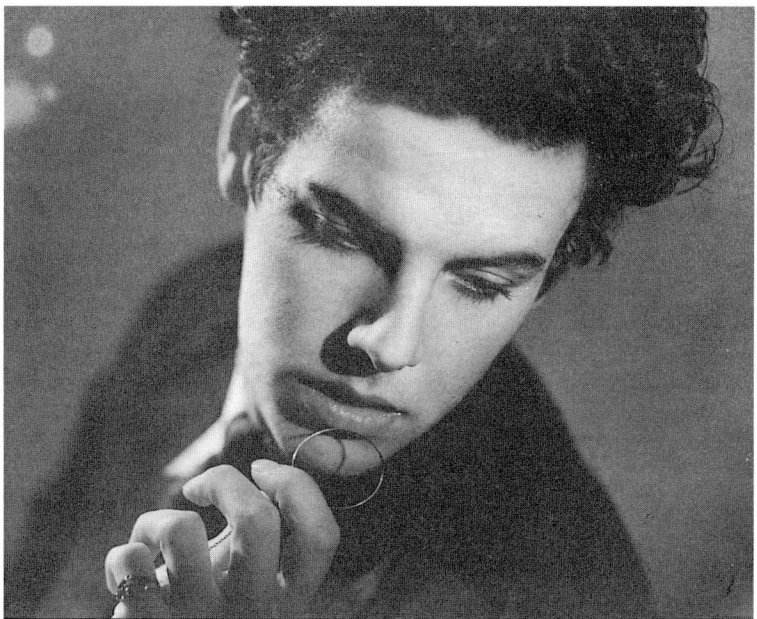

> portraits, that my face holds in it the two sides of my charac-
> ter. The left hand side, where I wore the eyeglass, looks quite
> wicked. The right hand side is totally different, almost angel-
> ic. There's even one he took of me in the nude, cropped off just
> above the pubic hair. Really, only Angus could have got a
> decent photograph out of my body. His lighting glamourised
> everything. He took a lot of nudes in those days, all very
> respectable as far as I know, without genitals showing.

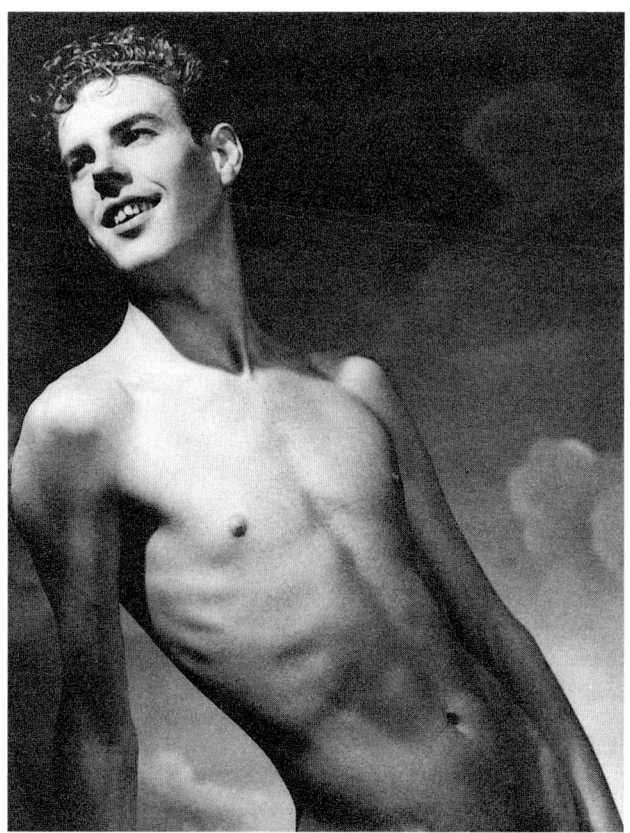

Over the next few years, McBean photographed a few of John's friends, among them David (who he posed as Nijinsky in *L'Après-midi d'un faune*). Shortly after John's visit, McBean was arrested for running a disorderly house and served a prison sentence.

Not everyone who met the 20-year-old John was so impressed. An unsigned postcard from 1940 contained some harsh criticism.

> Avoid being argumentative even tho' your superior knowledge compels you to join in. Make friends and cut out the idiosyncrasies that are especially John S.B., and commence with a

clean slate ... Keep out of the spotlight a little ... the bloke in the corner sees most. If, at any time, you need any help I can give you – let me know immediately, for you're not a bad chap deep down. All the best, and remember, cut out all eccentricities, for even as a pose, they elicited hostility and not admiration.

But there were plenty who were attracted by the loud-mouthed, loudly dressed young artist. John, who loved being at the centre of things, gathered round himself a group of friends who saw each other through the War – the 'Crowd', as he called them, a mixture of aspiring actresses, drag queens, middle-class girls roughing it and beautiful boys on the make. With his knack for seduction and his enthusiasm for show business, John was a magnet for the fame-hungry, love-hungry young people who were daring enough to stay in the West End during the Blitz. The complex inter-relationships of the Crowd became a source of endless fascination – he was still writing about its poignant minutiae 40 years later – and marked the happiest period of John's life.

The first character to latch himself on to John was Douggie Harris, known as 'The Wicked Feely' (a 'polare' nickname that roughly translates as 'Bad Girl'), a drag comedian who performed his act around the dying music hall circuit. He was a familiar figure around the West End clubs, and John described their first meeting in highly coloured terms.

Fat, pink and near-naked, Douggie Harris saw me talking happily with David. For all his perspiring lack of glamour, he behaved like a star. Douggie was a 32-year-old, short, balding, very stout, pink-fleshed male transvestite ... He lived with his very strange, bejewelled and even more grossly stout, orange-bewigged, white-faced, scarlet-lipped and foul-mouthed mother in a dilapidated lodging house off the Camden Road. The house belonged to the mother, while Douggie found the lodgers, all elderly queers, and a couple of skinny teenage boys who skivvied.

Here at last was the arch corrupter who John feared would lure David into the West End, away from his protection. But of far greater interest to David, and to all of John's subsequent boyfriends, was the crowd of vivacious young women whom John had taken to squiring around town. Dinora, Betty and Gloria were the first – girls who would spend the night with a good-looking serviceman, would take presents of cash or nylons from the officers and would even allow themselves to be kept in rented flats by well-to-do admirers. These were the 'good-time girls' who flocked into the West End in the 40s.

> They had polished to a fine point the business of being a whore without standing on a street corner. They never actually charged, they never made bargains, there were no financial transactions, they just said hello and laughed with the boys who took their fancy and kept them company till the morning, extracting as much as they could in the way of gifts, meals and drinks. Leicester Square was a seething mass of young men in uniform. The ones that were moving around were heterosexual, looking for girls. The ones that were leaning against the railings were trade, looking for men because they wanted to get paid.

All the girls loved John, the eccentric, attractive young man who encouraged them in their exploits, told them all how talented they were, advised them on their dress and was available for double dating if there were enough sailors to go around.

It didn't take him long to realise that the easiest way of picking up the good-looking, masculine men that he preferred was not by cruising the gay bars, but rather by frequenting the places that a serviceman on leave would go looking for female company. There the boys would drink, flirt and allow themselves to be seduced – by a man if they were feeling curious enough. It was a fantastically successful ploy, as much of John's wartime correspondence testified. 'My dear John,' wrote a sailor named Bobby,

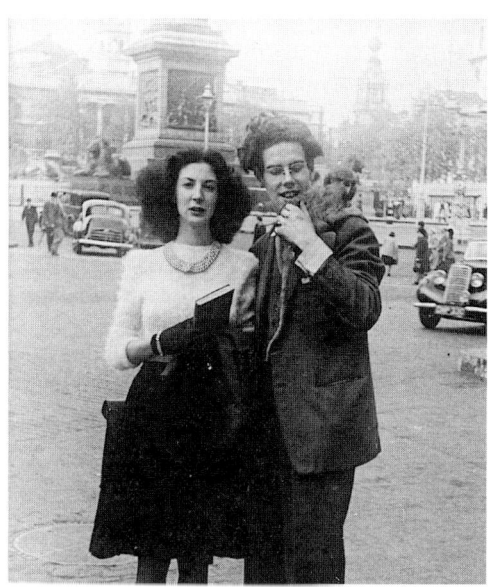

*With a wartime girlfriend
and their 'living accesso-
ry', a monkey named
Vision, in Trafalgar
Square. Vision belonged
to ballet impresario Leon
Hepner, who lent John
his West End flat in
return for pet-sitting.*

What a pleasant surprise to hear from you again – and many
thanks for the enclosed. Came at a very opportune moment I
must say – Well, I can always do with some anytime ... And
what's it like down West these days? Seems ages since I was
last up there you know John. How are all the crowd then?
Dearest Dinora, Mavis, Margot ... Please give my kindest
regards to them all will you John. I have missed you a lot you
know but by now I'm getting used to being away ... Well John
I wonder if its any good my reminding you of those photographs that you promised me so long ago. Apparently you
always forget, but really John I would like them you know.
They were a few copies of that profile of myself in uniform –
one of that batch of photographs that I had taken at Dinora's
– well you should remember ... And one photograph of Dinora
could I have? ... Anyhow I'm looking forward very much to
seeing you again John as we have got a lot to make up for
haven't we? Will you save one of those 'grand mysteries' for
me when I get leave again John?

John had perfected his routine. He picked Bobby up in the Café Royal, introduced him to the girls, plied him with drinks and took him back to one of the West End flats and offices that were his overnight stops. There he photographed him (some portraits, some nudes), had sex with him and sent him back to his ship with his horizons considerably broadened (and, as Bobby's letter shows, with a few extra pounds in his pocket). Another letter from 1941, from an airman named Ronnie, gives more insight into John's regular patter.

> The most interesting feature of our affair is that although I enjoyed our effort together equally, if not more so, than any woman I have ever had, I still never think of having an affair with a man, always with a woman. I learned quite a lot about l'amour with you, but I want to try the new technique 'par une femme' ... I have a confession to make to you. Something happened on our last meeting which I rather wish hadn't. I am referring to Margot. I'm sorry lad but I keep thinking about her. You certainly are a lucky beggar. Or should that last word be spelt with a 'u'? No, I remember you said otherwise...

Many faces came and went in John's wartime circle of girl-friends – some of them got married and gave up the West End life, some of them were killed in air raids. There were always plenty of new girls in town to take their place. One afternoon in the Coffee An' John got into conversation with a West London teenager who introduced herself as Micky Anderson, a mousy-haired waif from Shepherd's Bush keen to launch herself on the West End circuit with a view to a career in theatre or films. John took her under his wing, and within a few short weeks had transformed her from mousy Micky Anderson to blonde bombshell Miki Petty, soubrette singer and actress, whom he would launch on her theatrical career.

Smartened up by John and his girlfriends, Miki became the gayest of the group, the most amorally pleasure-seeking, the girl that all of John's boyfriends fell in love with, his ideal accomplice in the seduction of straight young men. 'If a girl walked through Leicester Square on a sunny afternoon,' he remembered, 'all the soldiers and sailors would whistle at her. Miki was one of the few who would whistle right back.' She was a great instigator: once she discovered a sun-lamp club in Ladbroke Grove and dragged John and his boyfriends over there for weeks of oily, goggle-clad tanning sessions. She would lead parties down to the Spielplatz naturist camp near St Albans where they ran naked through the fields and frolicked in the wooden cabins.

There was one more layer to John's London life during the Blitz. While not pulling dead bodies out of smouldering buildings or living it up in the clubs, John could be found relaxing in one of the city's steam baths. He had started going to the Central London YMCA on the corner of Great Russell Street to clean up after his ARP shifts, and had immediately discovered to his delight that the hot showers were crowded every afternoon with servicemen eager for relief, who wouldn't even cost him a few shillings in drinks and cab fares. Some of them he would take away to photograph; others he would quickly enjoy and move on. From the YMCA, he explored further: the Imperial Baths in Bloomsbury Square, the Turkish Baths in Regent Street, bath houses as far afield as Bermondsey and the Elephant and Castle. Some of the boys in the baths were interested in a bit of casual whoring, but rarely charged more than a meal and a bed for the night.

* * *

This strange idyll couldn't last forever. John had left the ARP at the end of 1941, and had taken a series of jobs at hospitals in and around London, claiming (as he had done from 1939) the status of a conscientious objector. But he knew that his call-up could not be delayed indefinitely, and finally on 9 August the dreaded brown envelope dropped through the door of his parents' home. He was summoned to appear before a Medical Board under the National Service (Armed Forces) Act. The examination took place the next day in Holloway.

The memory of that day, unlike so many others in the war, remains vivid. I arrived at a drab, spacious, artificially broken-up room, canvas and wood screens creating alcoves through which men were processed. The routine of passing from one alcove to another, after undressing and clutching one's clothes, is too familiar to describe again. Suffice to say that after bending, inhaling, exhaling, being tapped, told to lift arms and legs and bend over, I was told I was 'A1' and ordered to wait on a bench, dressed, till called to meet the man who would decide my fate and future.

It was about noon when I was told to sit at a trestle table opposite a small, well-built man of about 40, greying hair, a small moustache. I had not finished replacing things in my pockets, and was carrying my crocodile-skin wallet, which I put on the table before me, with my fountain pen. My eyeglass dangled from my neck on a gold chain, and I replaced my ruby and pearl tie pin and leaned my silver and malacca cane against the table. All the man had done was watch me. He smiled, took off his glasses, cleaned them, replaced them, and closed the file that lay open on his desk. He asked me what I did. I told him about art school, ARP, my show business connections, glamourising everything a bit as I went along. He nodded and smiled. I thought he was about to make me face up to the realities of the war and my duty.

Instead he told me that he was very fond of the ballet, especially the Sadler's Wells Company. Did I know any of the dancers? Yes, Helpmann, Lawski, Palthengi and some others, I replied fluently. I made it clear that I spent a lot of time socially and backstage at the ballet, in London and pre-War Paris. I dropped the names of Lifar, Mistinguett, Josephine Baker, Cocteau and Gide. His eyes widened and he drummed his fingers on the table.

I picked up my pen and put it into my pocket, and in doing

this my jacket cuff knocked my wallet on to the floor. It fell under the table, between our legs. He and I bent down to see where it had fallen. It lay nearer to me but the contents of one of its pockets had spilled out nearer to him. They were photographs. While I picked up the wallet, he picked up the photos, and laid them slowly face up one by one on the table between us. There were six: two of David, two of Vic, two of another boy called Eddie. All had been taken on Hampstead Heath in the men's enclosure. Only the two of David were not total nudes.

'Are these some of your dancer friends?'

'No, these are personal friends, but that one (pointing to David) is a very personal friend.'

He looked at the photos again and gave them back to me. I put them in my wallet and the wallet in my pocket. The doctor took a gold fob watch from his waistcoat, looked at it, closed it with a click and replaced it. 'Well, my boy, I don't think we have time to make a balanced assessment of your case before luncheon. Might it be a good idea to talk a little more over some food and wine?' He didn't wait for my answer, but leaned forward and said more quietly 'Meet me on the corner to the left in ten minutes, eh?'. He shuffled his papers neatly, stood up and walked from the table.

Ten minutes later a chauffeur-driven car drew up on the corner where I stood. The door was opened and I got in. The doctor patted me on the knee and said 'Good! I feel quite peckish! Here's my card' – Dr Otto May of Harley Street and Hampstead.

We were driven to a large restaurant and enjoyed a splendid meal. We talked a lot, mostly about me and my friends. I was quite open about my sex life and my interest in the kind of young men I expected to find in the forces. 'Oh, I don't think it would really be in the nation's interest to provide you with so much opportunity,' said Dr May. 'I think it might be better for us all if you continue your useful creative life in London.' He paid the bill and we returned to the examination hall, where, within a few minutes, he had given me total exemption from military service – on medical grounds! As we shook hands, he said 'If ever any of your young friends need help or advice, please feel free to put them in touch with me. It was a great pleasure meeting you, Mr Barrington.'

John was issued with his first Regular Unemployment Book at Camden Town. Free of any immediate worries, he settled down to enjoy the rest of the war – with another profitable sideline now in his command. Dr May proved as good as his word, and soon John was 'referring' young men to him as a way of securing their exemption from National Service. He charged a small commission, of course, for which he prepared a 'psychoanalytical report' testifying to his subject's mental illness or sexual deviation. Meeting Robert Helpmann in the Ivy one day, he found that the Sadler's Wells Ballet was in danger of losing many of its male *corps de ballet*; thanks to John and Dr May and their 'exemption service', Helpmann kept a number of his dancers.

* * *

John didn't have to fight, but he was faced with another immediate problem – he had to earn a living. In the early part of the war, he had barely thought about money, ekeing out his small art school grant with a few bob earned as a sketch artist around the West End cafés. But now, with art school finally abandoned, it became clear that he could not afford to keep up the life to which he had become accustomed without a job.

There were few legitimate jobs for which John was qualified or suited – but in wartime London there were plenty of semi-legal scams that suited him better. Bob Wellington, the driver with his ARP unit, had been involved in black market activities ever since the beginning of the war when he had taken to syphoning petrol out of the ARP vehicles and selling it as lighter fuel. When their team had broken up, Wellington went into full-time racketeering with his brother

Frank, expanding his market from lighter fuel into cosmetics. He opened a small factory in a disused studio in Goodge Place, where he rebottled cheap perfume (bought by the barrel and diluted with anything that came to hand) into bottles that he spray painted and labelled with forged brand names, particularly Yardley. John's involvement in the operation started off innocently enough, getting jobs for his girlfriends in the bottling plant and occasionally helping out; soon he was spending many days working there himself.

But flogging dodgy perfume was not good enough for John. He had never let go of his pre-war dreams of establishing himself in the theatre, and as more and more of his friends were beginning to pursue show business careers (David, under the tutelage of Douggie Harris, was now working as a dancer), John decided the time had come to get in on the act himself. He'd spent enough time in the West End clubs to make some useful contacts, and decided that he would be the perfect booking agent for the Soho circuit. He began introducing himself to people as an agent looking for talent, and even managed to find work for a couple of singers and variety acts at clubs where he was known.

Soon there was more to the job than simply acting the part. Through the Wellingtons, John met an American agent who was looking for an opening in London. Belle Avalon was middle-aged, a retired roller-skater who was now managing an act, the Four Renowns, that she was trying to get established on the music-hall circuit. John remembered her as 'a short, witty, common and coarse lady with superabundant energy, eternally optimistic, rather tubby, over made-up, exciting company and a heavy drinker', and the two took to each other instantly. Belle was a hard-headed businesswoman; John, with his cultivated airs, provided the perfect front for the business. They set up shop in Belle's Oxford Street premises, and he took a short lease on the flat above the office. As the destruction of London continued around him, John travelled all over town keeping an eye on the acts that he and Belle had booked (and always looking out for a

promising steam bath or servicemen's pub in every quarter
of the city that he visited).

As Bob Wellington's cosmetics business prospered he
began to pour money into Belle's agency. John, never one to
look a gift horse in the mouth, was delighted when Bob set
them up in offices in Great Newport Street and offered him a
personal salary of £15 per week – enough to live well, with a
little left over for the boys. In 1943, they moved to an even
swankier address – Cambridge Chambers, overlooking
Cambridge Circus at the heart of the West End. At the crossroads of Charing Cross Road and Shaftesbury Avenue, the
office was situated opposite the Palace Theatre where Ivor
Novello ruled. The rent was taken care of by the Wellingtons,
and John was given his own suite of rooms where he could
carry on his various business activities, spy on the comings
and goings of the West End from large windows, entertain
friends and lovers and take photographs. Inspired by Angus
McBean, he began studying camera technique more seriously, set up a makeshift studio and darkroom in his office and
practised on a succession of soldiers, sailors and airmen –
sometimes as many as three or four a week were brought
back to the office and photographed. In many cases, as John
recorded in his diary, the promise of photography was a
handy way of getting the boys out of their uniforms and in
the mood; the modelling was generally a prelude to sex.
From his delight in recording his lovers, John began to build
up a body of photographic work that would soon take his life
in an unexpected direction.

Headed notepaper was ordered, listing the companies
operating out of Cambridge Chambers as JB Advisory (a lay
psychoanalytic service, catering to reluctant servicemen),
various theatrical agencies including JB Enterprises and
Belle Avalon Productions, *Cinopaedia* (John was using this
title as a means of getting to press screenings) and Gay
News, a newsletter John was planning to circulate about the
clubs and bars of the West End. While Belle and John busied
themselves in the front offices, Bob and Frank Wellington

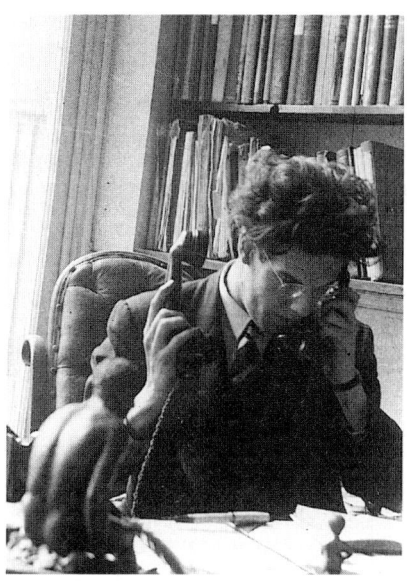

The impresario at work in Cambridge
Chambers, 1943

were expanding Peronia Cosmetics in the rear of the building, every so often asking John to sign and date receipts as
director of the company.

With money in his pocket and an impressive address on
his business cards, John took to the high life with a
vengeance. The Café Royal became a nightly haunt, and
when he was feeling particularly flush he would treat David,
Miki or the boyfriend of the day to dinner at the Ivy, the
restaurant on West Street that was a favourite watering hole
of Coward, Olivier and the theatrical aristocracy. Pursuing
Noël Coward became a full-scale obsession, as John felt his
improved social status might finally grant him access to the
Master's charmed circle. He bombarded him with letters and
accosted him in public – to no avail. 'He's so devilishly eva-
sive!' John complained to his diary. 'Last time we met was in
the Boeuf, during a bad blitz in April. Got nowhere."We must
meet again, dear boy!" and then whoosh! Gone!' On another
occasion he wrote:

Opening of lovely roof gardens last night on top of Derry &
Toms, Kensington. NC cuts the tape and drinks the first
champagne. After hovering I ask him a question or two. He
says he's writing the story for a film about the Navy, his
second love to the theatre, he says. I believe him!

On another occasion John caught up with Coward in the
gents toilets at the Café Royal. Coward gave him a big wink
and said 'Hello, dear boy, how's trade?'. John said, 'It's been
rough, but it's picking up.' Coward laughed and replied,
'Naturally old boy! Picking up's the thing!' Another wink,
and he walked out. Coward may have been beyond John's
mark, but there was one bona fide theatrical celebrity who
became a close friend and peripheral member of the Crowd
during the war: the critic, James Agate. The first encounter
had also been in the Café Royal gents one evening when
John was celebrating his birthday. A short, bald, cigar-smok-
ing man had offered him the single tablet of soap as they
washed their hands at adjacent sinks, and tried to engage
him in conversation. John left hurriedly, only to discover
later that the soap was being offered by none other than
London's most respected theatre critic, the scourge of the
Sunday Times and a prolific autobiographer, author of the
multi-volumed *Ego* series.

Thereafter John saw Agate regularly in the Café Royal,
where they would occasionally nod to each other and Agate
would size up John's latest uniformed conquest with an
appraising glance. By 1942, they were on cordial terms. 'You
do seem to have the most delightful young friends,' remarked
Agate one night to John, who proceeded to show him photographs of some of the sailors and soldiers he had admired.
'Agate has captured my nice Welsh soldier!' he complained to
his diary on 1 September 1943. 'No matter, I'd got him into
camera at 5pm!'

The friendship grew quickly. Agate knew everyone at the
Café Royal but nearly always dined alone, so he was an easy

target. At first they would have drinks together, then Agate started taking John to first nights and taught him the grand manner, of which he was a fine exponent. Agate would walk into the Café Royal and immediately start ribbing the head waiter, whom he called 'Archbishop'. 'I say, Archbishop, come here for God's sake, man, what are you hanging around for?' John drank all this in and incorporated it into his persona; even in his 70s, ordering a drink in relatively humble surroundings, he treated waiters in the Agate manner ('Bring me another glass of this bloody red ink you call wine!')

If John saw in Agate a mentor, Agate found John endlessly amusing, an eccentric type as well as a good source of soldiers. One night over whiskies in the Café Royal, they decided to concoct a dialogue between the critic and a 'Young Man' for inclusion in the forthcoming volume of *Ego*. *Ego 7*, when it was published in 1944, was full of references to John, most of them fictionalised versions of real conversations:

> MAY 28, SUNDAY. A week or so ago I again met in the Café Royal the young man with whom I had the extraordinary conversation reported in my entry for March 14. I said, 'All joking apart, how intellectual are you?' He said, 'Try me!' Whereupon I trotted out the old teaser about the three schoolboys with the three red and two white tabs. He said, 'I'll send you the answer tomorrow.' Two days later I got a note written in a really dreadful fist. I replied to this, saying, 'Not only have you taken the problem down wrong, but you have the worst handwriting I have ever seen.' When I got in tonight I found shoved under my door a letter written in unimaginably lovely copperplate, in which, incidentally, the young man admits that he cannot spell. Which is fortunate. 'Perumbulating' is a beauty. It looks as though John Shreeve Barrington and I are going to be friends.

John teased Agate with stories of his sexual conquests, showed him photographs and letters from his favourite sailor friends, among them the permanently randy Bobby, whom

Agate had admired in the Café Royal. 'My own Darling,' begins one with which Agate was greatly taken:

> I was thrilled to hear of your fun and games with Dinora. I should have been there with you and Din', that would have been something camp to remember! How about it John? We three on the spree. Christ, John, I'm nearly coming!!! I can see your mouth watering now. Here I am sitting on the couch by the window with the sun streaming down on me. It's really gorgeous darling. Makes me crave for you! To feel your lips upon my — ! I'd better toss myself off ... I do honestly enjoy writing to you John, especially in a camp tone!

One night in June 1944, Agate invited John back to his Alexandra Mansions apartment after a long night in the Café Royal discussing their respective sex lives. Agate's tastes tended towards rough trade, while John was still in pursuit of his aesthetic ideal made flesh. The evening ended with Agate giving John a blow job and commissioning him to provide a number of erotic drawings of negro models.

* * *

The summer of 1944 brought good news. '6 June: Invasion Day! Nice lunch. No one mentioned the boys dying on Normandy Beaches,' records the diary. But the aerial bombardment of London continued.

> 19 JUNE: Doodle bomb fell today on Jean's café where I ate last night. No friends killed. Saw it pass over Cambridge Circus, lunch time, from office window. Was going into details for forming a new ballet company, both of us so blasé that we hardly paused from talk as the engine cut off and the thing began to glide down Charing Cross Road. When the crash came we turned back to the cost of scenery, costumes and orchestration for *Les Sylphides*.

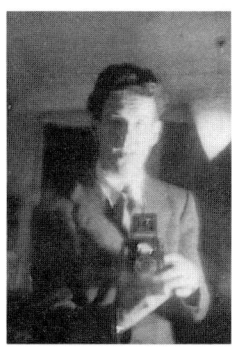 John saw out the summer of 1944 at Cambridge Chambers, where his theatrical clients that year included the actor Maxwell Reed, first husband of Joan Collins. Increasing amounts of time were spent in the darkroom, as John had started selling prints to a few friends, among them Agate. His interest in pornography was growing.

2 NOVEMBER: My birthday! Yesterday was very gay! At 2pm, after 12 days of extensive preamble, a very fat man called Slim – an ugly bastard – arranged to place in my hands 2,850 'magnificent' photographs of assorted nudes. The samples he produced were excellent. He wanted £150 for the lot. Raked the cash together and at 2pm took taxi with him to Park Lane Hotel. Parted with cash. Sat waiting for half an hour until I realised I'd been conned good and proper. A nasty, though amusing, blow.

14 DECEMBER: Completed an erotic book of 60,000 words and sold it in five carbon copies at £20 a volume. So add pornographer to my other accomplishments.

The international news was fast becoming cause for celebration. In May 1945, John wrote a lengthy account of his experience of VE Day – one last glorious fling before he had to contemplate the harsher realities of peace.

A rumour became a certainty. Gaiety began to invade the people at about 3pm. Met Margot and took her to see the film *Dorian Grey*. When we came out of the cinema VE Day was here at last. At 9pm Leicester Square, Coventry Street and Piccadilly were crowded beyond imagination ... Drink flowed. Many were already tight by mid evening ... We all loved everyone.

Margot and I had to move via back streets to the Café

Royal and then needed to bribe our way in. Champagne with Jimmie Agate. Then at 11pm back through the crush in Piccadilly Circus, kissing every soldier, sailor and airman I could meet. Watched the lights go on in Leicester Square for the first time since September 1939 ... Impossible to get into Corner House, crowds too great. So pick up superb sailor, take him to office and fuck him 'silly', an exceptional activity for both of us. Give him a bottle of whisky and £5. Then take the bus home to Tufnell Park. It thunderstormed and rained tropically. Everyone asleep.

Tuesday: VE Day official. To office by 10am. Worked till noon. Streets getting crowded again. Splendid view of crowds from office window. Open windows and wave to people passing down Charing Cross Road. West End is like a huge fairground with pictures of Churchill, King and Queen, Monty, Eisenhower etc. Coloured hats, streamers, men with movie cameras. Boys and sailors up trees and lamp posts, Americans at the Rainbow corner throwing french letters full of water onto crowds. Met Miki and Ricky (USAF) outside Café Royal 6pm. Went to St James Park, struggled through crowds in Mall. Left Miki and Ricky who felt like bed and sex (and he didn't want me) . . . At 3am tiredness crept over London. People just sat down and talked. A few made love. Young men in uniform with girls. And I also saw in dark doorways and in alleys and phone boxes sailors and kneeling men.

At 4.30am to the Corner House. Crowded, noisy, much like it was in the Blitz. Hot chocolate and scrambled eggs. Nice lonely sailor, never learnt his name, at same table. Big, tall, very masculine. Dark hair, blue eyes, olive skin, perfect teeth. Half an hour's chat. Established that he never had. Couldn't. Nothing a man could do would make him come, so what's the point. A real challenge. Took him – without much protest – to my office and persuaded him to show me his body. And then a rapid erection as he assumed poses. A little more persuasion and he lay on the divan, posing as a sleeping god. A jaw-aching, tongue-tiring hour resulted in his sheepish, grudging admission that everything is possible given the right time, place, incentive and partner. I'd like to have seen him again, but he wouldn't even join me for breakfast. Half a tumbler of whisky, a refusal to let me kiss his cheek, and he was gone into the now depleted crowds. Before he disappeared he raised his arm with a clenched fist, but he didn't look back.

THE MODERN IDEAL

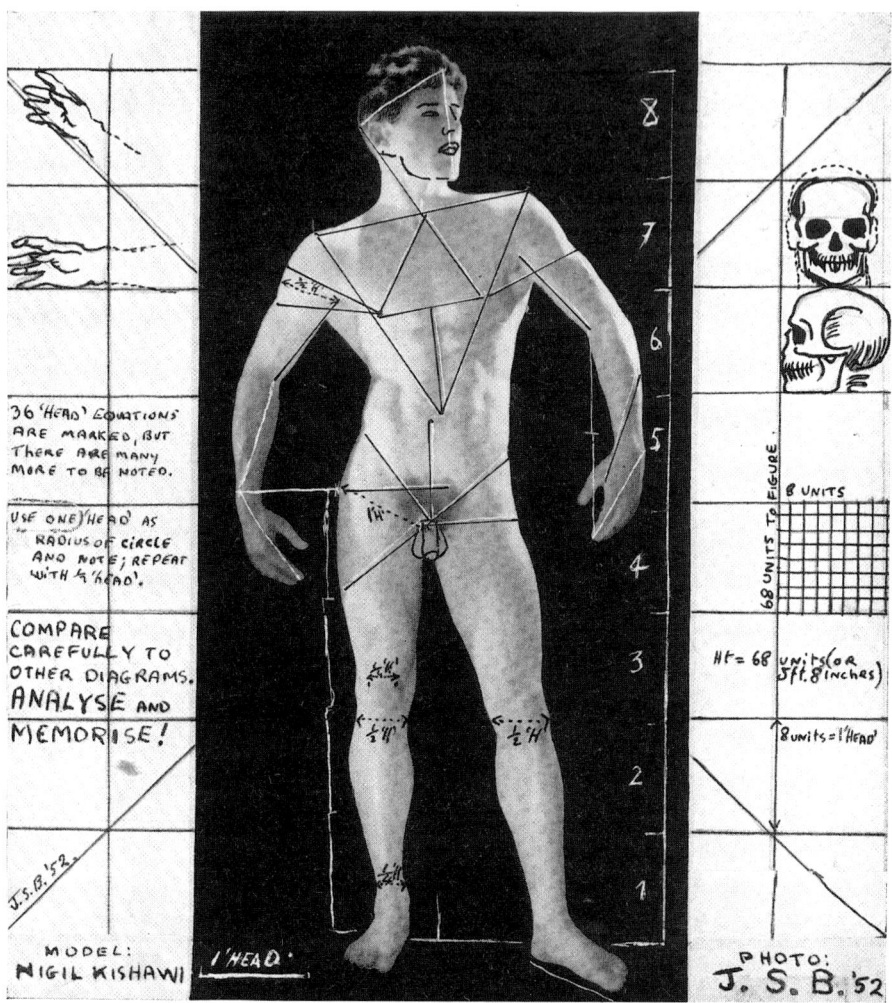

point will, with its base, give the base of the male scrotum and buttocks. The second division gives the base of the knee-cap and the fourth the level of the pubic symphisis. To establish the height of the shoulders construct a square of 1⅔ heads, the lower corners of which will place the armpits if the top forms the top line of the main square; this will give the broadest width of the clavicles and the shoulder line is so placed as to make the base of this square one-third of the distance from the nipple line (*division six*) to the shoulder line. From the navel describe a circle, radius five heads.

Now refer to diagram on page 46, and with a compass build up geometrically the whole male figure. You will discover—if your square is on a large enough scale—*that every curve and line required will be part of circles*, the centres of which will be points already marked, and the radii, one head, or multiples of 17 units.

47

A page from Art and Anatomy, expounding John's favourite science of anthropometry

Chapter Three
Art and Anatomy

For John and his crowd, peace meant facing up to the awkward questions that they had happily avoided during six years of sex, death and danger. John, at 25, had emerged from the war with little: his art studies had gone by the wayside, he earned pocket money from the black market and second-rate show business, and he'd had a lot of lovers, some of whom he'd photographed. Now there was the pressing need to establish an independent living.

Most of his friends were in the same boat. David had started serious dance training during the war, and was getting regular work with the various touring ballet companies that travelled up and down the country. Miki, no longer able to live on handouts from generous GIs, decided that the time had come to launch herself into a musical career. John was the only one who couldn't decide on a profession: in his own mind he was equally adept at art, costume design, journalism, photography, fiction and sculpture. One night in the Café Royal he asked the advice of James Agate, who had obligingly read the manuscript of his wartime novel *Dion*. Agate knew John was brilliant – the flattery of *Ego* was not entirely fatuous – but warned him that he would never be able to concentrate long enough on anything to bring it to a satisfactory conclusion. 'You're a jack of all trades, dear boy, and likely to be a master of none,' pronounced the critic.

John knew all too well the truth of the warning, but it didn't help. He wanted to work, but couldn't bear the idea of missing out on anything. He desperately wanted to continue the momentum of the war years, when anything was possible and an attractive new sailor could walk into his life at any moment. True, there were plenty of servicemen left in London after the war with even more time on their hands than before, and he availed himself of as many as possible. But try as he might, he could not ignore a greater truth: the free and easy days were over, and Britain – even Bohemian London – was returning to a sober normality.

During the war, it was easy to get away with things. While John had been a sexual adventurer, his partners in crime, the Wellingtons, were getting away with some serious financial misdemeanours. Their cosmetics company Peronia evaded thousands of pounds' worth of purchase tax; John, as a director, knew what was going on, but turned a blind eye. Thanks to the Wellingtons, he enjoyed the high life throughout the war with a decent salary, beautiful West End offices and the comfortable illusion that he was making his mark in the theatre. All he had to do in return was sign a few receipts and hand out the Barrington charm to clients. This dream came crashing around him early in 1945, when HM Customs and Excise, keen to clear up the black market, made their first appearance.

The initial investigations took place in January, when the diary records 'C&E making enquiries about last two years of cosmetic production and its too profitable sales.' Over the summer, the Wellingtons packed up the operation and disposed of as much evidence as possible, but it was too late. Customs officers had already seized accounts, receipts and invoices for the period 1943-45, and handed the case over to the CID. John made a statement to them over the summer, claiming that he knew nothing about the business. But in October, Detective Inspector Hannam of the CID tricked him into making a fuller statement in which he admitted that he knew what the receipts were for, although he still denied the extent of his involvement.

How was John caught so easily? During the summer of 1945, with his £15 a week salary from the Wellingtons cut off, he had thrown himself into a new role, that of ENSA producer, putting together entertainments for the forces overseas. He had been approached by the ENSA impresario Leon Hepner who suggested that John should get a show together to entertain the troops in the Far East, with a long rehearsal period and a guaranteed salary of £12 per week. He jumped at the idea, recruited all his talented friends and formed his own company. Miki, David and Douggie Harris joined a team of dancers, acrobats and musicians to star in a show which he was devising, a homage to the sophisticated revues that he had seen and loved in the West End clubs. Rehearsals for *Calling London!* were predictably fraught affairs as John and Douggie wrestled for control of the show while Miki and David (to John's dismay) embarked on an affair.

When the time came for the group to apply for passports, there was a hitch: John discovered that the CID had put a

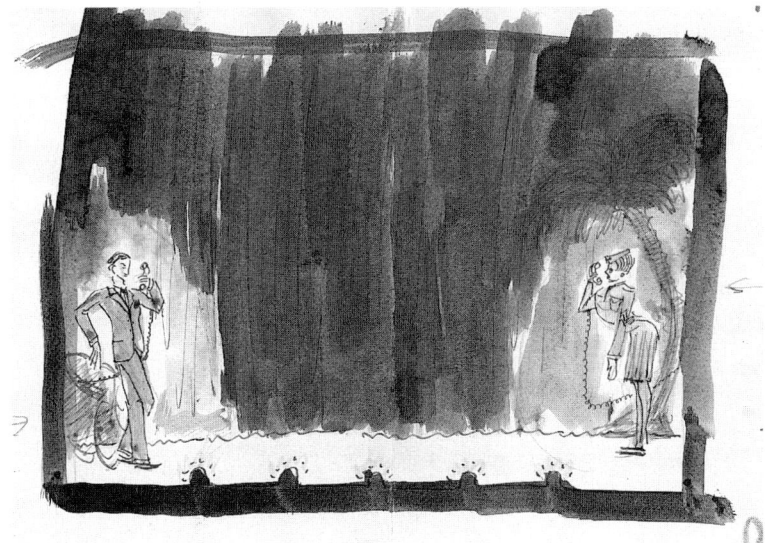

A sketch from John's Calling London! notebook

block on his passport pending investigations for fraud. Frantic that he would miss the tour, he stormed off to Scotland Yard to see DI Hannam, who promised him an exit visa if he made a further statement, which he did.

14 OCTOBER: Yesterday spent two hours at Scotland Yard being blackmailed into telling the truth about how Bob W involved me. I am now sure that I was very unwise, even idiotic. I admitted perjury and forgery and made a short statement revising my previous statement of March, which the CID had accepted after it had been backed up by others involved. Now they have a case of conspiracy to threaten me with.

Hannam was as good as his word and issued a visa for John to leave the country – but too late. By that time the ENSA company had already set sail.

Under this cloud of fear, John was restless and near to hysteria. He fell in and out of love with men and women at the drop of a hat and packed in as much sex as he could.

22 JUNE 1945: Have done two excellent case histories this week. One for Eddie B – very much a labour of love, if it works and keeps him out of HM Forces I'll have him on tap (literally) for a few more months. One for a Negro Ponce called Walton. He paid, but not much.

9 JULY: Went to Ponds and met Eddie J, who I've photographed every year since 1940. Again he wanted to be 'took', so I snapped while he dived and swam. Then I suggested that we go into the wood and take some nudes. He spent the walk to the woods talking about his girlfriend, how she would one day and then wouldn't the next. Took 20 pictures. Then the unbelievable happened. Never before had I done more than hint at my physical interest.

8 OCTOBER: Margaret of *Calling London!* company says she loves me and wants us to marry. To Café Royal to meet won-

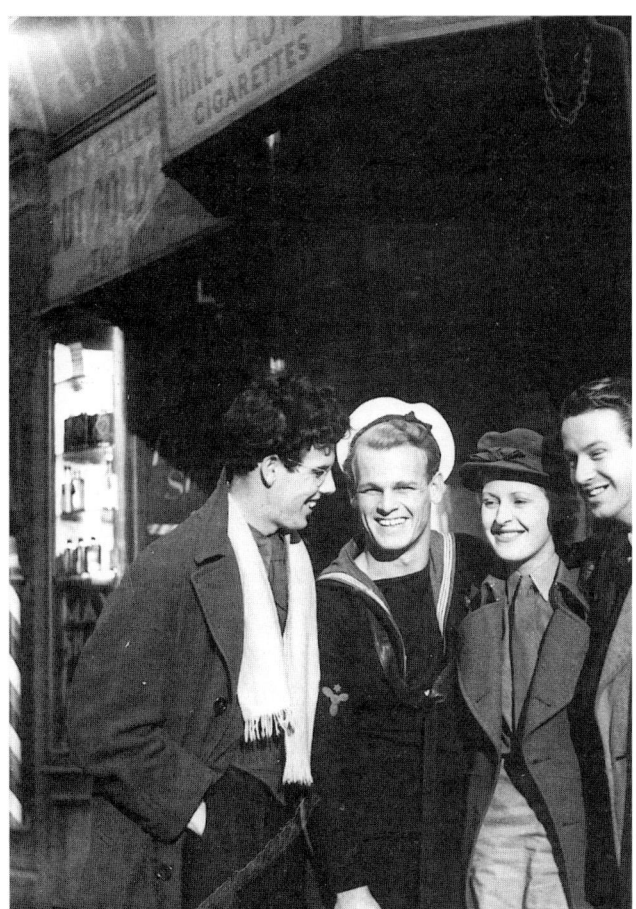

John and his 'blond paragon' sailor Donald with friends in the West End

derful new blond and beautiful RN sailor from Nassau, Bahamas, Donald. Met him yesterday in Charing Cross Road, looking at art books in Zwemmer's window. Adopted him totally all afternoon and all night till I left him sleeping with a note on his chest to meet me in Royal for dinner.

9 OCTOBER: After eating with Miki, Donald and Tony, we all feel very sexy and so hire taxi to take us off at 10pm to that convenient place to rent by the hour near Marble Arch,

Sussex Gardens. A mad night. If only Margaret had been able
to see me with Donald last night.

20 OCTOBER: Jimmie Agate agrees that Donald is 'quite the
most eye-catching young man I can recall seeing in uniform'.
Suggests I get Angus McBean to photograph him. Shall speak
to Angus. As I write I can feel India slipping away. Maybe
Donald is God's consolation prize to me.

3 NOVEMBER: Hair dyed black by Ivan yesterday. Better than
the mousy blond, everyone says. Margaret shocked by my CID
troubles. Policemen worry her more than pretty sailors. 'You
mustn't let mother know!' she keeps bleating. Still she's good
fun in bed...

The *Calling London!* company – including David, Miki,
Douggie and Margaret, John's 'fiancée' – set sail for India via
Gibraltar and Suez on 28 December 1945. John had resigned
himself to the fact that the show he had organised, starring
all his friends, would carry on without him. A few days later
Donald, his blond Bahamian sailor boyfriend, also left town,
leaving behind a few happy snapshots, bundles of passionate
letters and the beautiful portraits that Angus McBean had
duly taken. 1945 ended on a dying note.

31 DECEMBER: Piccadilly Circus, 1am, alone. Usual crowds,
usual opportunities, all ignored. Nice evening at the Royal
with Jimmie Agate and his crowd. Champagne, cigars, sincere
wishes to and from everyone. My heart is at sea...

John buried himself in work. In a new basement office in
Great Newport Street, he and Belle ran their agency by day,
while by night John smoked endless cigarettes and worked
on a life-size nude statue of Donald, which he submitted to
the Royal Academy summer exhibition. It was not accepted.
And he waited for his case to come to court. The Wellingtons
kept him on a £20-a-week sweetener, guilt money to stop him

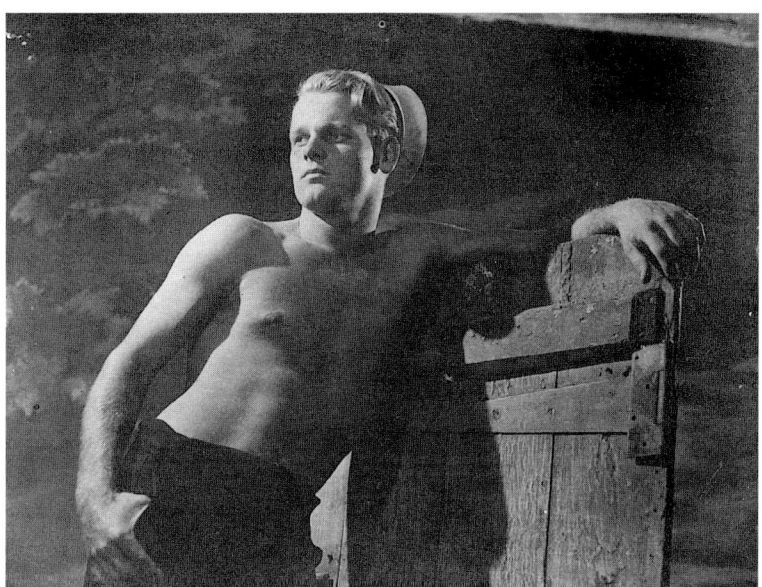

Donald photographed by Angus McBean

from making another statement to the police. Donald was back in Nassau, sending loving, passionate letters; the *Calling London!* company were having fun at sea (and Margaret wrote to declare that she had fallen in love with another). John consoled himself with a round of brief sexual encounters, using his camera more and more with each new 'model', as he now began to call his partners.

15 JANUARY: Go with new commando friend Roy to boxing match at Seymour Hall. Also take Billy and Cliff, both semi-professional boxers. Both boys are good fun in studio after pub crawl. Hope to make long-term model friends of them. First new faces this year. Both relax and pose naked, warmed by whisky and my hands.

23 FEBRUARY: Bermuda Club, Wardour Street, cocktail party. Went 9ish. Lots of lovely black men half dressed in the heat. Take three to supper and to studio for semi-naked photos, a dozen roll-ups of weed, two bottles whisky. One leaves at 1am,

one passes out, George and I do some nude studies, he gets very randy. His first time. Amusing breakfast in Soho.

To add to his emotional problems came a letter from ENSA Rangoon in May, from Douggie Harris, written in the same idiosyncratic way he spoke.

> It's 6am morning Rangoon the coolest hour of the day I'm rest-
> less cant sleep = David in other cot fast asleep looking like a
> Baby Fawn Bless his beautiful little face but not such a little
> cock = looking at him I feel Guilty and Ashamed Luring such
> a Beautifull Boy to the West End nightclubs Perverts.
> However he's come thru' it all Splendidly ... Incidentally He
> and Mike (My Boys Name For Miki) are quietly falling in love
> with each Other ... I feel Happy about it (How do you feel?) ...
> So Bela Barrington & Harriet Harris His Two Fond Aunts
> (tantes) David thinks you wont see the humour of that I think
> you will = Imagine two Dear Old Ladies a la Baddley and
> Gingold Black Tafeta Jet Beads Cream Lace Drinking
> Mazawatee Tea & fondly extolling there Dear Nephew's
> Virtues (vaguely jealous of each other) & all a flutter for Big
> Wedding Day etc etc ... Well cheerio kid Look After Yourself =
> Cant Wait to see You The Scandall!

John fumed at the insinuation that he and Douggie were two jealous old 'tantes' clucking over a beloved nephew, frustrated beyond endurance that the show – his show – was enjoying a great success in the Far East while his friends fell in and out of love without him.

David, Miki and Douggie returned to London, and John's case had still not come to trial. The reunion was strained and unhappy, overshadowed by legal worries and the collapse of David and Miki's romance. David went straight into a touring show, and Douggie got Miki a job singing in a 'sleazy Soho music club, 60 per cent lesbian and queer'. The Crowd that had so much fun just surviving the War was fragmented. To make matters worse, John lost his West End base in

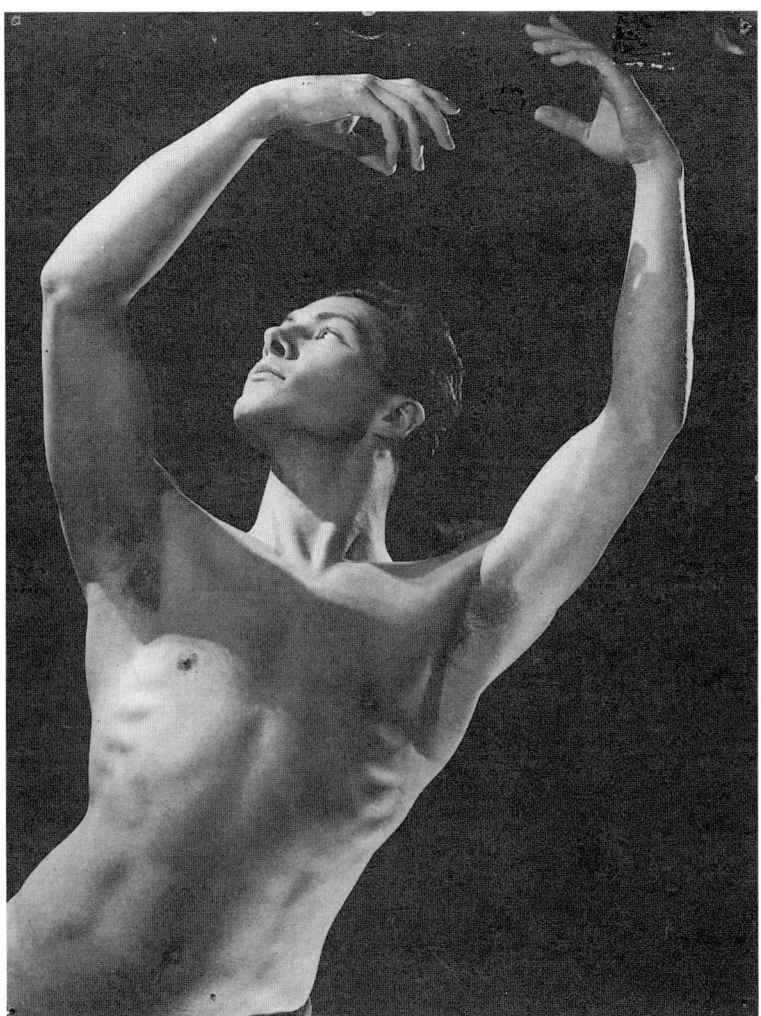

David Dulak photographed by Angus McBean

September and moved all his belongings back home.

The trial was adjourned again and again as the prosecution collected fresh evidence. John finally stepped into the dock at the Old Bailey on 11 November and, over the subsequent weeks, saw the charges against Bob and Frank Wellington dropped on grounds of insufficient evidence. Finally there were only two defendants: John and Jasph

Crandall, an elderly ballet entrepreneur for whom David had worked, a member of the *Calling London!* team who had signed occasional receipts for Peronia Cosmetics. The jury retired at 3.30pm on 24 November and returned their verdict at 4.45pm. Jasph was sentenced to three months in prison, John to 12.

* * *

After all the fears and worries of the past 18 months, John handled his time in prison very well. He was inside for 11 months, first at Wandsworth, then Pentonville; contrary to the advice of his friends and family he decided to appeal and to cause as much fuss as possible. At first the Wellingtons assured him that he would be out of jail in no time, but by the beginning of 1947 John finally admitted to himself that he had been a stooge in the whole Peronia business and that Bob Wellington, now beyond the reach of the law, had taken him for a ride.

He spent a cold but not unpleasant Christmas in Wandsworth ('I've already made a few young friends in prison who help to keep me warm'). He spent January writing reams of notes for his appeal, sketching in a notebook with a scratchy steel-nibbed pen, reading the Bible, masturbating twice a day. He wrote and received masses of letters from his mother, brother Michael, David, Miki and various sailor boyfriends.

His application for leave to appeal was refused, and he settled down to see out the rest of his sentence in Pentonville, whither he was rapidly transferred. On 3 April he received a letter from the Solicitor's Office, HM Customs and Excise, informing him that he was personally liable for the £2,100 owed to them, plus £17.19s costs. The Wellingtons had let him down again, and this time they had left the country. John vented his rage on the prison authorities by firing constant petitions to the governor's office insisting on his 'rights', mostly concerning the amount of correspondence and visitors he was allowed. He stole black wax from the workshops where it was used to toughen the coarse thread for mailbags, and modelled male nude figures which he hid in the water jug during inspections. Using blue ink, red brick dust and pencil, he executed two portraits, one of Christ and one of Donald, which he smuggled out of Pentonville at the end of his stay and hung, framed, in his home.

On 12 June, John received a letter from George Mathew, James Agate's best friend and executor.

> I expect you will have heard of Jimmie's death and when I tell you that he was very ill from early January to the end you will understand why it has been so difficult for me to write to you or to arrange to come and see you ... I asked him several times about books for you and he always agreed to send some after that first Boswell volume on Johnson, but he just always forgot ... Poor Jimmie's end was mercifully sudden. The telephone rang – I went to look for him to come to it to speak to his doctor – and after a long search found him dead behind his bedroom door. I had spoken to him five minutes earlier. I know you will be sad at the news.

Another link with the wartime high life was gone; an important one for John, who had relied on Agate to re-establish him in the literary and theatrical worlds.

By the summer of 1947, John was simply counting the days until his release. He stopped writing in his notebooks, stopped writing so many letters, and kept a low profile. On 15 October the longed-for event took place. Details of his return home, his reactions to his parents and friends, his adjustment to home life after nearly a year in prison, went unrecorded; for a while, he stopped keeping a diary. But he was determined that his new-found freedom would signal a personal and professional rebirth, and that the bittersweet memories of the War should make way for a new, respectable existence.

John's first action on leaving prison was to enter into a lengthy, fantastically naive correspondence with HM

Customs and Excise seeking to defer payment of the £2,100 debt. Bankruptcy proceedings had already been threatened, and he went into a panic. 'I agreed to acknowledge the debt under very clear conditions,' he wrote to a Customs and Excise official in November.

These were that I should be given the FULLEST FACILITIES to resume a respectable career and to re-establish myself in a progressive and respectable society and that when my financial position warranted the expenditure I should attempt, voluntarily and honestly, to repay in instalments this fantastic debt ... I pleaded not guilty to the charges made at the Old Bailey ... I appealed and still take the attitude that I am an innocent victim of circumstances ... Personally speaking I am so tired of the whole business that your department has my permission to do as it pleases, and I throw in gratis, my best wishes and all the compliments of the season! ... I believe that someone in authority is labouring under the hallucination that I have some money and that if I am worried enough I will produce it. Please rid that person, if they exist, of this CHILDISH idea! I do not mean that I am not well off, or that things are difficult, or that I am trying to make ends meet. I MEAN THAT I HAVE NO MONEY AT ALL! NO MONEY AT ALL. I shall borrow the twopenny halfpenny stamp to post this letter from my mother...

Amazingly, this rant (it went on for many more pages) had the effect of securing a deferment from the Customs and Excise official for 12 months, during which time he was expected to 'rehabilitate yourself'. He was triumphant; 'And I didn't have to pay stupid solicitors to represent me!' he scrawled across the top of the official's reply.

Belle Avalon took John back into partnership and gave him use of one room in her two-bedroom flat above Bond Street tube station. Back in the West End, John went into overdrive. He wrote letters to everyone he could think of, particularly friends of Agate's, announcing that he was back in circulation and available for work. He planned dozens of publications, among them *Out of Sickness*, a novel that he had been sporadically writing and rewriting since 1945. As a producer, he told friends, he was off to Berlin to put on *Pygmalion* for the Control Commission and had been approached by Leon Hepner to manage a series of ballet recitals. He was pushing a play he had written entitled *Grim Harvest* at anyone who would read it ('the drama of a film-crazed girl married to a soldier and the emotional tragedy that results from her catching venereal disease').

Way down a list of similar projects that John wrote in his diary in January 1948 is the only one that was to bring him any success: *The Male Nude in Photography*. He was planning a hardback art book of his work for sale in the Charing Cross bookshops, but had also decided to cash in on his now considerable collection of photographs by selling to private collectors. Remembering the advertisements he had seen in the back of magazines before the War, he attempted to place announcements in *Health and Strength* magazine offering mail-order sets of photographs of 'the athletic male nude'. *Health and Strength* declined the advertisement, suggesting instead that John should advertise his work in art magazines. *Health and Strength* did, however, buy 30 of his pictures in February 1949, his first sale to a magazine. But for the rest of 1948 he was content to swap pictures with other photographers and to sell prints to interested parties who visited his 'studio' in Oxford Street, attracted by adverts strategically placed in the windows of Old Compton Street newsagents. The January 1948 list of projects gives priority to the theatrical and literary; when these let him down in the following year, John found that he had a ready-made career waiting in the wings.

To underline the fact that the easy sexual atmosphere of the war had now evaporated, John had his first serious experience of queerbashing in April 1948. On the afternoon of 1 April, the diary records, he took two sailors to Belle's Oxford Street flat, photographed them and wrote '!!!' beside each name, his usual sex code. Later that evening he was strolling through Piccadilly Circus when he was stopped by two attractive guardsmen, who suggested he took them for a drink. He declined, but said that if they were at a loose end later they could find him at the Brasserie Universal on the other side of the Circus at 11pm. He dined with Maxwell Reed, with whom he was trying to set up yet another theatrical agency, and checked in at the Universal on his way back through Piccadilly. The two guardsmen were there, so John bought them a drink and agreed to put them up for the night in Oxford Street, as their barracks, they told him, had closed at midnight.

He hailed a cab from Piccadilly Circus, paid it off at Bond Street tube and invited the two guardsmen in. He was found the next morning by the cleaner, unconscious in a pool of coffee. The flat had been mildly ransacked, and £4.16s cash had been stolen. John was taken to University College Hospital where he remained for ten days, suffering from severe concussion, the effects of which he felt for the rest of the year. His handwriting and dancing, he said, never recovered. A spate of similar attacks were reported by friends throughout 1948.

Compensation was on its way in the shape of a new friend whom John met in Tufnell Park on 4 May, a short, charming, good-looking 17-year-old called Terry Parsons. John 'adopted' him for the day, took him back to the family home during the afternoon (everyone was out at work) and embarked on a pleasant affair.

> Terry wanted to be a ballad singer and his heroes were Crosby and Sinatra. He already crooned a little with a local band that occasionally performed at the Tufnell Park Palais de Danse above the big corner pub on Saturday nights. I agreed to help him get into showbusiness on a 'You scratch my back...' basis. He'd arrive most mornings at 9am, after my mother had gone to work, and we'd leave the house at 11am after a nice couple of hours, and make our way to London, me giving him advice,

making plans. This relationship remained stable through most of the summer until Terry went to do his National Service. In the early 50s, when he came out of the army, Terry changed his name to Matt Monro and began a swift climb up the showbusiness ladder.

Another reason why he was keen to keep Terry as a companion was nothing to do with his singing potential; he had one of the biggest cocks John had ever seen.

In the last week of June, London was host to the Katherine Dunham Dancers in the revue *Caribbean Rhapsody* which came into the Prince of Wales Theatre. John had been spending time backstage at the Prince of Wales on and off since coming out of prison, but the arrival of the all-black company gave him an extra incentive. Soon he had become friendly with one of the company's male leads, Wilbert Bradley, and persuaded him and some of the other dancers to pose for his camera. Throughout the run, John and Wilbert dined, drank and clubbed together with other Dunham stars, among them Eartha Kitt. Most evenings they ate at the Berengaria in Long Acre, where Kitt seemed to live entirely on ice cream.

* * *

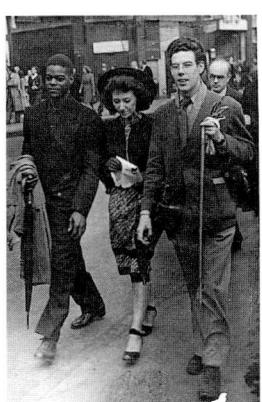

With dancers from the Katherine Dunham Company

Photography was growing from a hobby to a compulsion. John's attitude towards it was ambiguous: he realised that it offered him a living, but was unwilling to pay the price of being branded a homosexual pornographer, particularly in the chilly atmosphere of post-war England. He beavered away at his other, respectable projects, hoping for the lucky break that would take him from the sordid underworld that he saw looming at his feet. The break never came, and circumstances took him further and further down the path of least resistance.

In 1948 he met Dick Roberts, a wealthy collector of male nude photographs and keen amateur cameraman. Dick's handsome home in South Kensington was a convenient retreat where John was introduced to clients, models and some of his peers in the physique business.

26 AUGUST: Dinner at Dick's in South Kensington 7pm to 11pm. Philippino house boy in attendance. Splendid collection of very fine male nudes.

27 AUGUST: Meet Wilbert 10pm. Go queer clubbing – he impresses more than he's impressed. Spend early hours taking photos of him in nude dance poses, single photo-flood.

4 OCTOBER: Dinner with Dick. Show him my recent pix of Wilbert, Sonny, Vanoye, John D. He's impressed and rightly so. His prints are much better than mine, but my models and compositions are better. Already I'm convinced the model in photography is more important than photographer, camera, darkroom.

25 OCTOBER: Wayne RN 5.30 'audition'. Very acceptable lunch time discovery in Leicester Square. Take him to see Dick Roberts for dinner and photo session. Dick pleased. Wayne pleased and stays with D.

13 NOVEMBER: 2-6pm photography, Cris MN 19, Douglas RN

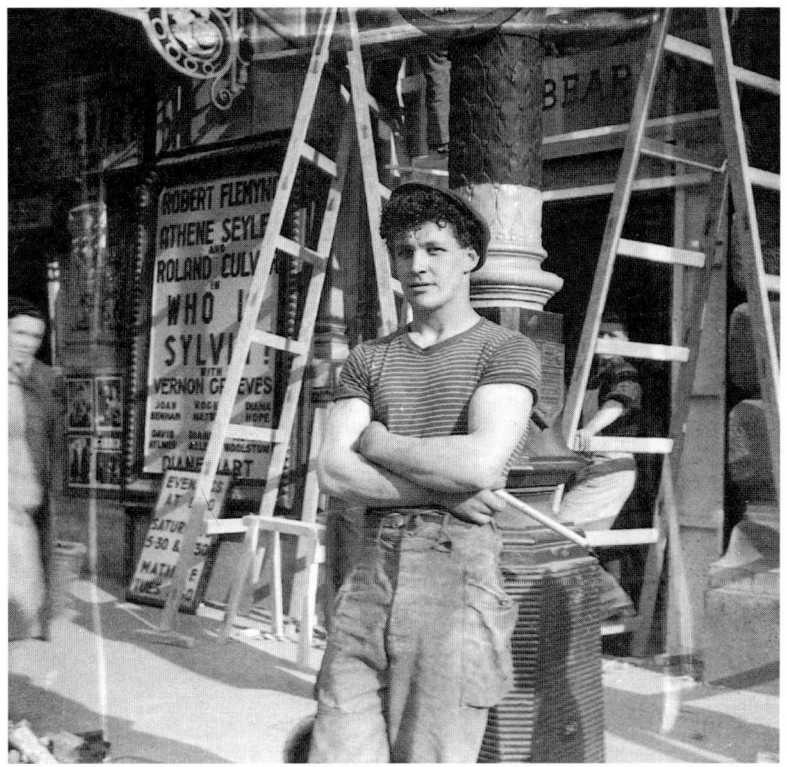

The streets of the West End were full of potential models

20. Lovely afternoon and very cheap – £9 between the two!

20 JANUARY: Put ads in three Compton Street shops for photo sets.

26 JANUARY: Buy second-hand enlarger after lunch, helped by Dick. Then to Bermondsey Baths for giggles with Lucky and John F, Soho pub crawl till 11pm. Wish I had a big central London flat to accommodate all these ships in the night.

5 MARCH: Photo sales building. Income very useful. Today is an excellent example: £14 by post from adverts in Compton Street.

8 MARCH: Register business names LENSART London and
ARTPIX London. 7pm hire big professional Holborn studio
with photographer Norman Larkin to shoot Jack Cooper as
Michaelangelo's David, Christ and Slave. Wonderful two-hour
sitting.

11 MARCH: Quality Inn lunch 12.30-1.45. Photo customers.
Also 5.30. Three more good sales. 'Lucky' RN noon. Keep him
as decoration for customers to oggle. They obviously wish they
could buy him. Both want pix of Lucky when available. He
doesn't mind. Both are too timid to suggest taking him out for
a drink. Give Lucky a small commission on sales.

12 MARCH: Spend day retouching Jack prints, deep sepia, as
good as McBean at his best.

Business built fast through 1949. Without a West End
base, John met models and clients at a handful of favourite
restaurants: the Quality Inn in Leicester Square, the
Brasserie Universal in Piccadilly Circus, Peter Mario's in
Gerrard Street and the Berengaria in Long Acre. In April he
compiled an album of sample photographs which he would
show to clients over lunch or tea. The adverts in Old Compton
Street were soon supplemented by announcements in *Sun
and Health*, *Health and Strength* and *Health and Efficiency*,
all part of the post-War boom in nudist titles. John's advert
began 'Designed for Aesthetic and Anatomical Reference by
Students of Art and Photography'. Income jumped from £31
in March to £75 in April as clients poured in; some of them
are named in the diaries for years to come. In May, he sent
out a circular to his best clients, apprising them of new
material and warning them that he planned to be out of the
country during the summer. At his busiest times, he was
auditioning or photographing two models a day.
    John was lucky. He had stumbled upon a market that was
not being exploited, and which was still almost totally under-
ground. A handful of other photographers in Britain,

America and Europe (Vince in London, Arax in Paris, Lon Hanagan in New York and Bob Mizer in California) were catering for a market that expanded in the 50s, then exploded in the 60s and 70s. But most gay men in 1949 were isolated, cut off from each other and from any material that reflected their desires. John saw that there was a growing demand; he also recognised that his clients, secretive and ashamed as many of them were, could be treated with less respect than mainstream business would ever have dared. While his photographs improved in quality, he regularly provided his clients with second-rate prints, misleadingly advertised and delivered late.

Most of John's material from this postwar period has been lost. A few prints remain (notably of the Jack Cooper-Michaelangelo session, styled by John but shot by Norman Larkin) but the negatives have been destroyed or turned to dust. In the early 50s, when he accepted the fact that male nude photography was going to be his principal source of income, he started to take better care of his negatives; what remains of his 40s work, and the descriptions in the diaries, give tantalising glimpses of a unique collection.

Such was the sudden success of John's camera work that when he visited Paris in June 1949, he found himself welcomed as an established artist. He had not been out of the UK since 1939, and after all the disappointments of the *Calling London!* fiasco and his imprisonment, was desperate to get away. Presumably with the blessing of HM Customs and Excise, whom he still owed a great deal of money, he took the boat train from Victoria on 17 June for a three-week holiday.

He found postwar Paris duller than the city he had first explored in the 30s, but full of new charms. Theatrical friends welcomed him as a guest at their shows, and he found comfortable accommodation in the Hotel Royal Pigalle, overlooking Place Pigalle, his Paris home for the next two decades. He visited Arax, the French physique photographer who specialised in athletes, boxers, bodybuilders and gym-

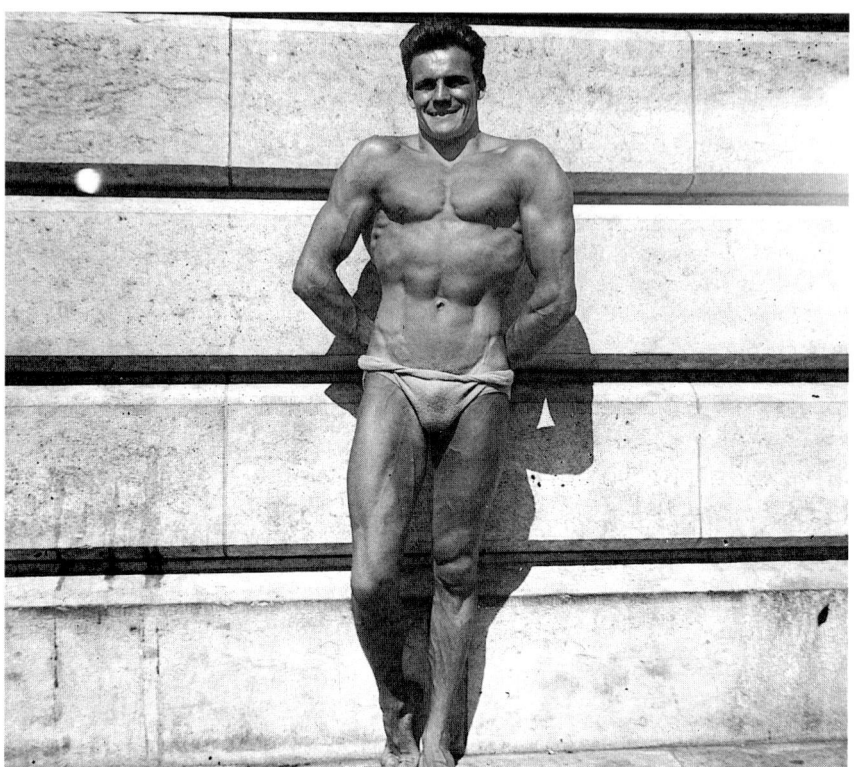

Jacques Pannier, John's guide to postwar Paris, June 1949

nasts. Arax introduced him to his two favourite models, Jean Merlier and Robert Duranton, already Mr Paris and Mr France and soon to become Mr Universe and Mr Europe. John took a dozen photographs, and made a date with another young Arax model, Jacques Pannier, who became his companion and translator during the rest of his stay.

With Jacques in tow, John visited Jean Cocteau in his Palais Royal apartment the following day. Attired in bowtie, monocle and malacca cane, with the decorative Jacques at his side, John attempted to chat to Cocteau about cinema and art. The interview soon deteriorated when Cocteau asked Jacques to strip, which he obligingly did. John then told Cocteau that he had photographed hundreds of other young men, at which point Cocteau got out his private 'refer-

ence' albums – full of photographs of boys kissing
and masturbating – which
he used for his erotic
drawings. John offered to
supply Cocteau with fur-
ther pictures, including the
ones he planned to take of
Jacques. When he revisited
Cocteau, again with an
attractive model, Edmond,
at his side, Cocteau insisted
on addressing John as
'Maître'.

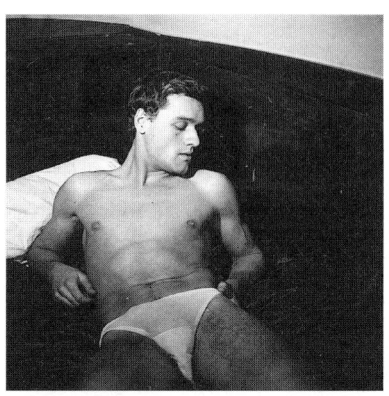

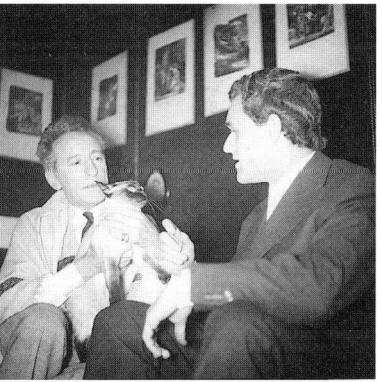

On my last visit he said,
'Maître, you are the most
magnificent photograph-
er of the male nude, I
want you to do me a spe-
cial favour. Take a photograph of me.' I thought,
'This is ridiculous, I can't
photograph Cocteau
nude.' His eyes were
twinkling, and he said,
'Avec mon chat nu.' So I
have a photograph of a
fully dressed Cocteau
and his nude cat.

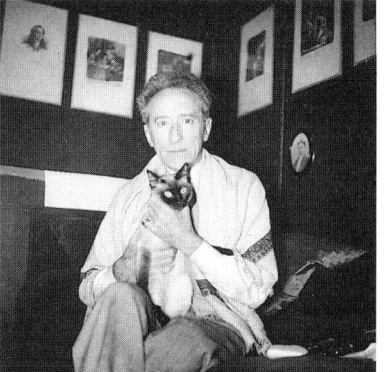

*John took his new Parisian model
Edmond (top) to visit Cocteau and his
'naked cat' in 1949*

John made another significant contact in Paris, 1949. While photographing Jean Merlier and Robert Duranton at a left-bank gym, he met a 19-year-old bodybuilder named Marcel James, who agreed to a private sitting at the Hotel Royal Pigalle the next day. James, as well as proving a co-operative model, became one of John's major international business associates when his photography operation expanded in the 50s and 60s.

* * *

If John's left-hand activities of taking and selling photographs had come on in leaps and bounds since his release from prison, his 'legitimate' career was faring less well. Since his unsuccessful VD drama *Grim Harvest* he had written two plays – *Laughing Parrot*, a screenplay which he intended as a star vehicle for Maxwell Reed, and *Horror!*, a melodramatic exploration of his interest in the paranormal (with predictable homosexual overtones). All he needed, as he kept bewailing to his diary, was a wealthy backer.

The day after his return from Paris he had a busy day of appointments with clients who were eager to see his new French pictures. Among these was a young architect called Nigel Westfield, a regular collector with family money who mentioned that he was keen to take up nude photography and publishing himself. It was all the encouragement that John needed. Within days, he was cultivating Westfield as his long-awaited patron, taking models to his Kensington apartment and trying to teach the nervous neophyte how to control himself with a naked young man in the room. For the rest of the summer, a steady stream of models picked up in the West End were making the journey to Redcliffe Gardens to pose for John and his new pupil. A delighted Westfield elaborated his plans to become an angel: he would produce *Horror!*, he announced, and would publish the wartime novel *Out of Sickness* and further titles.

By September, Nigel was bringing his own alarmingly young boyfriends home and asking John to photograph them.

'Warn him strongly about lads under 18' he wrote in the diary – hypocritically, as he had regularly photographed models as young as 16, if they met his criteria. Pretty boys notwithstanding, Westfield was as good as his word on *Horror!* and invested £1,000 of his own money to book the Chepstow Theatre in Notting Hill pending a West End transfer. A cast was found, and rehearsals commenced. *Horror!* was a strange play, recounting with full melodrama the tale of Sir William Fletcher, a middle-aged financier, who uses a medium to bring back the ghost of his dead protégé Peter. The final scene called for an elaborate theatrical effect, whereby the old man, in the grip of death, transformed into a living skeleton on stage. This was achieved with make-up, which the actor had to apply while ducking behind the sofa, and with the use of luminous face paint which only became visible when the lights changed.

Beautifully printed invitations and press releases were sent out to potentially interested parties announcing *Horror!... A Tragedy* 'produced and directed by John S Barrington'. 'Though the cast is fully signed and now in rehearsal we do not intend at this time to publish their names or the name of the author since all that we wish you to know is that though the play will most emphatically shock you, you will remember it for many years.' An article in the *Middlesex Independent* in November described the producer/ director as 'a novelist, film journalist and former set designer for the *Folies Bergère* in Paris'. Further pieces appeared in the *Daily Mirror*, *Sunday Dispatch*, *What's On*, *The Cinema Studio* and even *Psychic News*.

Rehearsals were going well, John's brother Michael had agreed to act as stage manager, when disaster struck – just as it had during the run-up to *Calling London!*, with depressingly similar results.

26 OCTOBER: Another long day. Start at 9am in West End, work in town till 6pm, over to Nigel's by 7. Talk over details. Leave at 10.10pm. Tube from Earls Court to Leicester Square,

then to Tufnell Park. Mislay ticket. Pay ticket collector, get a
receipt. Leave station at 11.10pm. Cross over to Dartmouth
Park Hill and walk rapidly up to bridge. Half-running foot-
steps behind me. A hand on my shoulder. 'Hey, stop, you
queer!'

Two men in civilian clothes identify themselves as plain
clothes policeman and tell me I am under arrest for importuning men in the public urinal outside Tufnell Park Station from
10.30pm to 11.10pm.

John was taken by car to his home in Brookfield Park
where the police made a search of his room, agreeing not to
disturb his sleeping parents. They found nothing: all evidence of his queer life was elsewhere. At the station, he was
booked with importuning for an immoral purpose and spent
the night in a cold cell. At 10am in Clerkenwell Magistrates'
Court he was charged, pleaded not guilty and granted bail.
Nigel calmed him down over lunch and persuaded him that
the show must go on, but for the rest of the rehearsals John's
delight at finally reaching the stage was tempered by anxiety
over his impending case.

Horror! opened as planned, and, thanks to a well organised publicity campaign, was widely reviewed. The pro-
gramme announced the author as 'John Esbeigh' (an occasional pseudonym, Esbeigh = SB). The critics were far from
delighted. 'Horror – but nobody shrieked' began one, going on
to report that 'the author ... unwisely made a curtain speech
and said that the play might get better later.' Another review
mentioned that the spectacular transformation climax, much
hyped in pre-publicity, had fallen flat because the violet-ray
spotlamps failed. The play completed its run, but the longed-
for West End transfer remained a dream.

On 31 December, after several adjournments, John's case
finally came up at Clerkenwell Magistrates. The result was
bizarre and unexpected: he was found guilty, and sent to
Brixton Prison for seven days pending a psychiatric report. He
spent the New Year, and began the new decade, back in jail.

For a week he brooded over the injustice of his lot: for all his many 'crimes' at this time when homosexual activity was illegal and often punished, he had never used public toilets for the purpose of meeting sex partners. On 6 January he returned to court, was fined £35.15s and released at 11am.

Within a couple of days he was back at work on a new project for Westfield – *Art and Anatomy*. John worked quickly, choosing the pictures and roughing out the text by the end of the month. Published in 1951, *Art and Anatomy* was a peculiar mishmash of learned text, drawings and photographs of the male and female nude. In the foreword, he wrote:

> You have here in your hands a reference work second only to the (impossible) possession of fifty exceptional models, always 'on tap', never tiring, interchangeable, ever-willing, carefully chosen for their variety – perfect examples of their anatomical types.

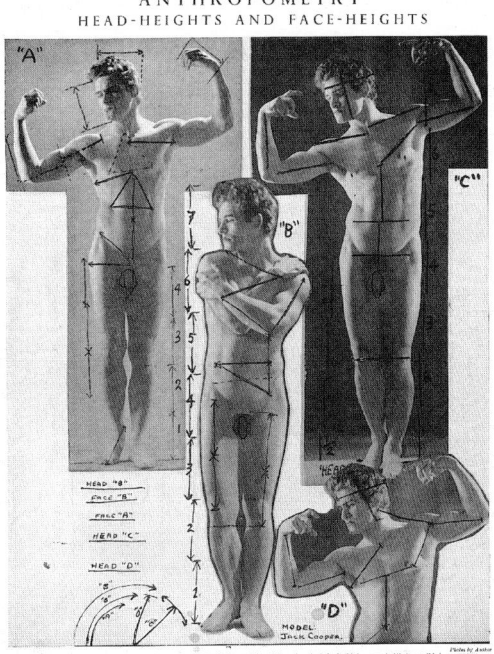

ANTHROPOMETRY
HEAD-HEIGHTS AND FACE-HEIGHTS

This model and Nigel Kishawi are the nearest to ideal proportions I have found—I don't think nearer in life is possible!

48

A long essay on proportion was illustrated by John's sketches, a chapter on anatomy was accompanied by Westfield's precise line drawings of bone and muscle. And finally, after all this, came the photographs. The female nudes, at the back of the book, were typical cheesecake glamour shots with no pubic hair, supplied by the photographers John A Owen and Douglas Webb. But the emphasis was firmly on the male. As well as John's photos there were pictures by Arax, Lon Hanagan, Athletic Model Guild, Norman Larkin and even Angus McBean (nudes of David Dulak and Donald). *Art and Anatomy* contains many examples of John's 40s work – domestic shots in Paris hotels and London flats, posed sessions in makeshift studios. The genitals in every photograph were obscured or erased.

With *Out of Sickness* and *Art and Anatomy* ready to be printed, it only remained for Westfield to sort out the business details and raise the cash from his various trust funds. John was delighted, so much so that he agreed to move into the house that Westfield had found on Ferdinand Street, Chalk Farm. It was the first time he had really moved out of his parents' home, apart from a few brief periods in the early 40s. With this new freedom, John, nearly 30, embarked on a furious search for love.

* * *

On a spring evening in Leicester Square, John met a young guardsman named Terry. After dinner in the Brasserie Universal, he was sufficiently interested in the intelligent, handsome, six-foot blond to write in his diary 'TERRY – I might fall!' Over the next few days, they were inseparable, spending nights at Ferdinand Street and days in the West End. A few weeks later, John resumed an affair with another of his seemingly unending supply of occasional forces boyfriends, and on 31 May met another young man at the Universal, Eric – '19, olive-skinned, very Spanish/Greek looking, near black curly hair, robust physique'. On 3 June he announced to the diary 'Who am I in love with today? ERIC!!!'

With Westfield and his latest discovery, John and Eric set off on a disastrous tour of France and Italy. The boys shopped up a storm while John and Westfield fretted over the budget all the way to Venice, where they looked in on the film festival. While John ran around trying to improve his acquaintance with stars and directors, Westfield was increasingly prone to drunken scenes and ugly scrapes with young Italians. The trip ended badly: John was mugged by two young boatmen he had picked up in Ventimiglia and taken out to a deserted clifftop for some open air photography and 'giggles'. They stole his jewelry and money; what they forgot to take was his camera, and the film it contained. When he developed it at home in London, it contained pictures of his assailants, naked in a rowboat, an hour before the attack.

They got home to find bound copies of *Out of Sickness* awaiting them, followed at the end of the year by *Art and Anatomy*. But by then author and publisher were arguing constantly, each leading an over-active sex life and accusing the other of irresponsibility and immorality. John was taking too much benzedrine, had his hair permed into tight curls ('I like it and so does everyone else!') and developed a taste for passive anal sex ('After all these years of saying no!'). Westfield was suffering a string of blackmail attempts and visits from irate fathers.

A week before *Art and Anatomy* appeared in the shops, Westfield 'sacked' John from the company, leaving him without the means to exploit his recent publications. Shamed and depressed by the whole episode, he moved out of the Ferdinand Street flat and took a room in Rowton House, Arlington Street, Camden Town – the famous doss-house. For the first time in his life he couldn't run back to the security of his family: Grace and Franz had sold the house and moved to Strobl, the Engljähringer family home in Austria, where they opened a small hotel.

2 MAY: My mother would faint if she knew where I was. The room is half the size of a prison cell, and not so clean. 800 men

live here. Could be interesting. Festival of Britain starts tomorrow. Can't find a place to store all my things.

7 MAY: Danny Kaye opens at London Palladium. Met DK, Bob Hope, Bette Davis, Judy Garland at party. From 3am to 6am at Corner House. Back to Rowton House in dinner jacket etc causing a minor sensation. I like contrasts, so I can't grumble.

9 MAY: Panzetta's bookshop in Charing Cross Road have a big window display of *Art and Anatomy* today! Another ambition realised.

12 MAY: After waiting three hours in queue, obtained £2.5s from the National Assistance Board. Humiliating.

The picturesque squalor of the doss-house soon lost its novelty, and John found himself better digs and a job (the first and only 'straight' paid job he ever had) at Autocheques Ltd in Regent Street, helping organise customers' holidays. Of course, it didn't last for long. 'I pity the wage slaves of the world!' he noted in the diary. 'I must leave this daily grind soon.' He stuck it out till August, then handed in his notice

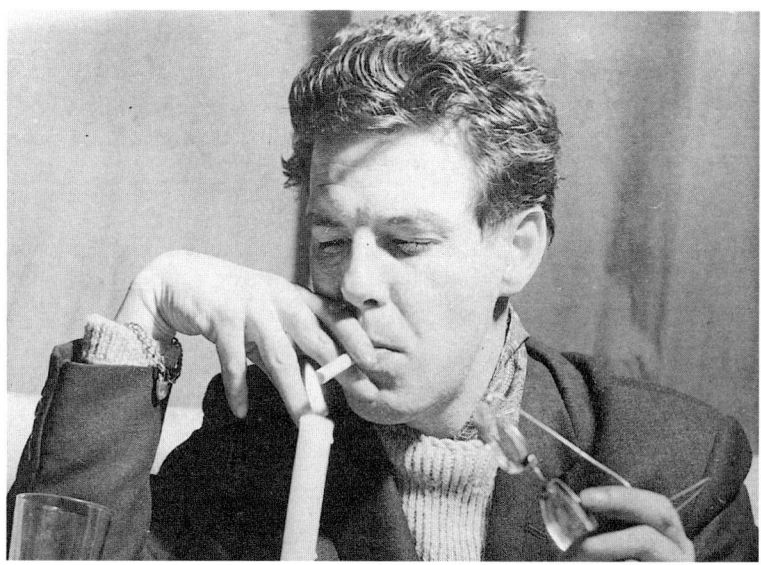

and rustled up as much money from friends and clients as he could. He pawned everything he wouldn't need for the next three months and booked reservations by train to Paris and thence to Austria. In August he was back on the boat train from Victoria.

One of the guests at his parents' hotel was a friend of Grace's, the Countess Ruby de Fleury, a colourful, heavy-drinking woman who took to John immediately. Travelling to Salzburg, John and Countess Ruby stopped off at a restaurant high above the city, ate lunch and drank a good deal of wine. During the drunken conversation that followed, Ruby informed him that Franz was not his real father. Pressed for further explanations of this bombshell, she changed the subject.

> The next day over lunch with Franz, I mentioned what Ruby had told me. He just said that I was bound to find out sooner or later, that I was not to tell Grace before I left, that I should leave the discussion for some other time. All I needed to know was that he had always loved me as a son, done his best for me, was proud of me and Michael, who was his real son. Perhaps, he said, one day Grace would tell me who my father really was, how and where I had been conceived. But Franz didn't know, had never asked, didn't want to know and hoped I wouldn't hurt Grace by asking her at the wrong time. Franz first met me aged two, when Dolly brought me back to the Willows. I decided that was enough for one afternoon. I left two days later.

The news of his parentage had no immediate effect; from Strobl he travelled to Innsbruck, and found what consolation he may have needed in the arms of a 19-year-old ski instructor named Gustav.

For the next few months, John travelled around Europe with his camera. He returned to London at the end of October, took rooms in Mornington Crescent and installed as flatmate his latest discovery, Ron, a merchant seaman turned art student. With the material that he had collected in Europe, John revitalised the photographic business: he had the pictures, and all he needed now was space and equipment with which to exploit them. Financially solvent for the first time in months, he got all his belongings out of hock or storage and looked about for suitable accommodation. Dick Roberts put him in touch with a rich young man who had just taken possession of a grand second-floor flat in Hyde Park Gate, overlooking the park, with a spare room for rent. John moved in almost immediately and spent Christmas Day 1951 fixing up a darkroom in one of the box rooms.

With his immediate financial problems out of the way and with a pleasant central London home, John redoubled his efforts to find himself a lover. Conscious that he had reached the age of 31 without having enjoyed a permanent relationship of any kind, let alone a *grande passion*, he started casting about for a suitable candidate with feverish determination. Terry, the ex-guardsman, proved too skittish for his needs, and too prone to run off with other (and richer) queers. What he wanted was a 'normal, healthy' straight young man, who had no interest at all in other men and who lived up to his by-now exacting criteria of male physical beauty. This person he would educate and mould, would introduce into a new world of sexual and cultural pleasures, and the beloved in return would be his muse, model and sexual partner. It was a doomed search: he clouded the issue with endless screeds in his diary about the nobility of friendship and the 'naturalness' of two men enjoying each other physically, but he could not face the unpleasant fact that the normal, healthy young paragon would be only too aware that John was a gay man in search of love.

For the first few months of 1952, John alternated his affections between Terry and Pam, his new £5-a-week assistant. Neither was a satisfactory lover; Terry kept disappearing, and Pam became too demanding and possessive. Models were 'auditioning' and being photographed at the Hyde Park

Gate flat more and more regularly, but John was neither happy nor satisfied.

Then on the evening of 25 March, strolling down Coventry Street with Pam after the pubs had shut, he caught the eye of a handsome young man in uniform. He wrote about the meeting in his next work of fiction.

> John and Pamela got off the bus at Piccadilly Circus. They crossed, arm in arm, through the crowds until they reached the front of the Pavilion Cinema, 'the Centre of the World'. Under its neon-lit canopy John came face to face with a tall young paratrooper, red beret askew. He too had a girl on his arm. Five long seconds passed as the crowds held the four immobile.
>
> They broke apart. Pam and John walked ten yards down Coventry Street. The paratrooper and his girl walked to the steps that led down into the Underground. John wheeled round and left Pamela standing still. He pushed back through those twenty crowded yards to touch the khaki elbow. The young man stopped and turned, one foot on one step, the other still on the pavement. The girl was already two steps further down. But she too turned, intuitively.
>
> People brushed past as the soldier grinned up at John. A threatening grin. But perfect teeth and dark eyebrows that met over hard eyes.
>
> 'Excuse me. Here is my card. How long are you on leave, may I ask?'
>
> The young man took the card but didn't look at it. 'A few more days.' The grin was half puzzled, suspicious but very polite. And very attractive, thought John.
>
> 'Do you live in London?'
>
> 'Yes. Why?'
>
> 'Well, it's a bit awkward to explain here. I very much want to see you again. For professional reasons. Please phone me any morning before noon. Soon as possible! It will probably be very much worth your while.'
>
> 'Maybe. I'll see. Thanks. Goodnight, mate.' He turned and was swallowed up in the downward tunnel.

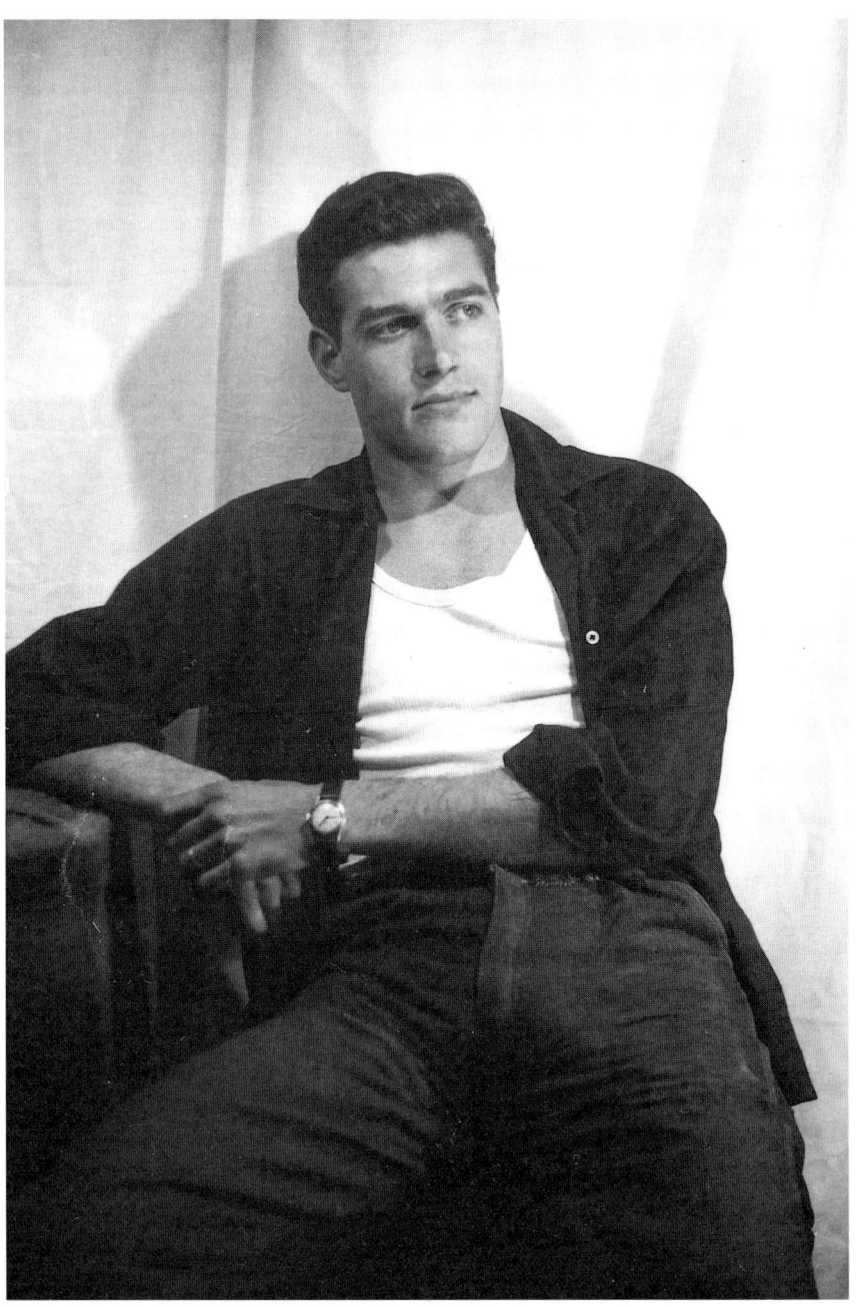

The greatest love: Peter, 1952

Chapter Four
'Dear Peter...'

When John was working on his autobiography in the 80s, he re-read his privately published novel *Dear Peter...*, a sensational but revealing portrait of the artist as lover.

> Although I can still agree with things I wrote, the actual character of Peter, the reality of the man, the human being that breathed in my company, that made me so unhappy and so ecstatically happy, doesn't exist. I've no recall of any kind of Peter. Just occasionally I have flash memories of him, and over the last couple of months I've had dreams about Peter – erotic dreams. I can't see him in reality. If I want to see him I have to look at a photograph.

John made a number of photographs and drawings of Peter, with his dark eyebrows, hooded eyes, large mouth and tough, masculine jawline. He is just the Barrington type, perhaps the one who epitomises above all others the qualities of butchness and availability that made John's models so popular.

The courtship was long and full of frustrations. For once, John was genuinely affected by his feelings, even though he never stopped taking pleasure wherever he found it. What follows is an account from various sources, some fiction, some diaries, of his first full-scale romance.

> The phone rang at 9.30am.
> 'Mr John Barrington, please.' The voice firm, young and unmistakable.
> 'Speaking.'
> 'This is Peter.'
> 'Peter who?'
> 'Paratrooper. You know. You gave me a card.' Of course John knew.
> 'I give away twenty or thirty cards a week. When did we meet? Where?'
> 'Night before last. Piccadilly Circus. I was with a girl. So were you. You said you...'
> Then John laughed and became his most charming. Soon it was established that the paratrooper was due back at the Bedford camp on Friday morning. There was only today and tomorrow in which to meet and talk. John explained who he was, what he did, how he wanted Peter as a top model for his next book on anthropometry. The word had to be explained.
> 'Sorry to have made such a mystery of it all' said John, 'but your girlfriend was looking daggers. Razor-edged ones.'
> 'Yep. She was pretty annoyed.'
> 'I can guess what she said. Did she?'
> 'She did, mate! But I told her I was old enough to look after myself. Well trained too. The paras don't fuck about, you know.'
> 'I do know, Peter.'

The young man crossed the square and entered the Quality Inn. He came to the table and shook John's hand, grinning. Very white teeth, very even. The eyes clear and friendly, the smile genuine, without threats. And he was punctual. It was just three twenty-five, March 27th, 1952. A Thursday.

Peter was not in uniform. He wore a well-pressed dark suit, a white shirt with double-cuffs, links, and a narrow Airborne tie – and he carried leather gloves. If he had dressed

for effect, Peter had succeeded in impressing – and further dis-
quieting the man. In daylight the paratrooper looked in every
respect better than the memory John had so often revived in
the last two days. Peter exceeded every expectation.

After a few preliminary questions and answers, Peter
agreed to come to John's flat for a spot of modelling.

The young man wandered around the large lounge admiring
books, drawings, photos, sculptures. The man was obviously
an authority on the male nude, and a copy of *Art and
Anatomy* on the coffee table proved he hadn't been giving the
paratrooper 'a line'. John was obviously what he said he was.

Without reminding or prompting, Peter surprised – even
shocked – John by casually undressing and unaffectedly wan-
dering around totally naked, modelling in uninhibited poses
the most perfectly proportioned, olive-skinned body John had
ever seen. With a whiskey and soda in one hand, Peter
allowed John to start posing him, touching him and measuring him with large and small wooden callipers, making notes
as he did so. They had talked as Peter posed, and at six
o'clock he got dressed, grinning a trifle sheepishly or, John
thought, perhaps teasingly. Part of their conversation went
rather like this:

'I've a fairly good idea of why you want me as a friend,
John, and the kind of friend you want me to be. First off, I'm
not another Terry, mate. I know all about him and his type,
that's for sure ... I'd like to be a friend of yours. Maybe we
could be pals. You said in the taxi you make quick decisions.
So do I, mate! I'll be your friend and a model for you, but I'll
be a straight model and a normal friend, John. See what I
mean?'

John agreed to keep the new friendship non-sexual, but
the way he wrote about Peter showed he was already
hooked. He dwelt on the erotic potentials of the relation
between the young model and the older artist, appreciative

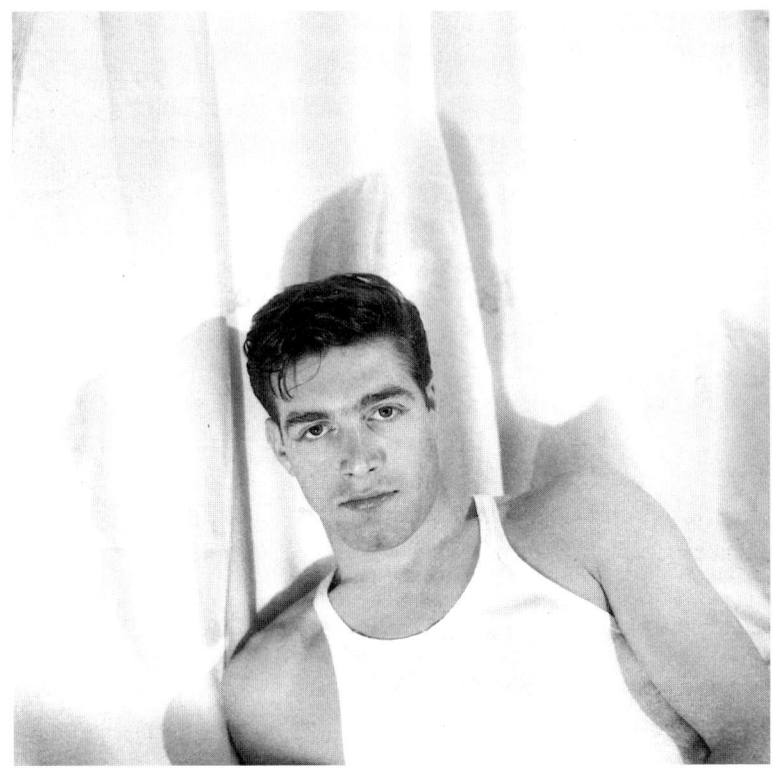

Peter poses for 'studies', 1952

but businesslike, recording and measuring his beauty. He
gave Peter the vernacular speech that he always ascribed to
the boys he fancied – the 'mates' and 'yeps' of his favourite
straight squaddie types. But how could John, the worldly-
wise sexual connoisseur, aesthete and jailbird fall so deeply
in love with a young man, however beautiful, on so short an
acquaintance? In fact, he was already in love with an ideal,
and Peter was the first person who embodied it. John decided without further ado that he was going to turn this relationship into a work of art. The reality of Peter, a simple,
ambitious soldier who was not interested in him sexually,
was not enough; he had to work it all up into high drama,
into fiction, into drawings and photographs – in order, perhaps, to persuade himself that he was feeling anything at all

other than the undisguised desire that he so feared.

The first step was correspondence. Shortly after Peter's visit to the flat, John wrote:

> I shall write to you very often. And I'll tell you why: not only will this future correspondence give me a great deal of pleasure, but it will also form the background of my next book – an idea that I have had in mind for some months, but one which I was unable to put into effect because I lacked the inspiration. However, last Thursday I found the inspiration I needed, so now I am all set to go! ... The name of my next book will be *Dear Peter...* It will comprise a collection of my letters and diary notes written to you during the next few months (I hope it will also include your replies... or is that asking too much?)

The rest of this long letter quotes authorities on friendship from Cicero to Wilde (via a great deal of Shakespeare, particularly the sonnets, much used by John in the 'persuasion' of young men). It finishes 'here ends the first 2,000 words of *Dear Peter...*, de tout coeur, John.'

The diary records a growing infatuation, as well as details of a still-active sex life that he omitted from his fictionalised account and certainly never mentioned to Peter.

> 29 MARCH: Am definitely head-over-heels! Maybe a little crazy too? Irish Bill 8pm to 11pm!!! No cause for frustration this week: Terry, Sheila, Leonard, Bill.
> 1 APRIL: Eight days to while away before leaving for Paris. I have completely fallen out of love with Terry, and I think he knows it too. Am instead head-over-heels with PETER, who promises to be a second Donald-experience. An ideal, *à la* Cocteau/Marais.

The longed-for reply finally arrived. Peter wrote in friendly, flirtatious tones; 'I don't think anything you say or write could bring about a delay in my answering your letters, or stop me from replying to them. It's what you might try to do that could bring an end to our friendship.' John wrote straight back, agreeing that they would be pals, nothing more, nothing less. Neither party could possibly have believed this for a moment.

> ... very much relieved to think and know that nothing I can say or write will damage this infant friendship. As to what I might try to do, on that ground I have no worries at all – and nor need you! For provided you always remember to say 'No!' three times you needn't think I'd ever risk so much for so little!

Enclosed with the letter was a copy of *Out of Sickness* – hardly guaranteed to convince the young paratrooper of the purity of the author's intentions.

Five days later John was off on his travels again, bound for Paris with Terry, selling photographs and brushing up celebrity acquaintances. The work was more successful than the play: within three days, Terry had abandoned him for richer admirers, and returned to the Hotel Royal only to pick up his suitcase and flaunt his new jewelry and shirts. John consoled himself by hobnobbing with Jean Marais and picking up Parisians before travelling south to Cannes, regretting that he'd left Peter for this fruitless escapade.

He got back to find a letter from Peter awaiting him. 'Since your bad luck with Terry in Paris, have you found anyone else to take his place,' asked the soldier, disingenuously, 'or are you leading a good clean and lonely life abroad?' Another letter arrived three days later.

> You may think me a little crazier than usual, writing and telephoning you on the same day, but I am quite forgetful, John, and there are so many things I want to say ... Yes, I think I want to see you again. Why? I – just – don't – know! Right, now, let's start.
>
> First, John, I want to write about us so far. As you say, we have only really seen and spoken to each other for about five

hours, but somehow I seem to read you a little better than most people I've known for months. I must admit that after that first day, as much as I enjoyed it, I meant never to see you again if I could possibly help it. I meant to write to you, but after the first couple of letters between us, would drop it ... Somehow things haven't worked out the way I intended them to, but I'm not sorry – yet I was a little afraid when Terry left you, because I was glad that you had other things to occupy your mind – and body. That is also why I was anxious to know if you had found anyone else to take his place, not as you thought, that Cupid's little stinger had slightly pierced my thick skin regarding you. I like you, John, but please understand this – that's as far as it goes from my end.

They were reunited in May. 'A very happy day and evening because at 3.30 PETER, paratrooper, arrives at Quality Inn. He is "ripening" splendidly,' John wrote in his diary. Peter returned to the army base at Bedford, fanning the flames with regular letters that he signed 'love as always, Pedro, X'.

I'd like to explain about the slight endearing phrases used in the last two or three previous letters. You said once that 'what was friendship but love?', and as you are a good friend of mine why shouldn't I put things like De Tout Coeur? Love as always, Peter.

During the summer John started work on a statue of Peter entitled *Airborne*, and sketched or photographed him whenever he could. The erotic overtones of their relationship were becoming more blatant.

19 AUGUST: Peter arrived at 7.30pm last night and left at 11.15 this morning! We had dinner, plus wines, at Corner House, walked and talked a lot. Back in my room we did a lot of platonic wrestling! A memorable night giving me much faith in our future friendship ... He modelled for some fine

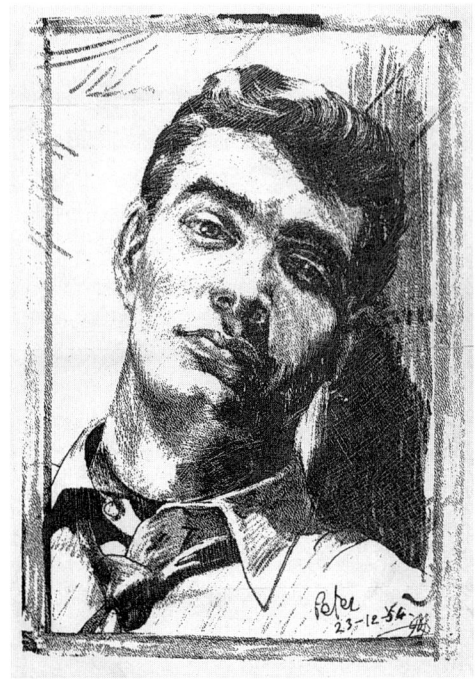

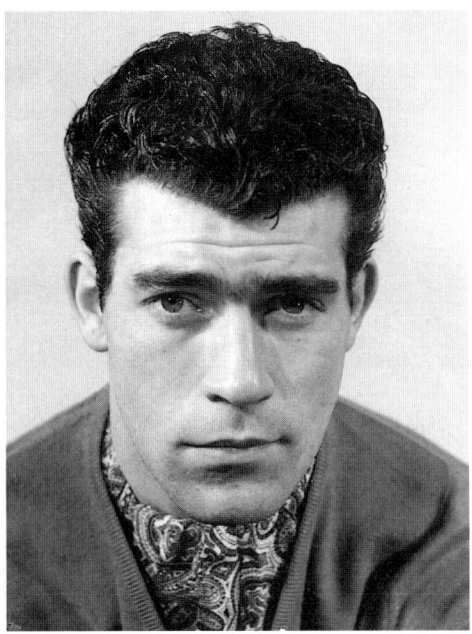

sketches, 'as long as you only look, John. Fill your eyes, mate, and dream what you like. Your dreams can't hurt me. You're welcome, pal!' So I do, and will treasure these pen and ink drawings forever.

Letters of increasing ardour passed between the two men while Peter was away; occasional meetings every few weeks brought them closer and closer to actual sexual contact. In *Dear Peter...*, John's preoccupation with the affair is total. The diaries tell a different story.

Work was keeping John busy – a hot summer had filled the streets of London with sparsely-clad young men who were easily tempted up to his flat and ended up in his expanding portfolio. Some of them were destined to feature in *Anthropometry for Artists*, his second book of nudes. Some of the models became regular visitors, filling in

Top: portrait of Peter by John.
Jimmie (right and opposite)
later made John godfather to his
children

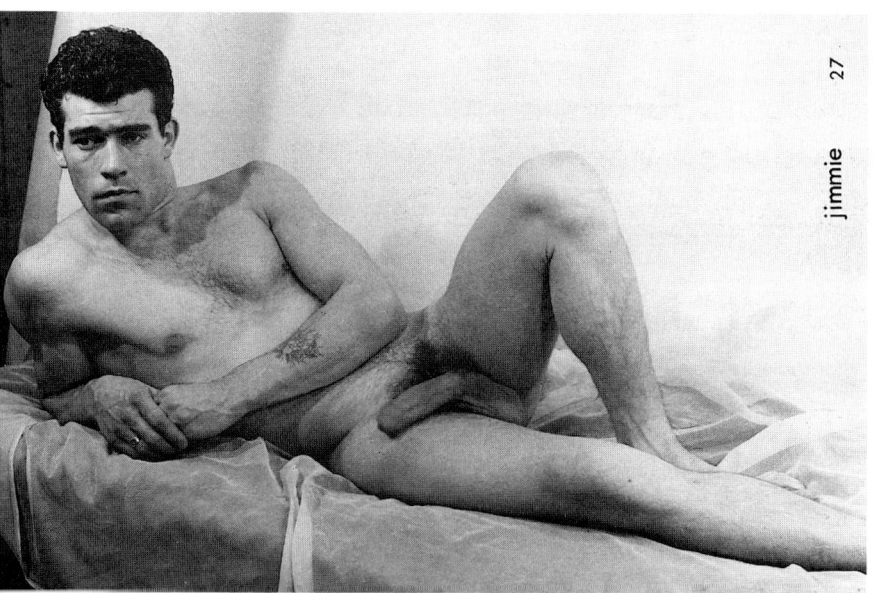

the time between visits from Peter, and helping John to cope
with the sexual frustration after he had left. Of the many
new names in the diary in the summer of 1952, one stands
out.

Jimmie Cranstone was an 18-year-old stagehand at Collins
Music Hall. Physically, he was another Barrington 'classic',
darker than Peter and more aggressively masculine-looking,
and, although straight, an enthusiastic model. His pictures,
taken over the next few years, were among John's most popular work. 'Would be much disturbed by Jimmie, were Peter
not always forefront in my mind,' he wrote. Jimmie was too
simple and straightforward; he did not appeal to the
Pygmalion in John, the part of him that loved to mould people to his own designs, relishing the resistance, the intellectual struggle that led to the physical surrender.

Just before Christmas, Peter visited London after a three-
month absence. John cooked him dinner in the flat, and
Peter opted to stay the night – on the spare divan, of course.
The following month Peter wrote to announce that he would
be out of the army within a week, much to John's delight.

'The big test now approaches!' he wrote, anticipating increased access to Peter and a speedy conclusion to the protracted seduction.

He invited Peter for dinner at his new flat on Putney Common ('On Queen's Ride! I like the name!) and spent the whole day buying and preparing food. After they had eaten he allowed Peter to read the manuscript of *Dear Peter*.... Peter was touched and impressed by the amount of time John had spent on him, and rewarded him with a friendly kiss before disappearing on the bus. Two weeks later, the invitation was repeated, and for John the game of cat and mouse was becoming almost too much to bear.

23 APRIL: From 6.30 to 11pm, Peter comes round to eat, read, drink, talk and model for me. This evening is so important in my life I must go into more detail. Laughter, talk, meal-cooking, drinking, eating, drinking again, the 'please can I get into something more comfortable on a hot night' from both of us, ending in towels round our waists at 9pm. The room candlelit, with two diffused table lamps. One over the bed where Peter reads the latest chapters of *Dear Peter*... I replenish his whisky straight. He gets up, naked, poses, stretches, moves around the room and then suddenly grabs me, pushing me to the floor in some expert unarmed combat tackle. I lie on my back, he naked on my chest. His knees painfully pin my outstretched arms as in a crucifixion. The record on the turntable has stopped. Total silence. Just his heavy breathing, his chest inhaling and expelling, his abdominals superbly hard and defined. I can count the hairs on his chest. His forehead perspires as he grins down at me.

The details of rising, drinking, looking at each other, the first words, I cannot now remember, though only a few hours ago. His grin I can never forget. I am enslaved and he knows it. Within the hour, we were back at the 22 bus terminal. When I attempted to get on with him, Peter stopped me. 'Go home,' he said. 'And don't write any more nonsense.'

I was just about to go back to Queen's Ride. Two local boys

stood by the bus terminus, just back from town. Nobby and Albert, both 20, both attractive, presentable, Cockney 'cheeky chappies' of medium height. I'd met them twice before in the George in Putney where they do a bit of weight training. 'So where do we go, mate?' asked Nobby, grinning. 'Coffee, or...?' I asked. 'Got anything 'arder?' said Albert. 'We 'ave!' said Nobby, laughing, poking his finger in my ribs.

Nobby and Albert left my room at just after 1am, having provided the orgasm Peter denied me, and with much less pain, each richer by 10s, agreeing to model for me soon.

The fictional account in *Dear Peter...* was a much more romantic affair. The two friends spend an evening at Lyons Corner House discussing life and love before Peter, sickening of the 'degenerate company', asks to return to the flat.

In the flat, now three in the morning, they undressed, drank a glass of cool milk each, and John turned back the covers of both divans. 'Don't bother with that one, John – we'll only need one.' They got into bed, they lay on their backs, finishing cigarettes. John turned out the light and the moonlight etched the room silver and black. Peter raised himself on an elbow, looking down at John. 'I hear your heart beating more loudly than my own,' he whispered. 'You're quoting, Peter.' 'Something from schooldays, a poem I copied from a book to give to a girl.' 'By Laurence Hope, *Indian Love Lyrics*.' 'That's it, Mr Encyclopaedia!' Then his head lowered. 'This is the knock-out, pet,' he said in John's ear. 'You mean you throw in the towel?' John whispered. 'No, it's a clean uppercut. I'm beaten. You can start counting me out.' Peter expelled the air from his lungs with a great sigh. His weight on John lay heavy, warm. He lay heavier and heavier.

The two spend the night in chaste sleep. The next morning John receives a telegram from Paris congratulating him on the first half of his novel *Dear Peter...*

* * *

The happiness that followed was short-lived. Peter stayed overnight at Queen's Ride more and more frequently; John, in return, lavished gifts on him: an electric razor one day, a gold chain the next. As spring turned to summer, Peter was visiting once a week to the satisfaction of both parties.

4 JUNE: Another perfect evening. I love him more than all the past put together; oh, past friends, please forgive me!

5 JUNE: Am so happy about last evening, so happy!

6 JUNE: I am ready, if asked – but only if asked – to become part of a mutual commitment with Peter. But he isn't, and will probably never ask; it would offend his estimation of himself, of course.

12 JUNE: Use my last cheque, overdrawing account, to buy Peter two shirts (£4) and a new toothbrush. His teeth are so perfect, they must be kept at their best! Peter again decides to spend the night but without sexual embraces or even familiarities. He sleeps, I doze till 6am. Happy? Oh yes! Frustrated? Not at all.

14 JUNE: Billy, ex-RN, settled in as a very good 24-hour companion-helper since Friday night. Much Peter-tension relieved!!!

With money in his pocket from a publishing deal he had struck with a firm in Harrow, John presented Peter with two tickets for Paris in July. They booked into the Hotel Royal, and spent the days visiting John's favourite haunts. In the hotel room Peter posed for photographs and occasionally wrestled. But there was still no sex, and when Peter returned to England to do his annual ten days recall with his paratroop regiment in Norfolk, he left John confused and exhausted and, uncharacteristically, celibate.

When they met again in London, Peter announced that he'd been doing a bit of 'pussy penetration' just to prove to himself that he was 'still normal'. John was upset, 'eating badly, not enough, smoking much too heavily, masturbating

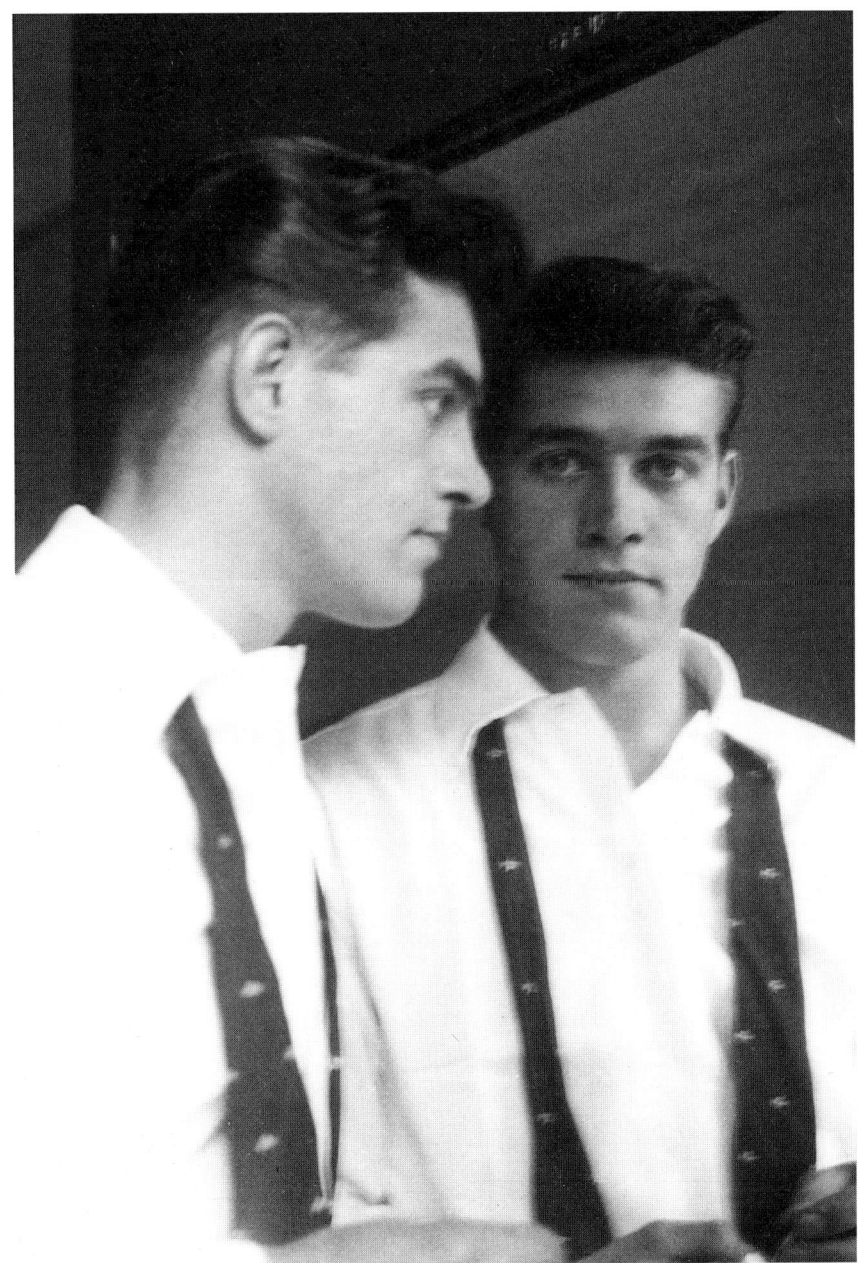

Peter in his RAF tie, Paris 1953. John loved mirror shots; nearly all his
models posed for them

too often'. He wanted Peter all to himself; the casual friendship with a straight man was no longer enough. In an unsent
letter, written as a diary note, he poured his heart out.

On Friday morning, when you left, I was so depressed by the
hopelessness of it all, of your cruelty and toughness of
Thursday night, of the great distance away from the fun and
laughter and affection of Paris and those nights at Queen's
Ride, that I just went to bed and cried (what an admission!)
till I slept exhausted. My first crying since 1941! All Friday
afternoon and evening I went among my friends putting your
case, trying through them to understand you ... to each I put
your side of the picture, arguing against myself ... To all those
friends, I couldn't find the rational reasons to excuse you, to
explain you; to them all you are just being plain bloody self-
ish, mean, unfriendly ... So Friday night I picked up three
very decent, fine-bodied sailors, as much like you with your
kind of background as I could estimate ... I brought them
home, made a big meal, lots of drinks and told them about the
same as I told my friends. And I defended you! The toughest
one, Sid, 6 foot 3 inches, wanted to give you 'a bloody good
hiding'. I got around to photographing these lads, and they
ended the night and saw in the dawn with all the sympathy
and friendship I so urgently needed! And as much for their
own pleasure, I assure you, as mine!

Conscious that he was never going to get the longed-for
commitment from Peter, John began to look around. He
wanted to settle down; at nearly 33, he feared becoming a
lonely, middle-aged man who had to pay for boys, even if he
called them 'models'. He wanted to let go of Peter but couldn't.
He was sexually obsessed by him, comparing all other lovers
and finding them lacking. Then a new strategy occurred to
him. Peter had admitted that he found their 'queer affair'
depressing and disturbing, and was openly distancing himself from a sexual relationship by sleeping with as many
women as possible. It was just as John had feared; as soon as

he allowed himself to become emotionally involved with a man, the relationship inevitably went wrong. He thought he could make himself more acceptable to Peter if he played down his homosexuality, and hit upon a bright idea that was to have unforeseen consequences.

> 29 SEPTEMBER: Depressed. An idea! Would Peter accept me more easily sexually and as a pal if I were more heterosexual? If I had a regular girl-bedmate, even one that he too fancied? Is my homosexual life, my dalliances since we met, a bit too much for him to accept? Could very well be. I'd find no difficulty in switching my casual interests to one or two nice girls – I know enough who'd be happy to accommodate me, after all.

It was another of John's habitual attempts to adjust reality to fit his schemes. This time he was creating a new role for himself, that of the bisexual lover who shared adventures with a male pal, who could compare notes on 'pussy penetration' in between bouts of husky man-to-man physical pleasure. Peter's noisy return to heterosexuality convinced John that it was a good plan. In November, Peter asked him for the loan of his room for the seduction of a girl; John obediently stayed out all afternoon, and on his return was introduced to Peter's girlfriend Anne.

> 14 NOVEMBER: She's a very nice, rather pretty-plain young woman. She thinks he shares the flat with me, noting the beds on each side of the room. What he's told her up to now I don't know. Sitting there watching them have tea I feel so much older. She's supposed to go back tonight.
> 15 NOVEMBER: Must stick to facts only! Anne and Peter still in flat, still in bed! She missed her train. Probably Peter made her? I tried to be jolly, broadminded and polite. She very much embarrassed, Peter thinking it all a huge joke! Got into my bed and switched off lights. For the first half hour I cried (stifled), but a new experience – dry tears. Oh what a debt he owes me now!

As John's relationship with Peter deteriorated to this humiliating pass, he saw the child of their recent past, the novel *Dear Peter...*, spurned and rejected by a series of publishers. Gollancz returned the manuscript with a curt letter of rejection; WH Allen were a little more polite (they felt they could not publish 'the story of the protracted seduction of a young man') but equally unhelpful. He decided to publish *Dear Peter...* himself as bound proofs, for sale to his trusty mail order clients who were already familiar with Peter from pictures.

The crisis was approaching. As 1953 drew to a close, John was constantly on tenterhooks, emotionally unstable, barely able to tolerate Peter's flagrant disregard of his affections. But he knew, too, that he'd got what he asked for; he longed to love a normal, straight young man, and now Peter was behaving exactly according to type. It was time for change, and John went about securing it with a reckless fatalism.

4 DECEMBER: 1pm Peter. His girlfriend not coming to London today after all. I wonder what he'd say if he knew that I can't get her out of my mind? I certainly do now wish that I could find a sweet girl. But would I like her and want her if Peter hadn't had her?

5 DECEMBER: Peter and Anne arrive midday. After an hour's chat I leave them to enjoy the room. Eat alone and go club crawling to places I've not been to for nine months. All rather too drab and queer.

8 DECEMBER: Letter arrives from Anne to Peter. After much mental debate I steam it open to discover she feels 'three's a crowd' – not at all surprised. But she also writes with a 'desperate love' for Peter.

11 DECEMBER: From 4pm to 11pm Dodo, my new mistress, and I amuse each other with something akin to abandon!!! Nice, an art student, a bit intellectual Bloomsbury, 5'1", excellent figure, uninhibited love-maker. She'll do.

14 DECEMBER: Meet Peter for lunch. Can't resist telling him about Dodo, but he won't believe a word of it. 'When I've had

her and watched you have her after, then I might believe you, mate,' is all he'll say before changing the subject. Spent the rest of the day with Mark, new model ... Dodo rings right in the middle of activity, so I talk sweet nothings with her while Mark does to me what she is incapable of doing.

17 DECEMBER: Mark poses for Dodo and I. His line and form captivated her, and she raved over his torso, fingering the muscles under his velvet bronze skin, and fascinated by his erect nipples. Nor did his hard-on embarrass her, tho' she wouldn't touch it.

18 DECEMBER: Peter arrives 2pm. We talk till 3pm when Dodo arrives. Peter says, 'Oh so you're the girl John's been raving about. The best sex in London, he says.' Dodo smiles wonderfully and says, 'If he says so, I suppose it must be true. Do tell me about yourself. John hasn't mentioned you at all!' When he leaves, Peter's handshake to me is the warmest two-handed grip he's ever given me.

23 DECEMBER: Lunch with Peter, now behaving inexcusably badly.

25 DECEMBER: Nice luncheon with my brother and his wife ... Peter didn't even send me fifty fags in an Xmas box!

30 DECEMBER: No mail from Peter, nor any from Dodo, neither sent late cards or New Year cards. I sent out over 80!

31 DECEMBER: Have photographed 43 young men in 1953, with many of whom there has been more than one sexual encounter. Some as many as ten times.

1 JANUARY: Have made a resolution – the obvious one – to recapture Peter!

6 JANUARY: Took a chance and phoned Peter, because there's a letter for him from Anne, two days old (he's also been neglecting her). Find him friendly and 'happy to hear your voice, John!' Says he's been much occupied with another female.

7 JANUARY: Meet P 1pm Quality Inn. His neglect of Anne makes the situation very drab. As to Anne, he says, 'She'll be okay. I'll write her nicely. I can write nice letters, John. You should know!'

9 JANUARY: Lord Montagu arrested. The whole of W1 is scared

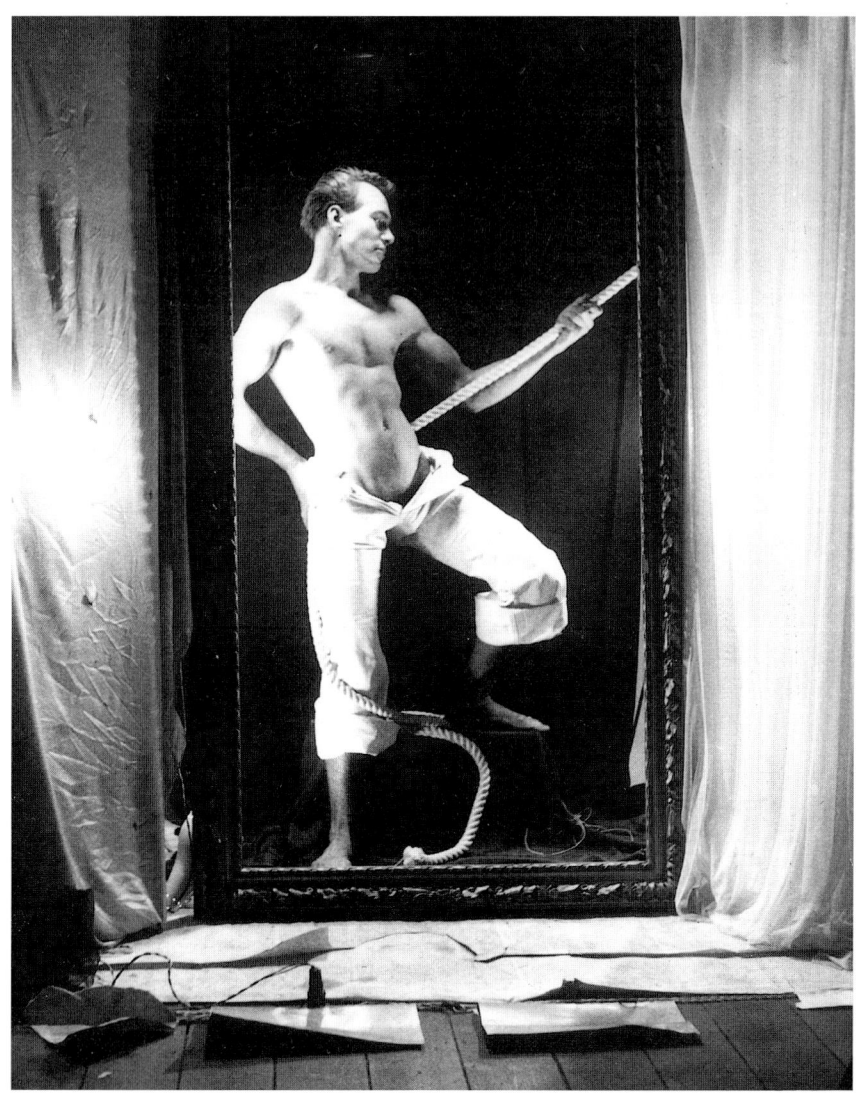

Merchant seaman Ron in a makeshift McBean-inspired studio devised by John, 1954

to death. Will now be the biggest case since Wilde's.

10 JANUARY: Peter arrived yesterday pm with Anne and they stayed till 4.30pm today. Ron also stayed the night!!!

3 MARCH: Peter for dinner in room at 7pm. Friendlier than he's been for months: is there still hope? He's on train at 11.15. Ron in when I get back to house. He's waiting for me in bed as I write this.

25 MARCH: Peter for dinner, he stays and poses too. When Ron comes in, I expect Peter to get dressed and go, but he just wraps my dressing gown around him and says, 'I think I'll stay if that's all right with you two love birds'. He's grinning his head off.

29 MARCH: Very polite notice from landlord to leave flat within two weeks.

10 APRIL: Find a nice room on Rosslyn Hill. Ron to move in with me.

What was Peter up to? He certainly saw John as a reliable source of money – he tapped him for cash and accepted all the presents offered. But there was more to it than that. With John's encouragement, he had decided to try his hand at professional modelling, and needed contacts and advice. And so they continued as friends for the rest of 1954, while John busily used his camera to make money. 1955 saw the final act of this strange relationship.

Anne had disappeared off the scene in the autumn, when a pregnancy scare sent Peter running for the hills, refusing to communicate with her even when she found it was a false alarm. John, however, was a better friend, and sent Anne a Christmas card. She replied with a short, friendly note in early January; John invited her to London.

29 JANUARY: Anne comes to town – her first visit in 12 months! Pleasant afternoon talking about ourselves, and Peter, inevitably. I enjoy her company, am surprised by how much.

30 JANUARY: Am flabbergasted! By 2am last night Anne and I were in bed together. I feel amazed and very young, very silly and very happy. Anne and I understand each other so well,

and our sentimental, physical and emotional rapport is complete. Hope it will last – this thing I've prayed for so long, this normal and healthy and jolly relationship with a girl. Walk together on the Heath hand in hand this afternoon. She leaves at 5pm and leaves my life very empty. But a complete solution of the Peter problem after two and a half years. I'm tentatively accepted as her future husband.

1 FEBRUARY: Peter takes the news in a rather jealous manner, and is more than a trifle coarse in his humour.

13 FEBRUARY: So much love last night and this morning. The decisions to be made exhaust me. A Jekyll and Hyde battle. Anne says repeatedly that she loves me.

19 FEBRUARY: A very old-fashioned day. Meet Dennis in Charing Cross Road. In evening, meet perfect model Tony, 24, boxer, ex-paratrooper, 12 stone, intelligent, co-operative, not sophisticated. 10pm meet Greg, blond, 18, very attractive and simpatico. And at 1am outside Belsize Park tube meet Ken, 6'2", 14 stone, so we spend till 2.30am in my room!!!

25 FEBRUARY: Took Peter and Anne to Casa Pepe, Dean Street, for dinner. All went in most civilised manner. I love Peter for behaving so well to Anne. And Anne loves him too, 'tis obvious. And Peter loves himself.

4 MARCH: Anne writes to say we'll leave things as they are for the time being – which means I've got a mistress rather than a fiancée. Much better! And so much more convenient especially re my private activities. Ron is back.

13 MARCH: Horoscope in paper reads 'Cut out your present hesitancy, Scorpio, and make a go of it!' Will do! I feel very much like marrying Anne. Will I ever find a better wife? Boy, you aren't as young as you once were, are you?

16 MARCH: Peter phones, all the old aches return. He's doing very well in modelling.

3 APRIL: Feel very eager to marry Anne. The only better hope would be the impossible one of 'marrying' Peter. But to marry Anne and have Peter as best friend, both for life, ah! But would Anne agree?

8 APRIL: Fly to Paris with Anne. 12.30pm to Hotel Royal

Pigalle, Room 12, the same I'd shared with Peter. A very sentimental night, undisturbed by the ghosts of others in chambre douze.

19 MAY: Peter tells me he is now attending cocktail parties at the Dorchester, film premieres at the Empire and receptions at the Strand Palace Hotel, plus girlfriend. Am glad he's working towards the world I always saw him in, but am also hurt that he is entering that glamour world without me. Now he's doing it with others. Which others? Queer ones most likely.

5 JUNE: See Anne off at Liverpool Street. 5pm to 10pm, Jimmie Cranstone. Could Jimmie become the next Peter? Not really. All the subtleties are missing. Take some fine studies of him today.

7 JUNE: Feel bad about being unfaithful to Anne last night, night before last and tonight. But had to. Will try to be faithful for the next week, unless very tempted.

19 JUNE: Anne and I have a wonderful weekend, stay in till 4.30pm making love.

John saw Anne nearly every weekend throughout the summer, filling in his weekdays with dozens of models, all carefully recorded in the diaries and in surviving photographs. Their affair, relatively carefree till now, began to get serious.

5 SEPTEMBER: A perfect 24 hours with Anne. I mean now to concentrate on reforming, socially, sexually, morally and financially. Will try to work harder, give up boys, especially layabouts. I will be faithful to Anne. Must find a flat and install her as a wife.

5 OCTOBER: Find a delightful two-room flat in Richmond. Pay deposit, to move in next week. Faced with prospect of living with me as my mistress, Anne has the quakes, so I offer to marry her as soon as she wishes – and may force her to do so. It would be the best thing for both of us.

12 OCTOBER: Move into new flat with Anne. Spend evening

decorating it, and it looks wonderful. Around a nice fire we sit on a nice sofa in a nice room after a nice meal cooked by Anne in a nice kitchen, open a nice bottle of wine and have a nice talk. Then at 9pm Anne proposes to me and I accept! We decide to marry on the 31st – Peter's birthday!

13 OCTOBER: Tell Jimmie about my engagement last night, after which we celebrate!!! No guilt feelings, just sadness that my life is swiftly splitting into two very separate parts which may never join again.

14 OCTOBER: Lunch with Peter. He takes my marriage plans very well, but won't agree to be best man.

18 OCTOBER: My new daily schedule: rise 9am, clean kitchen, leave house 11am. Town for lunch to meet folks and do business till 4pm. Home by 5pm. Make up coal fire, get in coal for the evening, peel spuds. Anne arrives sixish, we cook a meal and eat 7pm, wash up, sit in lounge and listen to radio till 10pm. Then I see her home to her room further up Richmond Hill, because she has decided not to sleep with me till after 31st!

26 OCTOBER: Meet Peter, 4pm, Quality Inn. Gives me £2 of £20 he owes me. Whatever was between us is, I fear, irrevocably gone. I really think he is wounded by me going so far with Anne.

28 OCTOBER: Mother sends money present for wedding.

30 OCTOBER: Last bachelor day. A lovely weekend with Anne in Richmond. 100% romantic.

31 OCTOBER: Peter doesn't turn up at Caxton Hall, so at 2.30pm I call in two strangers from the street to witness my marriage to Anne. Then a hand-in-hand walk past Buckingham Palace and down the Mall for tea at the Quality Inn. Manager and waitresses provide a nice wedding gateau and sincere good wishes. But where are all my friends? No matter.

Even in his wildest fictions, John could never have imagined that he would finish his relationship with Peter, the greatest love of his life, by marrying his discarded girlfriend.

Nor, perhaps, could either John, Anne, or Peter have imagined that the marriage would last for 35 years. He had escaped from the lonely middle age that awaited him. And it was just as well, because at the end of 1955 he needed all the love and support he could get. On 8 November, after little over a week of married life, John was arrested by a plain clothes police officer on 24 counts of sending obscene material through the post.

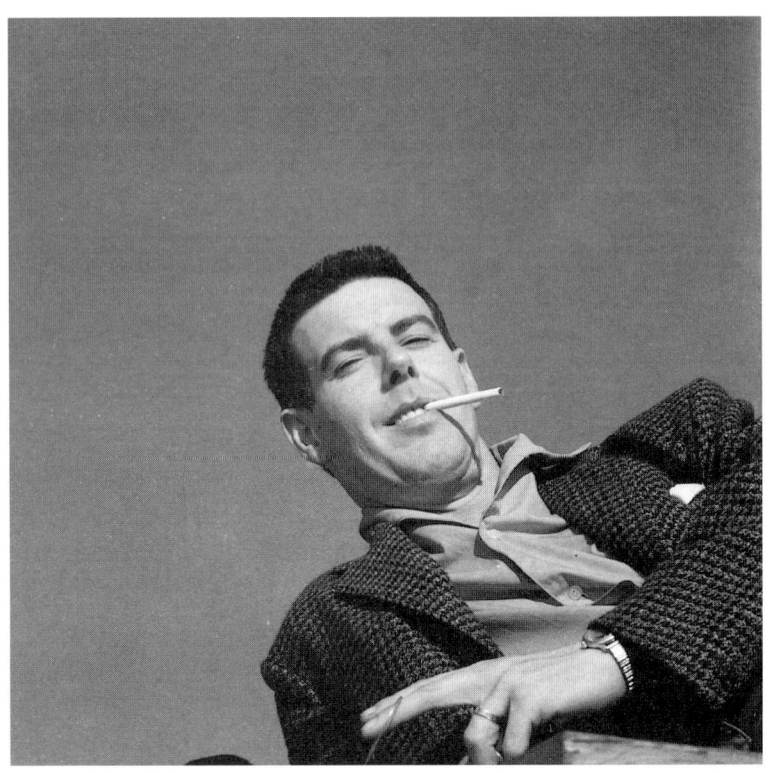

John with his Laurence Harvey crop, c 1960

DIARY NOTE 1990: For 350 nights each year for 30 years I have shared a midnight bath with my wife and we have both slept naked together. We made love (very approximately) 7,000 times, more than three times as often as I made love with men. How do I sexually define myself?

Book Two: Married

1955 – 1991

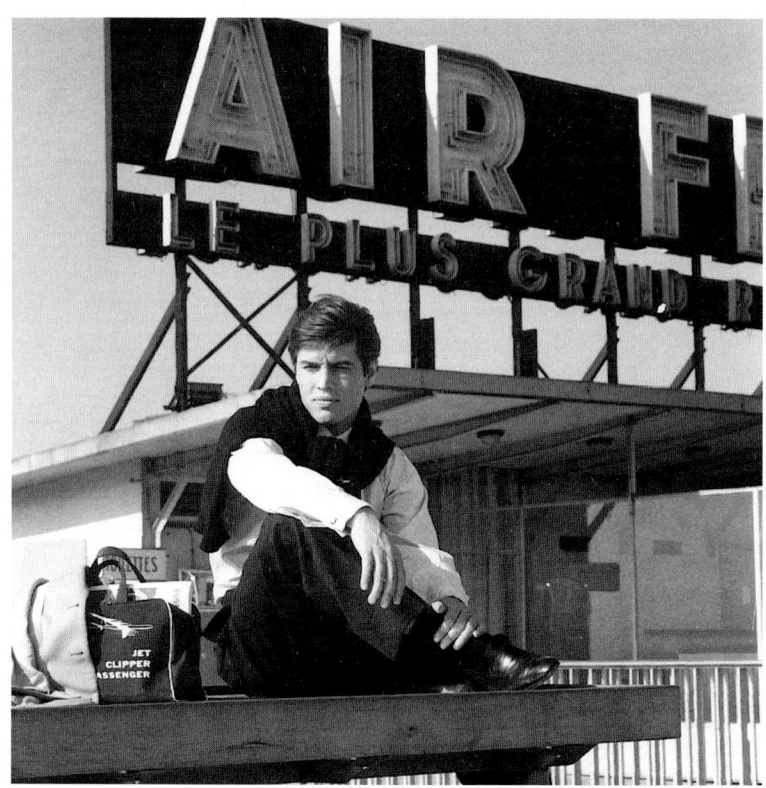

Giancarlo, John's favourite 50s model, at Nice airport

Chapter Five
To the Riviera

The CID had been preparing a case against John for some time. The climate in England had been one of growing hostility to homosexuality; the Montagu case proved that the tolerance that flourished in the war and its aftermath was over. John had been careless. As usual, he thought he was above the law. He had been sending out photographs left, right and centre without really knowing what his legal position was; he can hardly be blamed in this, as the whole area of pornography and postal regulations was even more muddy in the 50s than it is today. In 1956, he paid the price for his carelessness and learnt his lesson. In future, he would be much more secretive.

The police's interest in John's professional activities had begun as early as 1952, when he had received a summons to Bow Street Magistrates' Court to face charges of sending obscene photographs through the post. The case, postponed until January 1953, was mercifully brief. He opted to defend himself; luckily, the prosecution's case was shoddy and relied mostly on insults. The magistrate was sympathetic and dismissed the case; John took this as carte blanche to carry on regardless. He should have heeded the warning, but was too busy pursuing Peter to worry about it.

The coast was clear until 1955, when the police once again

visited his rooms in Rosslyn Hill, investigating photographs that had been sent to a customer in Swindon, Wiltshire. They took nothing, but asked to see him again in ten days' time while they made further investigations. At this time, John was running the business from an office on Tottenham Court Road – which the police didn't yet know about. Everything went quiet until April, when the hammer fell: John was served with a summons alleging the sending of indecent material through the post, the court appearance scheduled for May ('Will handle own defence, of course!' he wrote in the diary). The magistrate found him guilty and fined him £50 plus £5.5s costs or three months prison. His marriage plans were set back for a few more months, but the worst was over. There was very little publicity, the fine was small and John stayed out of jail.

But the police weren't satisfied. On 30 September they were back, and much more determined. A mail order client in the Midlands had been prosecuted over involvement with a teenage boy; during a search of his premises, the police had found pictures by John S Barrington with the painted-on slips scratched off, exposing the model's genitals. It was all they needed; they returned to Rosslyn Hill, ransacked the place more thoroughly and confiscated dozens of negatives. The summons served under the Obscene Publications Act 1857 itemised a 'list of property traced to John S Barrington

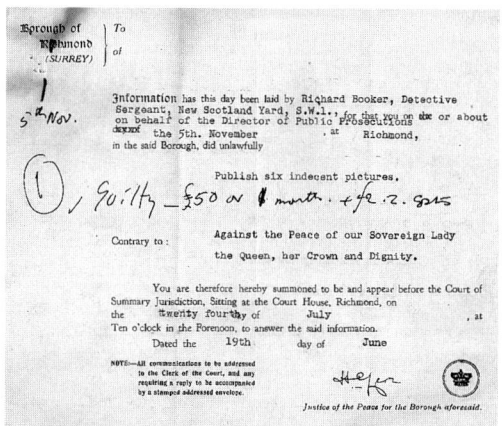

... for which a destruction order is sought'. Included were 'Book entitled "The 120 Days of Sodom"', 'Book entitled "The Rosy Crucifixion"', 'Sketch book contaning 8 drawings of males', 'Glass negatives of nude male', 'Indecent photograph of nude male' and, to cap it call, '1 Dill Doll'. As John and Anne prepared for their wedding, the CID were preparing their case.

He was arrested on 8 November 1955 and spent the night in Tottenham Court Road police station before being taken to Clerkenwell Magistrates' Court where he was granted bail. But he was unable to raise the necessary £200, and was transferred to Brixton prison. The following morning, Anne arrived with other friends to stand bail. John was out, but not for long. When the case finally came to court on 13 December, he found himself with inadequate defence and faced with a hostile judge who, in his summing up, became 'almost hysterical' before finding John guilty on all charges. The sentence: three months in prison and a fine to the company of £250.

John and Anne spent their first Christmas as man and wife miserably, knowing that their separation could not be postponed indefinitely. On the first page of his 1956 diary, he wrote 'Resolution: to do everything I can to keep Anne in love with me.' Four days later, after a nightmare of delays while his appeal was dealt with (and refused) he was taken to Pentonville.

* * *

Since he first started placing advertisements in newsagents' windows on Old Compton Street in 1948, John's career as a purveyor of male nude photographs had expanded rapidly. At first he was a fortunate amateur, gifted with a knack for picking up good-looking young men and sweet-talking them into his studio to be snapped and dispatched. The financial rewards that he enjoyed were a pleasant perk, nothing more. But during the early 50s, he became more businesslike – partly through his own awareness that there was serious money to be made out of pornography, but also through the encouragement and financial backing of other, more experienced players in the field. Nigel Westfield had been the first of these 'angels', but he, too, was a dilettante whose interest in the camera was mostly for fun rather than profit.

In November 1952, just before the police first started showing an interest in his business affairs, John met a photographer and pornographer called Basil Clavering. Clavering was older, wealthier (he was in the film distribution business) and better connected. John's on-off guardsman lover Terry had met Clavering during one of his West End whoring sessions, and took John to meet him at a cocktail party at Clavering's impressive Pimlico flat. During the course of the evening Basil showed him his extensive collection of military uniforms (they were displayed all over the flat) and flattered his literary ego by suggesting he was just the man to take over a pet project, a history of corporal punishment in the army and navy that Clavering had been researching for many years. Escorting John round his collection of boots, helmets, whips and spurs, he outlined the terms of collaboration that would begin with an immediate 'goodwill' payment to be followed by £10 per week salary. Work on *Under the Lash* began straight away and carried on sporadically through 1953 (it was eventually published by Torchstream Books in 1954).

John's introduction to Clavering marked a rapid increase in the amount of photographic work he was producing; Clavering seems also to have encouraged him to exploit the market by providing his clients with more explicitly erotic images. In January 1953 he began photographing 'wrestling duos' – a popular device in early physique photography for getting two men naked and in physical contact. As the political and moral climate in Britain was becoming more repressive, John was becoming more daring.

Suddenly he was overwhelmed with projects. While his courtship of Peter preoccupied his personal diaries, he was filling in the time between each passionate encounter with a

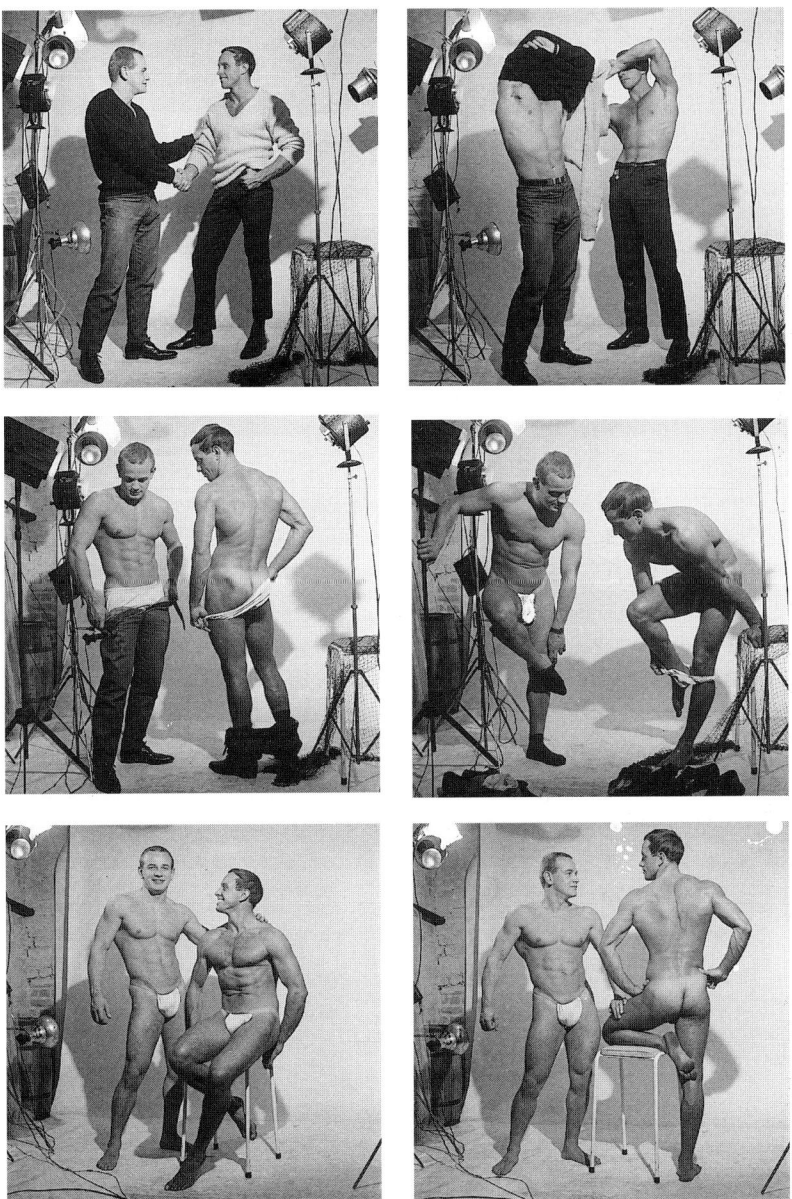

Regular Barrington models Vic Heywood and Roy Scammell strip off for some
'dual studies'. Vic's genitals were inked out (middle row, right) on the original
negative

huge amount of work. In June 1953 he approached Samuel Sidders & Son Ltd, the printers of *Art and Anatomy*, with a business proposal: Sidders would invest the necessary capital to print and bind his next photographic book *Anthropometry and Anatomy*, cutting out the necessity of a third-party publisher (a particularly welcome arrangement as it finally freed him from business connections with Nigel Westfield). Sidders, after seeing the dummies which John had prepared, gave him a contract and an advance of £300. The first pages came off the press in November, and bound copies from the first print run of 5,000 were delivered by Christmas. It sold out quickly (significantly, many of the orders were from his growing list of American clients) and was reprinted almost immediately. *Anthropometry and Anatomy* was a handsome volume, large format, 112 pages, retailing at £2.5s, containing much of the material from *Art and Anatomy*, but greatly expanded and more open in its appeal to a homosexual reader (there were far fewer pictures of women). There is more of John's work in the book, small pictures crammed in a dozen or more to the page, recording the lovers and photographic techniques he had acquired since 1951. A feature on portraiture used pictures of Peter – including two nude oil paintings with exaggerated muscles and genitals that John had executed from photo-studies.

In February he was approached by the publishers WH Allen with a view to producing a glossier, sanitised version of *Anthropometry and Anatomy*, provisionally entitled *The Nude in Art*. He was delighted, and went to work straight away, happy even to oblige the managing director who insisted that there should be plenty of shots of naked women to counterbalance the male nudes ('He's a tit-enthusiast,' noted John). A contract and £50 were forthcoming, and John buried himself in the British Museum researching sculpture photographs, and had daily meetings with contacts who would supply him with the required female nudes. In March, however, WH Allen got cold feet. It was hardly surprising; even airbrushed and full of naked women and Greek statuary, a John S Barrington book on the nude was hardly a safe publishing prospect in the cautious atmosphere of 1953. He was philosophical; Allen let him keep the advance and even paid him a further £40.

But less cautious investors were waiting in the wings. One client offered £500 capital to set John up in a proper photographic business in West End premises with some decent equipment. A company was registered in August under the name Lensart Limited, the letterhead boasting 'Publishers and Camera Artists for Theatre, Films, Press and Culture-Physique (Pose Plastique)'. Office space was found in Tottenham Court Road, next to the YMCA, at £440 per annum. For the first time since the heady days of the war, John was back in business in the West End, convinced that Lensart would provide him with a secure income as well as giving him a way into show business. He fantasised about getting back into agency work, of establishing himself as a second Angus McBean photographing the stars, of writing journalism and books.

There were other operators in the physique field, but none as prolific. As his market expanded, John responded by getting more and more models in front of his cameras. Sometimes, he had so many models competing for his time that, after a couple of sessions, he would hand them over to other photographers, notably Basil Clavering (who was also building up a photographic business under the name Hussar Studios, specialising, needless to say, in guardsmen). When John returned to London from his French holiday with Peter in October 1954, he got straight to work on Lensart's first publication, planned originally as *Lensart Monthly* but published under the title *Male Model Monthly*. Sidders printed 2,000 copies in November, and John set about selling it. Many went to his regular mail-order clients, but a substantial number were sold to newsagents too.

Male Model Monthly was the first magazine of its kind in the UK. Physique publishing was in its infancy, and still cautious: there were no genitals or pubic hair to be seen in *Male*

Model Monthly, certainly nothing that could suggest to the innocent purchaser that this was a homosexual publication. But interested parties could easily find out where to get more photographs of the beautiful young men they saw in the pages of the magazine. Business boomed at Lensart, and John's financial situation improved rapidly. By the time he married Anne in October 1955, he was well set up as a provider.

Contact with other photographers and publishers also provided opportunities for profit. John, never the most scrupulous of businessmen, had already been selling copies of Jean Cocteau's erotic drawings which he had photographed on to copy negatives during a visit to Paris (these were among the negatives that were seized from Rosslyn Hill). In February 1955 he visited the Zurich offices of the Swiss gay magazine *Le Cercle* which had been publishing Barrington photographs for some time. John hated Zurich but was delighted by what he saw in the *Cercle* picture library. 'Mostly stupid camp and arty pornography,' he wrote, 'but some good pages, especially von Gloeden's studies. Copy them on to three rolls of film. These negs may make the trip to Zurich worthwhile.' And they did. John immediately offered his British and American customers copies of Wilhelm von Gloeden's turn-of-the-century studies of Sicilian youths, and made a tidy sum. He would do the same with the work of many other photographers and artists over the next few decades, even, on occasion, passing off their work as his own.

So when the police finally caught up with John at the end of 1955, it was no small-time operator that they were after; he was a serious pornographer, making a considerable amount of money. His photographs were tame enough, but full-frontal nudity and wrestling were sufficient to land a man behind bars in 1955. But he never exhibited the slightest remorse. Many times over the years he expressed the desire to move out of the male nude market, not because he thought it was immoral or illegal, simply because he wanted to be respected and acclaimed as a serious artist or writer.

It was during his time in Pentonville that John began to think seriously about writing his autobiography. Something of the singularity of his position – a newly married man, married to his best friend's ex-fiancée no less, in prison for dealing in homosexual pornography – had obviously struck him.

The first page of his prison notebook bears the title 'NOTES; dedicated TO MY WIFE ... being some unoriginal imaginings by John S Barrington, author of *Horror!*, *Grim Harvest...*' and some dozen further titles including *Dear Peter...*, *Under the Lash*, *Art and Anatomy* and *Anthropometry and Anatomy*. There follow thousands of words on his relationship with Anne, how she changed his sexuality and saved him from misery; there are notes of dreams (particularly about Peter) and of his prison reading; even the draft of a letter to Noël Coward requesting a meeting. One page bears a remarkably accurate pencil sketch of Anne executed one night in his cell ('which reminds me of drawing Donald, July, 1947! – only 50 yards away!' he noted of his earlier stay in Pentonville).

At the back of the notebook are some preliminary autobiographical jottings that outlined the ideas John was to pursue for the rest of his life. 'Idea – two diaries "edited" by JSB – on a schizophrenic basis – one a good, enquiring, curious, Christian soul, an artist; the other a pagan, "what I would be if I could" adventurer and sexual decadent.' Ever since he had first considered marrying Anne, John had written about his fears that it would mean a split in his personality, a strict division of his activities. At first, this was a practical reaction to the contradictions implicit in his marrying a woman at all; but as he dwelt on his circumstances in prison, he began to develop it into an artistic idea. From January 1956 onwards, John regarded himself quite coolly as two different people: one the respectable married man, an artist, draughtsman and publisher, celebrity-hunter and philanthropist; the other a promiscuous gay pornographer, unscrupulous in business, amoral and pleasure-seeking.

He was released from Pentonville on 3 March, and went home to Richmond and a waiting Anne. They had a quiet meal and went to the cinema, where they saw Peter's giant smiling face on the Odeon screen advertising Aspro.

* * *

As soon as he was out of prison and over his immediate personal problems, John was back to his old tricks. He took studio premises in Richmond in partnership with a couple of professional photographers who specialised in weddings and christenings, and set to work on two projects that required his immediate attention – a book and a magazine – which both demanded the urgent acquisition of more pictures. How much of his previous work had been destroyed subsequent to the police raids in 1955 John could never remember, but there is very little that ties up with the names and descriptions before that time; after 1955, however, there is masses. As he moved more seriously into international gay publishing, he needed a constant supply of new pictures, so as soon as possible he organised a trip to the place where he knew he would get them – Cannes.

In August Anne and John took their first trip together to the South of France, a belated honeymoon. Armed with business cards boldly proclaiming connections in 'Paris, Rome, New York and Hollywood', John was ready for some serious talent-spotting. Days were filled with long coastal drives, sun-bathing and sightseeing, nights with expensive meals and romance – but for two or three hours every afternoon John would wander off with his business cards and camera at the ready. On this visit, he was mostly content to take snapshots of the beach boys as they strutted around in their *slips de bain*, happy to show off for the eccentric Englishman with the Agiflex. But the results were remarkable. The bright sunshine of Cannes, the tanned bodies of the boys, provided a huge contrast to his studio-bound London work. The boys he met on Cannes beaches over the next 20 years were the subjects of his best, most collected pictures.

When he returned to London, John had enough new material to complete his immediate projects. The first was a magazine, more ambitious and less discreet than *Male Model Monthly* – the first issue of *Manifique*, a title he was to use over and over again, which reproduced some of his best London work to date with a smattering of Cannes pictures. The second was a softback book, *Youth in the Sun,* boasting over 100 of the Cannes photographs, some of his line drawings and a certain amount of pirated work, most notably the paintings of the American artist Quaintance.

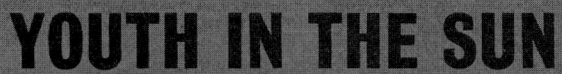

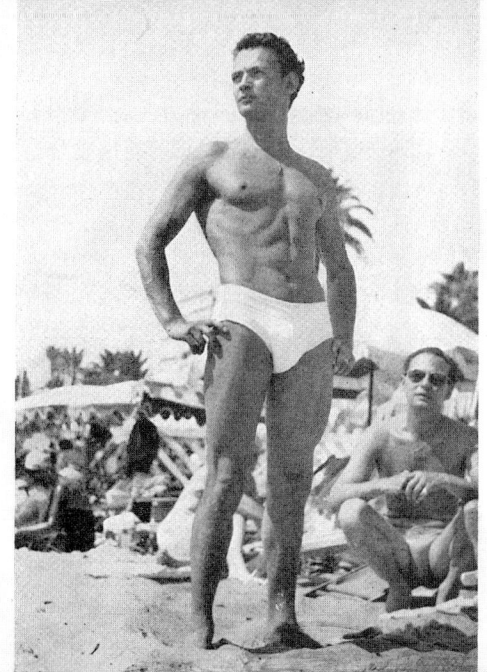

John was enjoying the fruits of his marriage, basking in his rediscovered prosperity, once again in contact with the celebrities he adored (he had recently added the name Alan Searle to his list of regular photo-clients; Searle was W Somerset Maugham's companion). He was also delighted, if slightly apprehensive, at the news that Anne was pregnant. All seemed simple until another of John's regular clients called to say he had met a young man whom the great photographer might like to record.

> 22 SEPTEMBER: Out of the blue comes THE MOST PHYSICAL-LY BEAUTIFUL YOUNG MAN I HAVE EVER SEEN! Andreas, Greek Cypriot, whose brother was recently killed by the British in Cyprus. A physical culturist athlete of 19 with a truly Greek God head ... and an olive-skinned physique that Praxiteles might have swooned over ... with a smile that beats even Peter's – because unlike Peter he has no idea what his smile can do to others.

Andreas was something special, and John wasted no time in getting him into the Richmond studio where he stripped and posed. Like most of John's model-conquests, Andreas was flattered and turned on by the idea of nude photography, and he found himself enjoying, and repeating, an experience that he would never have considered without the presence of

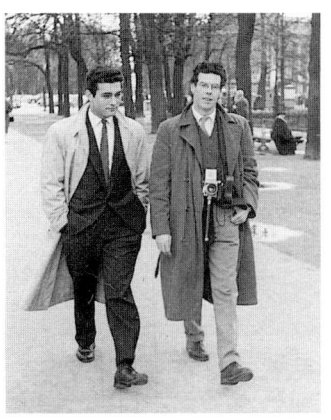

the camera. John was discovering that his new role as a married man and father-to-be had distinct advantages. Discussing the situation man to man with Andreas (insofar as his limited English allowed) John was able to impress on the model that his

Left: Andreas and John (with ever-present camera) step out.

Opposite: Andreas, 1957

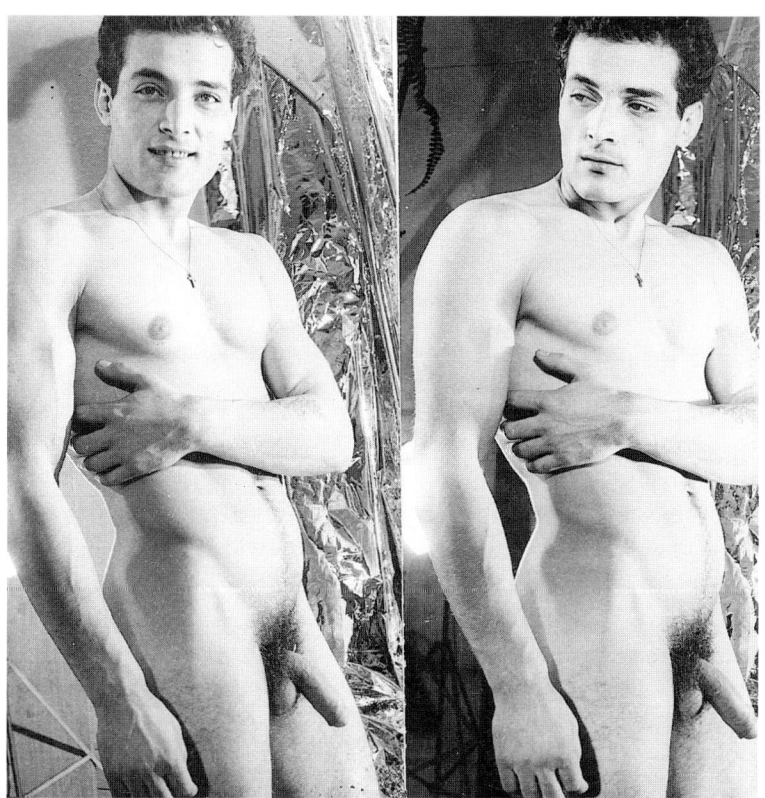

friendship would be strictly casual, that they were both really straight and that any 'giggles' they might have in the studio were an added bonus to the business of taking pictures.
The ploy thought up as a desperate attempt to get Peter back
was turning out to be very useful.

For a few months Andreas was visiting Richmond two or
three times a week. In March 1957, on his way back from a
visit to Austria where his mother, Grace, was nursing the
terminally ill Franz, John had a tryst with Andreas in Paris.
His pockets full of money received from a Paris client, John
treated Andreas to the full Paris experience, ending, of
course, in chambre 12 of the Hotel Royal Pigalle. They
returned to London after two days.

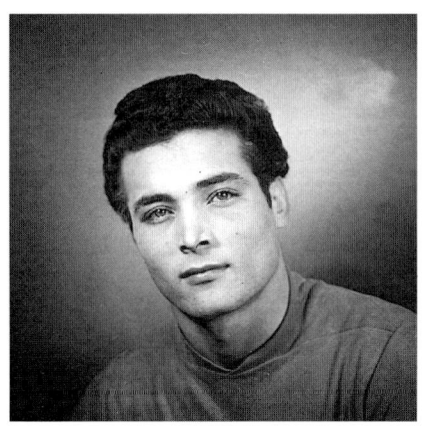 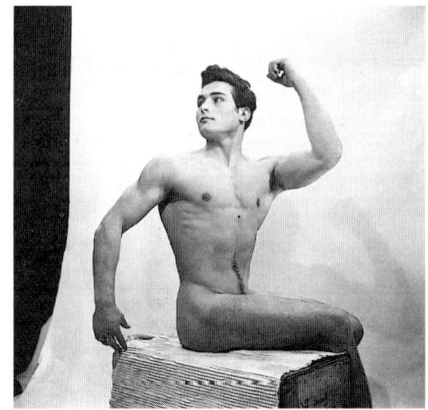

21 MARCH: Last night I told Anne about meeting Andreas in Paris – 'by chance'! Of course she was jealous and upset, very unhappy, but wonderful about it and said she trusted me...

A few weeks later, Anne was taken to hospital, where she gave birth to twin daughters.

* * *

On 26 July, this advertisement appeared in *World's Press News and Advertisers' Review*:

EDITORS TAKE NOTE!! Aged 36. Established author (8 titles), publisher (own periodical with International sale), photographer (very frequently published), illustrator and commercial artist. 12 years free-lance journalist and publicist. Subjects: Cinema, Theatre, Art, Fashion, Photography, Literature, European travel and tourism, Personalities and Social reporting, sociological reportage and demi-monde coverage all over Europe, Athletics, with a personal 'angle' and 'in' to almost every subject covered by any International Daily or Weekly. Wants to write and illustrate own controversial column on variety of subjects, preferably for syndication. ...ANY SUGGESTIONS? Interested only in large-circulation periodicals and newspapers!

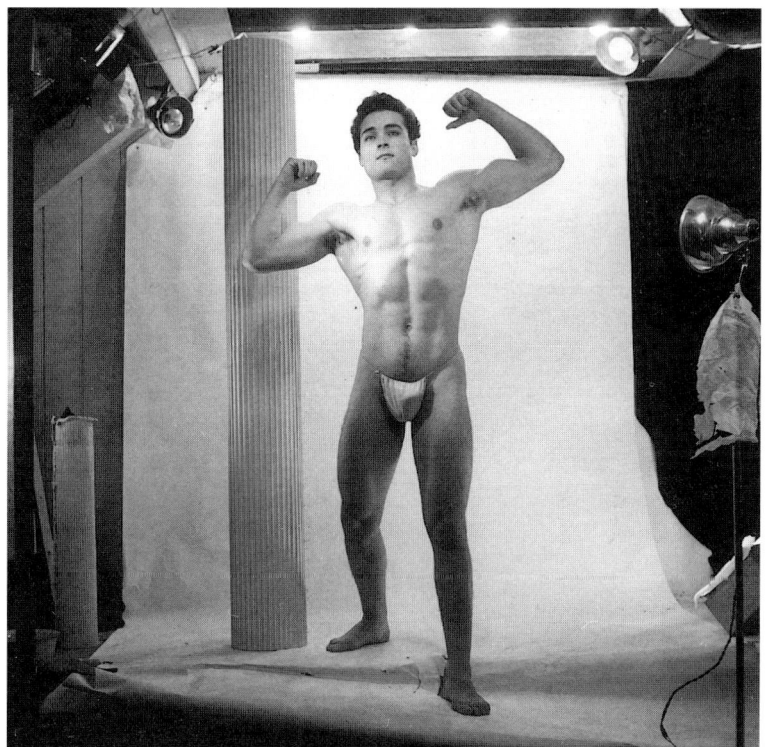

In American physique magazines at the same time, the following announcement was appearing:

AN ARROW INTO THE BLUE!

In an age of ballistic missiles, arrows may seem a bit out of date – but if one is out to aim too high an arrow may well serve its purpose! The distance this is being aimed is three to five thousand miles and may well fall on stony ground. Anyway, wealthy Americans are invited to correspond confidentially on new, unique, cultural, and exciting enterprises. Please supply some financial bona fides in first letter to: John Barrington (personal)...

John was wrestling with the same old problems. On the one hand, he was still trying to break out of pornography and into respectable journalism. On the other, he was a man with

Best Value CHEST PULLS

For massive chest, shoulders, arms and back development. World's Best Cables.
HERCULES MODEL. Something new! Graduated cable strength. Every cable differently coloured for easy selection of poundage. Check increases as your strength grows! SIX super cables with fast snap locks for rapid changing. **27/6**
STANDARD MODEL. A super-power 10-strand kit. Suitable for advanced Bodybuilders. Beginners and medium-advanced men also benefit through its progressive poundage scale. Live rubber cables help you achieve maximum development in record time. Only **51/-**
JUNIOR CHAMPION. The famous Junior Champion Chest Pull is ideal for young lads. Special cables enable the weakest to train for power. **15/-**

Overseas postage 3/6 on any model.
Body Sculpture Chest Pulls incorporate all modern features, specially designed for speedy bodybuilding progress. Noiseless in use—ideal for the man who trains at home.
EXERCISE CHART FREE WITH EVERY OUTFIT
Obtainable only from:
THE BODY SCULPTURE CLUB,
The Manor House, Worcester Park, Surrey.

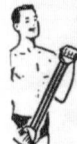

YOUTH IN THE STUDIO

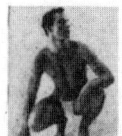

200 exceptional camera studies of finely proportioned male models in a great variety of inspiring poses. Ten Photo-catalogues of 12-16 assorted studies, plus complete lists, for **7/6** Per Catalogue.

JOHN BARRINGTON
18a Hill St., Richmond
Surrey, England
Double professional fees to above-average models

ART FIGURE PHOTOS

Over 300 studies, varied models and poses, to suit students, artists, designers, connoisseurs, etc. Classic and draped.
Printed catalogue and two samples, p.c. size, for only 3s. 6d., from:—

ANNETTE PRODUCTIONS (MW),
24 MADRAS ROAD, CAMBRIDGE

64

A small ad from Man's World, a British physique magazine, 1956

new responsibilities who had to bring home the bacon, and saw a plentiful supply of that in the growing gay market – if only he could raise the capital. Books and magazines were selling well, but the most lucrative arm of his operation was being run from Paris. Since his trouble with the law in 1955/56, he had sold his photo-sets through a Paris office, run by his friends Marcel James (an ex-bodybuilder and sometime model) and Jerry Weinstein (a barrister working for the United Nations). None of the business was transacted in the UK, and nothing could be traced to John – who nevertheless made hundreds of pounds a week from these sales. James, Weinstein and John worked under the collective name Jean-Paul David – yet another pseudonym.

As John moved in his private life closer to the norm – married, with children, living in the prosperous suburbs, rarely venturing into the West End – his work was taking him deeper and deeper into the gay world. As a married man, it was easier to pick up models, and this paradox amused and delighted him. Since his marriage, John's appearance had changed significantly. He abandoned the more obvious affectations (walking canes, monocles, flowing scarves and chamois gloves were all discarded; two of his more 'form-fitting' suits were mothballed), cut his hair to the regulation 50s short-back-and-sides, started wearing conservative spectacles. He was altogether a less alarming sight to prospective models than the theatrical apparition of the 40s, and the wife and babies were the final touches that completed the image.

One afternoon in August 1957, John realised the possibilities of his new, super-straight appearance.

> If a date in my metamorphosis can be pinpointed, it might well be 5 August 1957. An ideal summer's day. I, my wife, her younger sister, walked along the promenade at Richmond beside the Thames, me wheeling the big double pram. Camera round my neck, of course. We met a real discovery! Don, 5'9", athletic, superb physique, half-Australian, well-tanned, crew-cut beach boy and merchant seaman, handsome and unat-tached. We adopted Don for the day. As a pram-wheeler he was perfect, freeing me for photography as, half naked, he angled his torso to catch the sun like a professional model.
>
> Don was the first of a new breed of very masculine young men who I met for the first time while with my wife and daughters. Only later did these virile youngsters discover the sort of photographic modelling and friend-ship that I auto-matically expected. The normality of my appearance, my expen-sive cameras, the laughing, happy babies, disarmed young men who would otherwise never have accepted the cards I gave them.

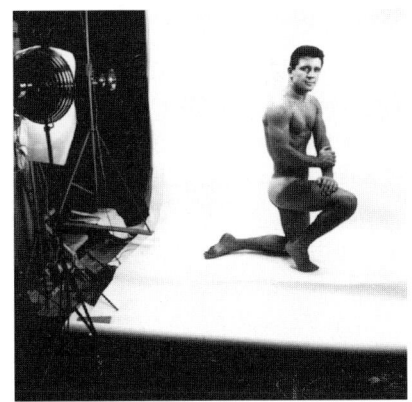

Don in Richmond, 1957

At a later date in his Richmond studio, after their first photographic session, John introduced Don to the additional dimension of their new friendship. Don was surprisingly cool; he already had, it transpired, two other 'good friends' who kept him in pocket money, and two girlfriends.

In April 1958, after spending the winter diligently exploiting his most recent photographic crop, John moved lock, stock and barrel to the Riviera for three months. He needed to replenish his portfolio – clients were already waiting for the latest batch of Barrington pictures, and a growing readership of *Manifique* and *Formosus*, his new US title, were demanding fresh material. Many clients had paid him in advance, trusting that he would return in the summer with suitable material. But in order to finance the family's stay in France, he came up with one of his boldest schemes, a 'tourism service' for wealthy Americans visiting Europe that he called The Gay Bachelor.

John said he was making use of his contacts with showbusiness, with clubs and hotels, to help American visitors enjoy their stay in Europe with congenial company, and that the financial rewards to himself were slight, usually in the form of gifts. In fact, The Gay Bachelor was a discreet escort agency. American clients (recruited through *Manifique* and *Formosus* and other means) would pay a fee, in return for which they would be introduced to Cannes gay bars and, crucially, to a handful of the beautiful young men they had seen in photographs. By the early 60s, The Gay Bachelor was doing thriving business as John met more and more sophisticated young gigolos who were happy to be introduced to wealthy new friends. In 1958 and 1959, the idea was just dawning on him. A prospectus for the service was a masterpiece of innuendo, promising:

> ...an entrée into the gayest social life of each town ... Take Paris or Cannes, for example. Young, good-looking, interesting friends will meet you – and they will be the sort of friends you will request before you leave the USA – and they will show you all you want to see, help you do all you want to do, speak for you and protect you! When you want to be alone you can

do as you please, but when you want your young genie he will
be there to help, advise and to amuse...

The Gay Bachelor was a great success. As a travel agent
and tour organiser, he enjoyed the hospitality of many
Cannes hotels, restaurants and night clubs for free; his
clients paid him, and from them he recruited new customers
for his photographs and magazines. Word got around Cannes
fast: the beach boys were eager to play ball with John, knowing that the friendly Englishman with the camera was the
key to untapping a lot of potential earnings.

On arriving in Cannes, he was careful to secure two separate accommodations. While Anne, the children, his mother,
brother and sister-in-law were settled in an apartment just
off the Croisette, John took a room at the nearby Miramar
complex that served as a studio and retreat.

The focal point was Eden Plage, the main beach where
families, celebrities and beach boys sunbathed side by side.
For a photographer it was a happy hunting ground; boys
would 'audition' on the beach or on the Croisette, then, if
they seemed responsive, would be taken back to the Miramar
or up to the rocky pinewoods just above the beaches and
hotels where John was fond of taking al fresco nudes.

Eden Plage was also a good place for celebrity-spotting,

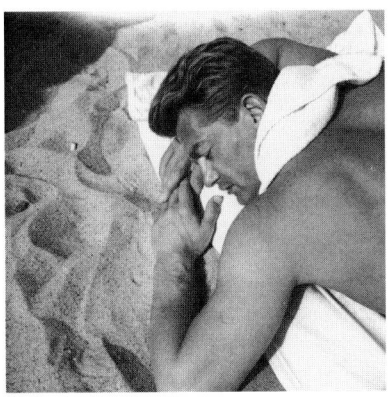 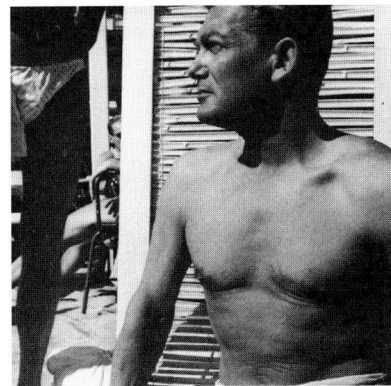

Jean Marais in Cannes, 1958

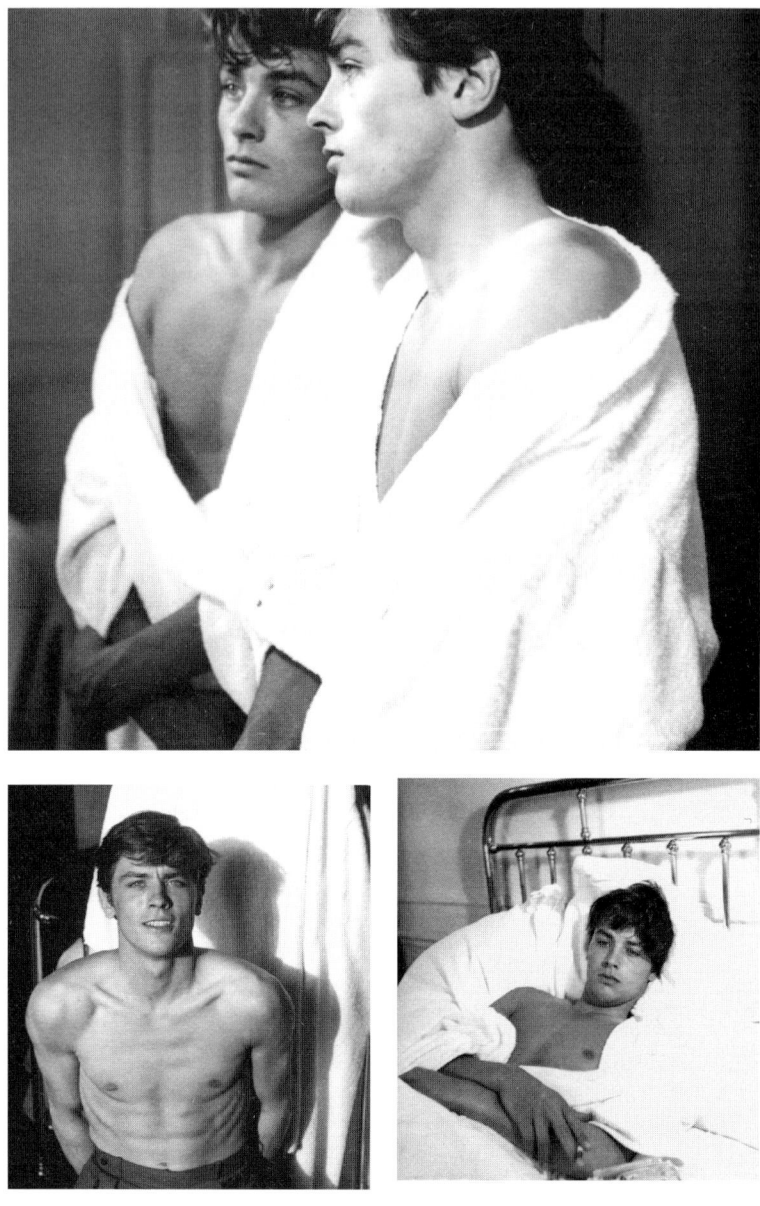

*Alain Delon, Cannes 1958, (above) and on the cover of a 1962 Manifique
(opposite). Rudolf Nureyev and Pablo Picasso both posed for John (opposite).*

particularly at festival time: in
1958, he was rubbing shoulders
with Cocteau and Jean Marais,
whom he photographed lying in
the sand in an echo of the famous
still from *Orphée*. Also in 1958,
John met one of the scores of
young actors in town to promote a
film, was charmed by his good
looks and ready smile, and took a
roll of photographs of him lying
topless on the crumpled sheets of
his hotel room. In later years, he

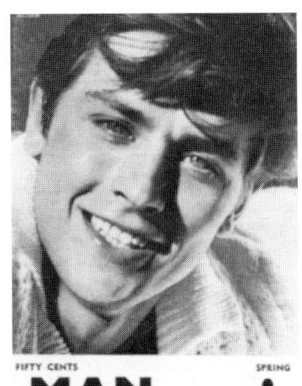

realised these pictures were valuable as the actor in question
– Alain Delon – became more and more famous. As Delon's
fame grew, John sold the photographs to magazines whenever he could, and regularly featured them in his own gay-ori-
ented publications. Delon was not amused: homoerotic pictures were bad publicity for the macho star. John faced an
irate Delon in Cannes and entered into heated correspondence with his management who threatened legal action.
'I've given Alain terrific publicity in the States!' he responded, wounded, and carried on publishing the pictures whenever he could.

Celebrity-spotting was a large part of the attraction of
Cannes for John, as enjoyable, if not as lucrative, as young
men. His files are full of snapshots of celebrities visiting

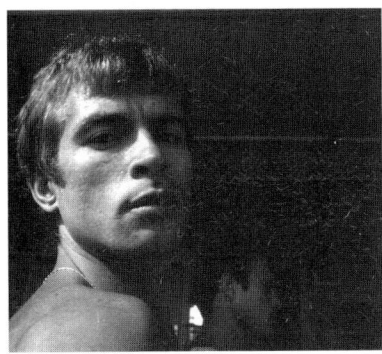
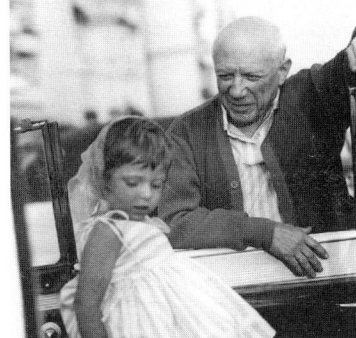

Cannes – Charlie and Oona Chaplin, the Beatles, Rudolf Nureyev (with whom he struck up a brief friendship), James Baldwin (with whom he argued about civil rights on the beach), Cliff Richard, Andy Warhol. In 1960, Pablo Picasso joined the family on the beach to build sandcastles with the girls; John was in seventh heaven. Just like the 16-year-old boy who sent cheeky propositions to Bernard Shaw and HG Wells, the adult John was delighted by celebrities and introduced himself whenever possible. Some of his claims were far fetched – John delighted in telling the story of how, one afternoon in Cannes, he had met Rock Hudson at a party and accompanied him to his hotel room where he had 'earned' a pair of the star's blue jeans by giving him a blow job.

One afternoon during their 1958 holiday, the sunbathing family was approached by a young beach boy who strolled over and introduced himself.

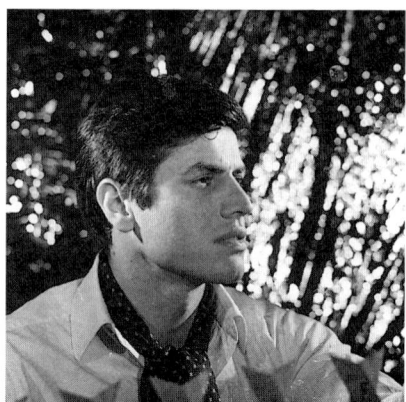

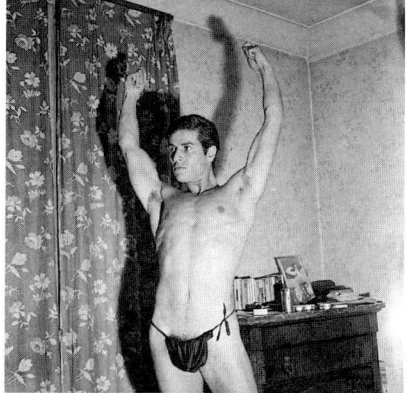

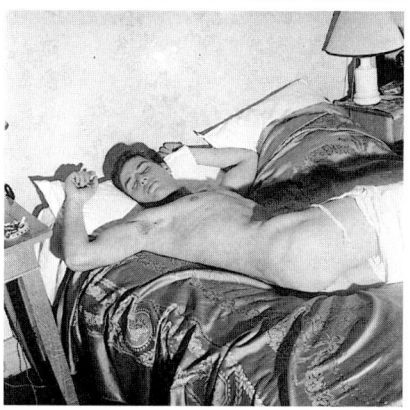

Giancarlo in Cannes (top) and in John's regular Paris retreat, the Hotel Royal Pigalle. Opposite: on a visit to London

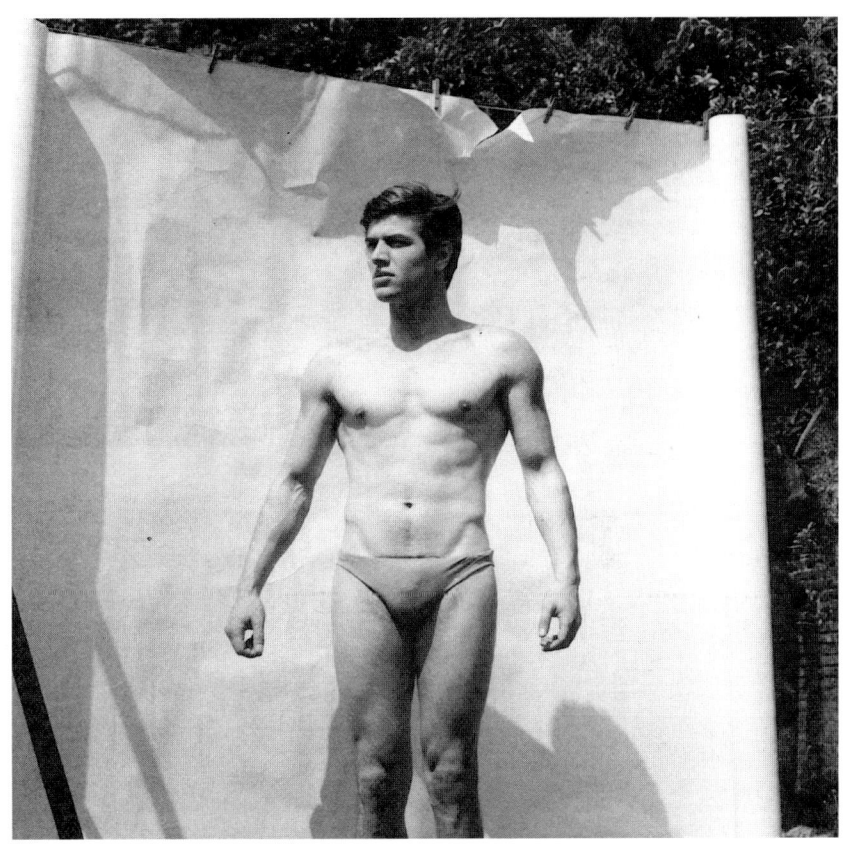

25 MAY: Excellent day on Eden Plage. This afternoon I make a
very major discovery: Giancarlo Zampetti. A young 21-year-
old Roman, a sportsman, actor, dancer, fashion model, world-
travelled, sophisticated, incredible charm and smile and quite
the most perfect physique I have ever seen. A friend of Alain
Delon and Claude Aragon. His personality is devastating. And
to Anne, the twins and myself molto simpatico...

Giancarlo spent the rest of the day with the family, flirting
with John and Anne and playing with the twins. The next
morning, John tracked him down at his hotel.

26 MAY: Giancarlo!!! Visit him at 10.30 in his room at the
Savoy and start photographing him even before he gets out of

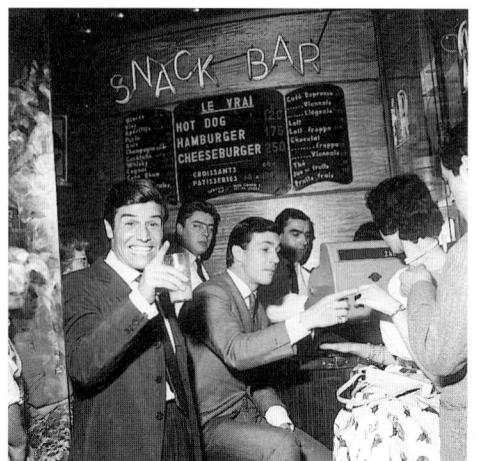
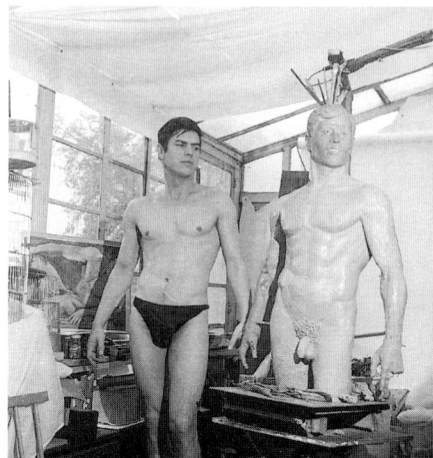

bed. Superb three rolls of film, and he most co-operative and
eager to please me and the camera – which he does!

Over the next five years, John photographed Giancarlo
again and again, selling his photographs as fast as he could
take them. Giancarlo never received a modelling fee. 21
years old and very conscious of the benefits his good looks
could bring him, Giancarlo was the perfect 'friend' for the
Gay Bachelor clients. He also became a close friend of John
and his family, the subject of hundreds of drawings and
sculptures. The pictures John took of him that first spring in
Cannes are among his best work. When a retrospective volume of his work was published in 1988, a photograph of
Giancarlo, naked on a blanket above the beaches in Cannes,
adorned the cover.

* * *

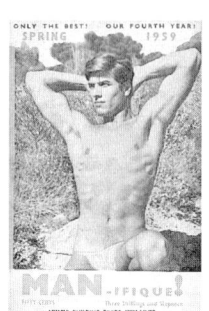

When he returned to Richmond John was in high
spirits. His three months in Cannes had been
more successful than he had ever imagined. He
had photographed dozens of models, real
Barrington classics, and it was just as well: his
office was piled high with orders, mostly from
America, sending money and demanding new pic-

tures. There was more legal trouble to face (he was fined £50 for publishing six indecent pictures) but this was swiftly dealt with. Pictures were despatched to his American outlets (notably *Trim*, *Tomorrow's Man* and *Grecian Guild Pictorial*) and to Marcel James in Paris. The reaction to the new pictures, particularly those of Giancarlo, was excellent, and new orders poured in. Sometimes up to 60 new orders were coming in from the States every week, each containing a $10 bill and requesting John's latest list. He started putting together regular brochures of his

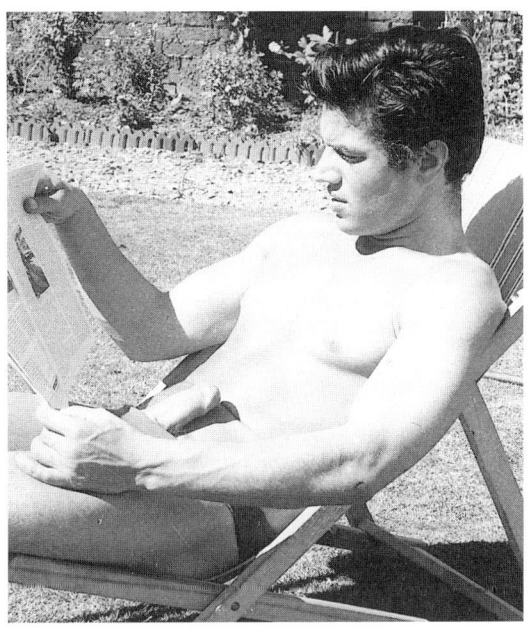

Giancarlo gets some sun in John's back garden (above). At large in Cannes (opposite left) and posing with a statue cast from his body, then finished by hand (right)

work – usually headshots of his new models, or postage-stamp-sized reproductions of recent sittings – which he would mail out to clients. These catalogues, for which he used the title *A Camera Life Class*, continued for the rest of his life, and in their pages appear all the young men he photographed from the late 50s to 1990, some of them returning over and over again.

Not everyone was delighted with John S Barrington. A client in Montreal sent a furious letter in 1958:

> I have received in today's mail another few circulars advertising new collections of 'exceptional, exciting, and thrilling … photographs of exceptional beauty in the young male physique'. I am sure you will recall that last September, I pur-

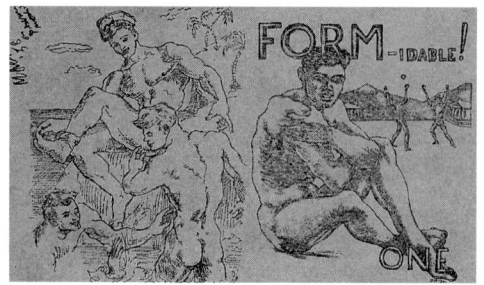

chased a series of these so-called 'superb photos' ... and chucked them down the incinerator. The set of some 24 photos which I received satisfied none of the glowing adjectives used to describe them. The photography was not only amateurish, but the prints were atrocious ... Never have I seen a collection to compare to the one sent to me. It was the complete reverse of what I had been led to believe from your hysterical advertising. I have in my possession several line drawings (very amateurish) and some 10 pages of your high-pitched (and utterly false) advertising. Nothing would give me greater pleasure, gentlemen, than to forward these to the American and British, and perhaps even French postal authorities as I pass through those countries on my summer tour. I imagine that the receipt of same would cause an uproar only to be equalled by the dropping of an H-bomb on the White House...

The criticisms of John's photographic technique aside (he never claimed to be a great technician) there was a lot of truth in this letter. The prints that he was sending out were poor – he used the cheapest, quickest methods of reproduction, assuming that most of his clients were too timid to complain. His advertising was 'hysterical' and 'high-pitched'. The line drawings to which the client refers are almost certainly those published in a sorry little volume entitled *Form-idable!*, which he had produced on a Gestetner machine. *Form-idable!* consisted of 14 sheets of foolscap, stapled together, each sheet bearing reproductions of some woeful drawings. 'It has proved quite impossible to make the publication a folded booklet without sacrificing plates,' the editorial apologised, 'but there is nothing to stop you folding it and stitching it yourself.'

John travelled alone to Paris to spend a week working with James and Weinstein on refining the mail order business. One night in the Café Flore, he moved in on a handsome young man who was sitting alone at the bar, drinking and looking miserable. John bought him beer, showed him pictures of his daughters and got him talking. Yves le Coadou (below), 24, from Brittany, until recently a jet-fighter pilot fighting in Algiers, was drunk and depressed. Traumatised by the war in North Africa, where he had seen many comrades killed, he was missing his family, had lost out on a promised civilian job and was broke. He hadn't even booked into a hotel for the night as, he revealed after several more drinks, he had considered killing himself. John talked the young man out of this plan and took him back to his apartment where Yves showed his gratitude 'in the only way

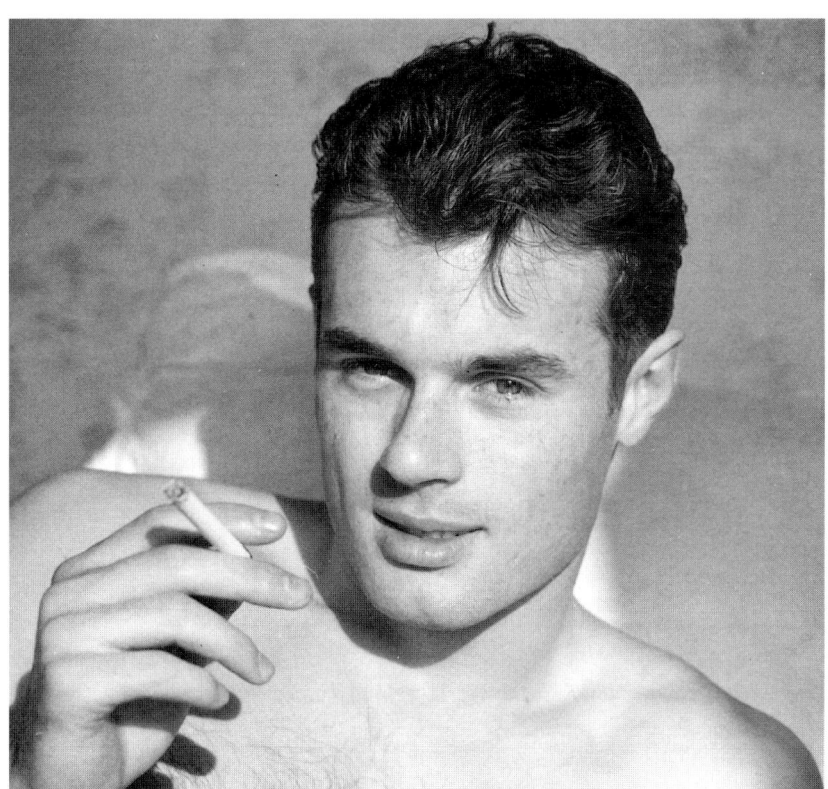

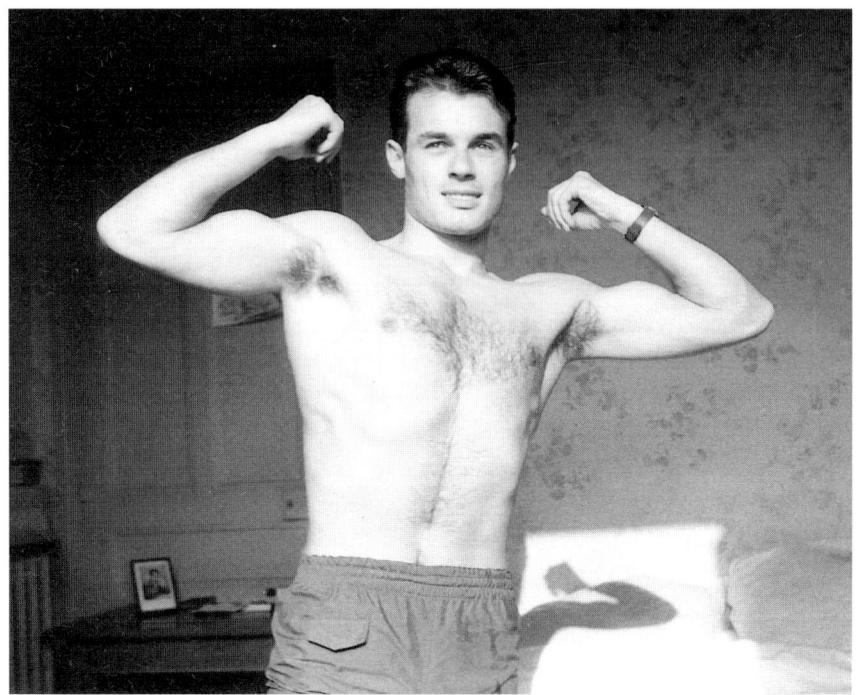

he could under the circumstances'.

For the rest of the week Yves was John's companion and model. Later in the year, as the family prepared for Christmas, Yves turned up in London as an unexpected guest. He gladly accepted a makeshift bed on the couch, and travelled down to Leigh-on-Sea to visit John's parents, who had by now returned from Austria. Occasionally he and John would walk up to the studio where they would take more photographs and repeat the intimacy of their time in Paris; on Boxing Day, John, Anne and Yves left the children with a babysitter and went dancing at the Whisky à Go-Go on Wardour Street.

John was developing a curious ménage. His model boyfriends were not just gigolos who posed, pocketed the money and left; many of them became regular visitors and, even more surprisingly, good friends of the family. He had the knack of inspiring loyalty, and gave advice, shelter and

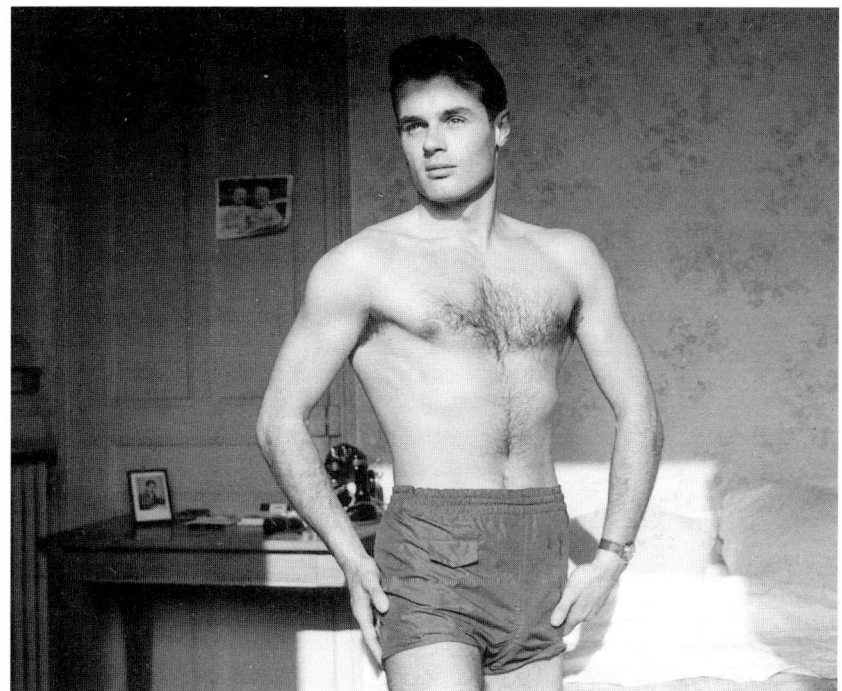

Yves, Paris 1958

money in return. In the years to come he took in dozens of waifs and strays who had commenced the relationship by posing for pictures and ended up staying for years, intrigued by the sexual adventures and the money but also dependent on John as a friend. By the 70s, he was godfather to the numerous offspring of former models who invited him to their weddings and called on his help in times of trouble.

Andreas, Giancarlo and Yves – the Barrington superstars of the 50s – remained close throughout the 60s. All three continued to enjoy occasional modelling sessions, and as the years went by their poses became more and more explicit. Whether they realised how far John would exploit their photographs is unclear; certainly they saw only a tiny fraction of the money. Most likely, at the end of the innocent 50s they were just horny, vain young men whose pride was tickled by the attentions of the man with the camera.

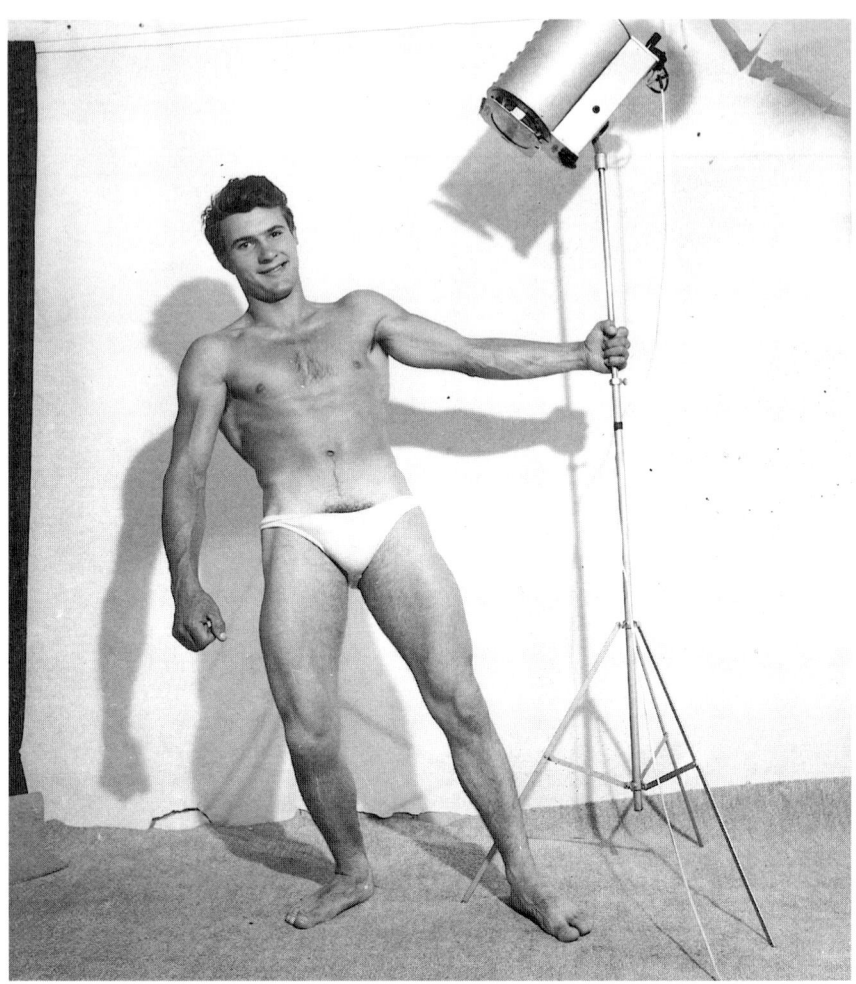

Tibor, 1963

Chapter Six
Physique

During the 60s, the small, closeted physique market exploded. New titles were launched, and photographers began to
flood the bookstores and mail order outlets with their work.
For John, this was a mixed blessing. He was uniquely placed
to exploit the new market, with his extensive back catalogue
of photographs, his current roster of star models in Andreas,
Giancarlo and Yves, and with his reputation bringing him
new clients and models in droves. But as gay publishing
went overground, standards were raised. It was no longer
enough to send out poorly-reproduced photo-sets or shoddy
pamphlets of line drawings to uncomplaining clients. The
competition, particularly from Scandinavia and the States,
was producing professional, properly distributed work in
comparison with which John's output was amateurish, a cot-
tage industry.

It was beyond his scope, both financially and temperamen-
tally, to become a smooth operator in the market. He liked to
get his stuff out quickly, to keep the money rolling in, always
looking forward to the next project that would make his
name and his fortune. His talent was for finding and photographing models; he was never a good publisher, writer or
editor. The best medium for his work were the new physique
magazines, where John S Barrington photographs were pre-

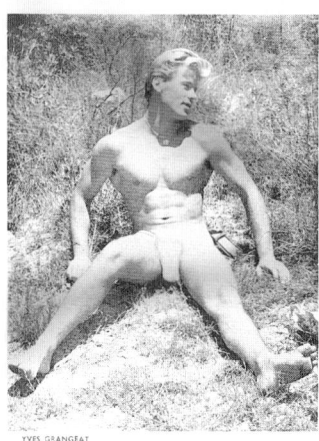
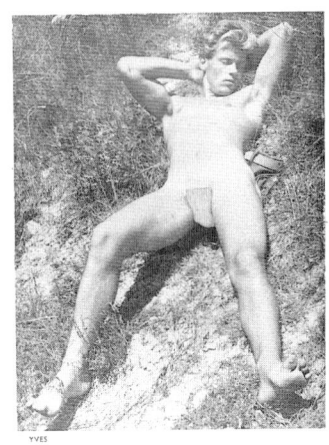

YVES GRANGEAT

Yves, 17-year-old, 6' tall, 182 lbs., was the model who got the biggest reader-reaction of Issue 8, so we are printing three more studies of this truly superb youth in this issue. A ship's carpenter in Cannes, Yves has two hobbies: weight-lifting and girls—in that order! Enlargements, 6½" x 8½", of Yves are 5/- each from Paignton Publishing Co. Ltd., or One Dollar each from Physique Publishing Co. (Addresses: pages 4 and 39).

10

YVES

"FORMOSUS!"

A new quarterly, edited by John Paignton, devoted entirely to large photo-graphs of exceptional models. Best art paper, exclusive illustrations ! 8¼" x 5 , 40 pages. No public sale in U.K.! Subscription: £1 for 4 issues, post paid. From: Physique Publishing Co. 18a, Hill Street, Richmond, Surrey, England. (U.S.A.: from the newsagent where you bought "MAN-IFIQUE!") Order "FORMosus!" To-day ! ! !

11

Ship's carpenter Yves Grangeat, another popular Riviera model, in a spread from 1959. The posing pouch was inked on; mail-order customers could send for 'unspoilt, uninhibited' prints

sented in good layouts, properly printed and appreciated by a critical audience. *Eos* in Copenhagen ran his photographs regularly in the early 60s (an edition in 1962 featured Yves on the front cover and a selection of John's work inside) as did *Physique Pictorial* in America. John's American publishing partner Louis Elson, who was using Barrington work in his own title *Tomorrow's Man*, was also publishing and distribut-ing John's titles *Manifique* and *Formosus*, his occasional *Youth* series and others. 'Magazines in the USA clamour for my photo-studies, especially Andreas, Giancarlo, Don and a few others,' he noted in his diary at the end of 1959.

As the decade progressed, his contribution to foreign mag-azines became more and more popular. For the USA, he started to produce colour slides (although his preferred medi-um was always the black and white print), responding to the increased use of colour printing in the porn market. At the end of his 1961 diary, he made a list of all his new models for that year, a total of 41. 'With all of them I broke the UK laws on sexual behaviour,' he later wrote,

> ... but I was never 'horizontal' with any of them and for all of them it was their first experience of fellatio. The cost of these sittings and the brief adventures was £72.15s. Twenty of them provided studies that are still collected and exhibited in 1988, and were often published.

Such was the income from Jean-Paul David in Paris to John S Barrington in London that he could afford to move to a comfortable house in south-west London where he lived for the rest of his life. He invested in a litho printing machine that enabled him to print his own magazines at home – a major contribution to his income. On that machine and bigger, better ones hired or bought throughout the 60s, he produced dozens of titles in small editions (sometimes only as many as 100), sold at a considerable profit (up to £15 a volume) to his mail-order clientele. These strange little limited editions were typical of John's independent productions – shoddy and full of mistakes, but more daring than mass-produced magazines could be, and the ideal advertisement for his more explicit photo-sets.

John was more reckless than his competitors. In Cannes in 1962 he met Bob Mizer, then the leading light of American male photography through the Athletic Model Guild and its publication *Physique Pictorial*. Mizer had already made a brief visit to the Richmond studio to buy some pictures for publication, and in Cannes the two photographers met on a shared quest for models. John offered Mizer the use of his car, introduced him to boys and drove him to the secluded locations above the town.

> The lads were amazed when Bob insisted that they wore tiny posing pouches, because he was frightened to take nudes, even on negatives, back via the New York customs! Troll the

gay bars in Cannes after dark, pick up hustlers and gigolos, all this Bob would do, but to photograph a nude in Cannes was beyond him.

By the end of the 60s, after years in which his work had been so far ahead of the competition that he was internationally recognised as a gay photographer, John found himself struggling to keep abreast with unforeseen developments. The sexual revolution took him by surprise; a married man and father, moving into middle age (he was 45 in 1965), he suddenly discovered that the repressive moral climate in which his work had flourished was being swept away by a new freedom. He was never in step with the political and social changes of the 60s. By the time the younger generation seized on the idea of openness in all things particularly sexual, it was too late: John had made a lifestyle of ambiguity and duplicity. And he was never sympathetic to the idea of gay liberation.

While he privately regretted the changes he saw around him, John recognised the need to keep up with the market, and concentrated his efforts on more explicit material. The colour slides that he was selling in the States were raunchier than the black and white studies that he reserved for the UK market, and when he saw competitors like Basil Clavering and others producing porn 'duals', he jumped in on the act. His photographs of men having sex together were never his best work – in fact, he frequently denied having taken any such photographs – but they were money-spinners. He took his first in Cannes in May 1969, in his suite at the Martinez Hotel, and was amazed at how co-operative the two models were (they received around £6 for their efforts). John was quick to put this new discovery to work, and decided that his next move would be into pornographic movies.

A few days later he took the models to the more deserted Île St Honorat, where he shot some Super 8 film and took hard core shots on colour transparency film, intending to produce a short film for the US and UK markets, the former with the still shots inserted at key points, the domestic version without full sex and aimed at the naturist market. The result, entitled *Gull Island*, sold well over the next few years through mail order, and provided another entry on John's CV. When he was feeling particularly confident, he would list 'film producer' among his jobs and cite *Gull Island* as one of his features. On another visit to Cannes he recruited a new cast of models, took them up on to the roof of the Martinez Hotel and shot his second feature, *Boys on a Hot Tin Roof*.

* * *

John's life settled into a pattern. With Anne and the twins as a constant source of domestic security, he made his annual trips to Cannes, sold his photographs and attempted occasional, disastrous forays into other fields. From 1958 to 1968, he produced his best work, creating his own roster of 'supermodels' each of whom had an enthusiastic fan following. But who were these young men who posed so willingly for John's cameras? How did the experience affect his, and their, lives? The story of the 60s is the story of his involvement with a parade of beauties.

John's best photographs have not dated. In the late 90s they look contemporary to gay men in London or New York. Andreas, Giancarlo and Yves share a timeless quality – but the model who embodies it best, and who was possibly his most popular model ever, is Tibor

T i b o r

Tibor was an 18-year-old Hungarian refugee; he had machine-gunned his way out of Budapest, he said, and had somehow arrived in England in the summer of 1962. Basil Clavering was the first to photograph him when he passed through London en route to stay with friends in the West Country. Basil sent his photos to John with a note enclosed ('He's far too pretty for me, dear boy. Much more your cup of

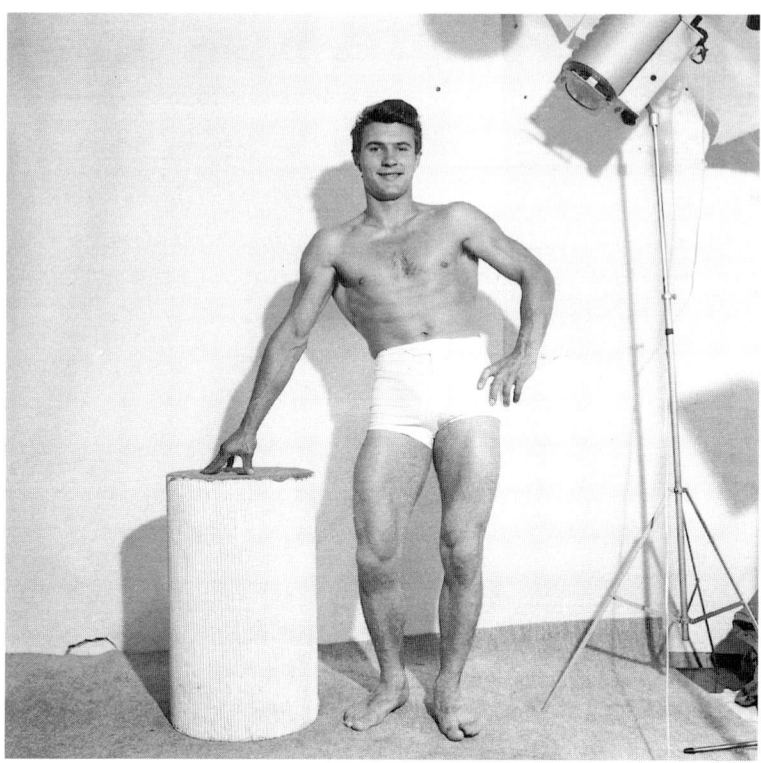

tea, I think') and suggested they meet. Tibor returned to London and proved a patient, willing model. John took him under his wing, helped him with money and fatherly advice (Tibor was already married), and photographed him every time he visited London. They remained friends for nearly 20 years

John never fell in love with Tibor, although he admitted in the diary that had the model's English been better, he might have been a more attractive proposition. Whatever his feelings towards Tibor, though, he recognised that he was a magical model. Clients demanded more and more of his photographs, and John reproduced them in line drawings and paintings to satisfy this obsessive demand. In the late 60s, Tibor even agreed to feature in some more explicit pictures: there is a photograph of him in one of John's low-budget porn

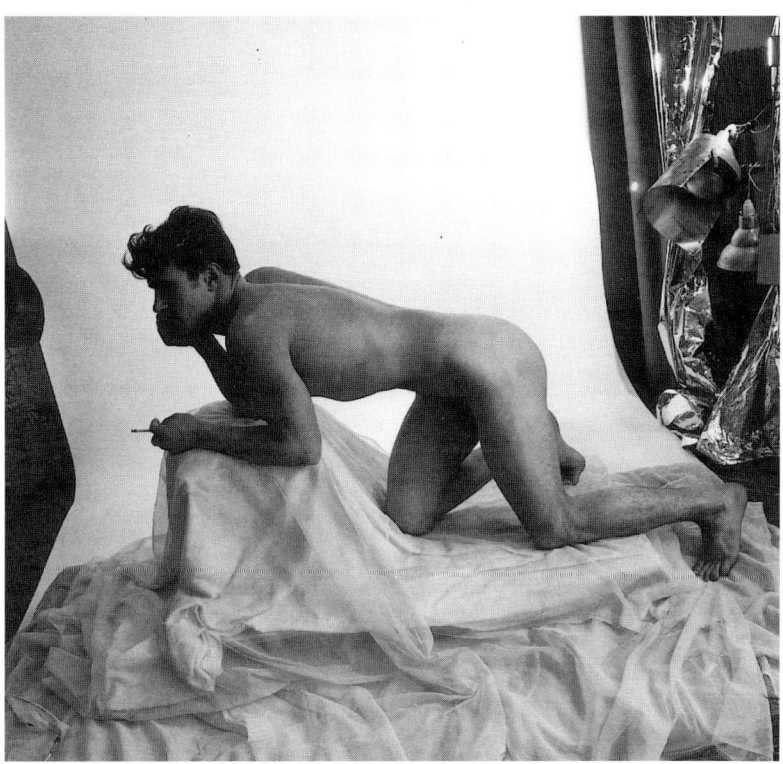

publications having sex with another model.

Tibor was not the most handsome or glamorous of John's models – that accolade would probably go to Giancarlo, Andreas or Yves, the beauties of the 50s – but he was possibly the sexiest. He met all John's exacting physical, 'anthropometrical' criteria, was masculine-looking and well hung, but he also projected a vulnerability and innocence that contrasted strikingly with his butch looks. In many portraits, he is pensive and distant, melancholy, particularly in comparison with other models, who usually take care to look seductive, teasing or playful.

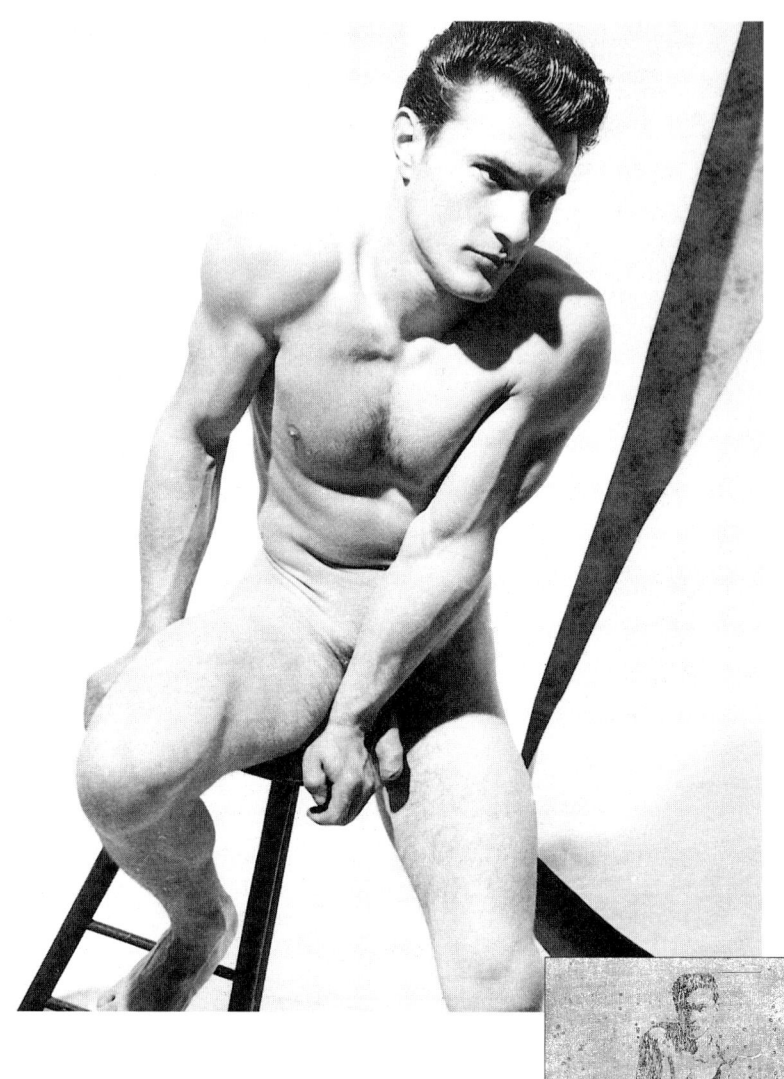

*Tibor poses on a stool – one of John's most popu-
lar sets of pictures, reproduced in etchings (right)*

Bill David

Models like Tibor remained part of John's social circle for many years after their first appearance; others crossed paths with him for only the briefest of moments. Of these chance meetings, the one who made the most lasting impact was a young American named Bill David who met John in Cannes in 1964. Only two diary entries record that meeting.

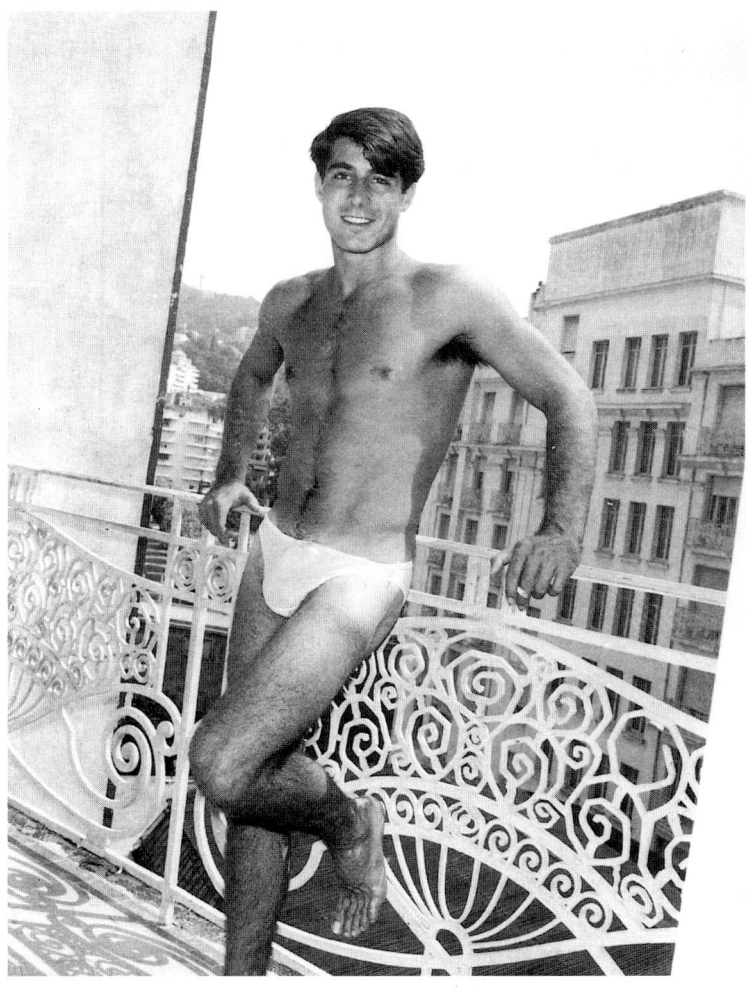

4 AUGUST: Bill David, young motorcyclist from New York touring Europe. Immediate rapport. Another Yves! Absolutely
superb in every possible respect. A good omen for the vaca-
tion, I hope.

5 AUGUST: Bill David!!! More superb pix. Unfortunately he left
Cannes tonight, but spent all day on beach with us. Hope to
keep in touch with him.

They met on the Croisette, where Bill was soaking up the
sun and posing with his motorcycle. The whole of their relationship is told in the series of photographs that John took
that sunny afternoon. The first shots show him on the
Croisette, a handsome, clean-cut topless beach boy wearing a
pair of frayed, cut-off jeans. He sits on his Triumph bike,
lounges in a deck chair and perches on a wall, his legs
crooked to thrust maximum crotch at the camera. The next
photographs are indoors, in John's apartment, where Bill,
still in his shorts, lies against the pillows and smiles coyly at
the camera. The rest of the pictures, taken the next day

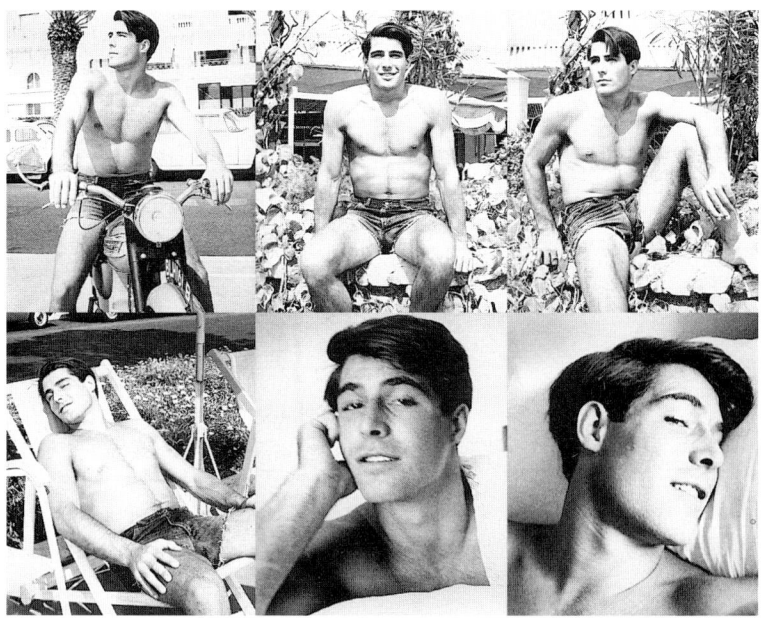

when the two men had better got the measure of each other, are more direct, less flirtatious. Bill poses on the bed, on the edge of the bath, even on the balcony with a cup of coffee in one hand, displaying his erection. He spent the rest of the afternoon on the beach, left Cannes that night and was never seen again. Did he ever see the results of those two afternoons? Did anyone ever recognise him from a Barrington publication?

Jean-Pierre Martin

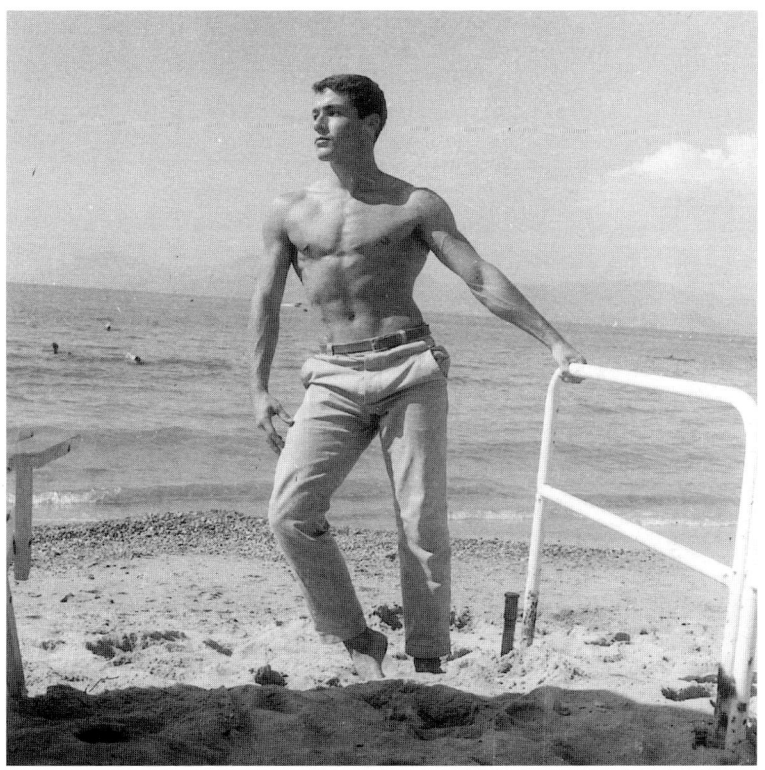

The most poignant story from John's catalogue of 60s conquests is that of Jean-Pierre Martin, the 19-year-old French paratrooper he met on the beach at Antibes in August 1961.

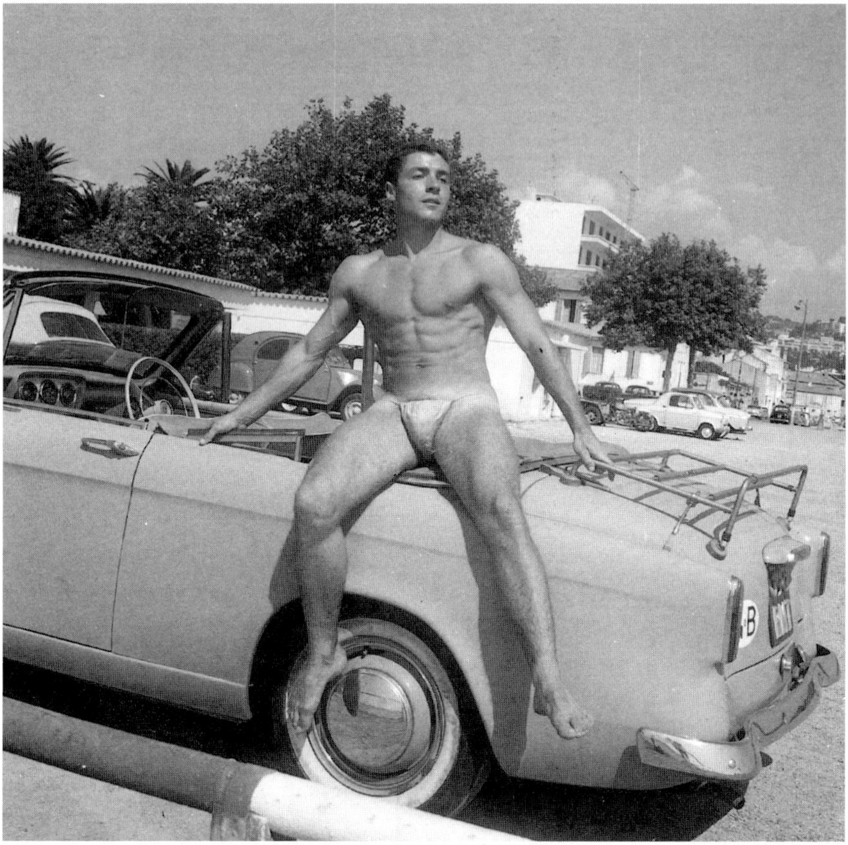

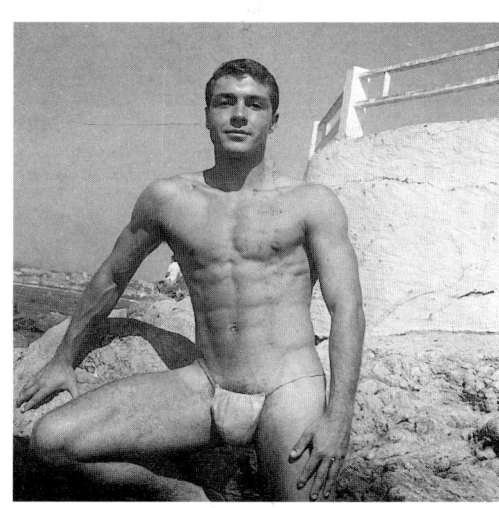

'One of the most physically beautiful and mentally attractive young men I've ever known,' John wrote in 1990. 'I have published him a hundred times and he still looks down at me as I type today.'

John had discovered the military camp at the Old Fort in Antibes in 1960. On the beach that ran alongside the camp, the soldiers would sunbathe, swim and, occasionally, accept the propositions of the visitors who cruised there. Within 48 hours of arriving in the South of France in August 1961, he had made his way to the Old Fort and met Jean-Pierre, a slim, boyish character who enjoyed being photographed and was willing to be adopted by the Englishman with the camera. John managed to get Jean-Pierre some leave at short notice, persuading the military authorities that he was needed by the Cannes tourist board to model for promotional material, and introduced him to the family. He photographed him in the pinewoods above Cannes, in the sea and in his car. After posing for photographs in the bathroom, Jean-Pierre insisted on taking John to bed and becoming his only 'horizontal' lover of the year.

The following summer, after John had successfully sold his studies of Jean-Pierre taken in August 1961, the two men met again at the military base at Nîmes.

> We climbed a small hill into a cyprus and fir woodland. There, in the hot and dappled sunlight, I took some of the finest studies of Jean-Pierre and with happy naked embraces we said goodbye, promising each other much longer intimacies in a future that we both sincerely expected to share in the months and years ahead. Outside the paratrooper's camp, Jean-Pierre kissed me and waved as I drove north.

Six months later, on a beach outside Algiers, Jean-Pierre and two comrades were ambushed by Algerian liberation forces with machine guns. All three were killed. It took two months before John discovered why Jean-Pierre's letters to him had stopped so abruptly.

John Hamill

Most Barrington models were opportunists who limited their photographic activities to John's camera and those of a very few others. John Hamill was a notable exception.

When John met Hamill in 1965, the 17-year-old blond was already the holder of several junior bodybuilding titles with eyes on the West End and Hollywood, willing to use his charms if necessary.

> 12 MAY: At Roehampton pool meet a stunning blond lad, showing off his diving. Annoy his girlfriend by giving him a card. Dream-boy type, ideal for US clients.

A couple of weeks later, Hamill made an appointment and posed for the first of many modelling sessions. 'During two hours of studio work he co-operated with uninhibited laughter. We talked over an extended luncheon for three hours, planning his future career.'

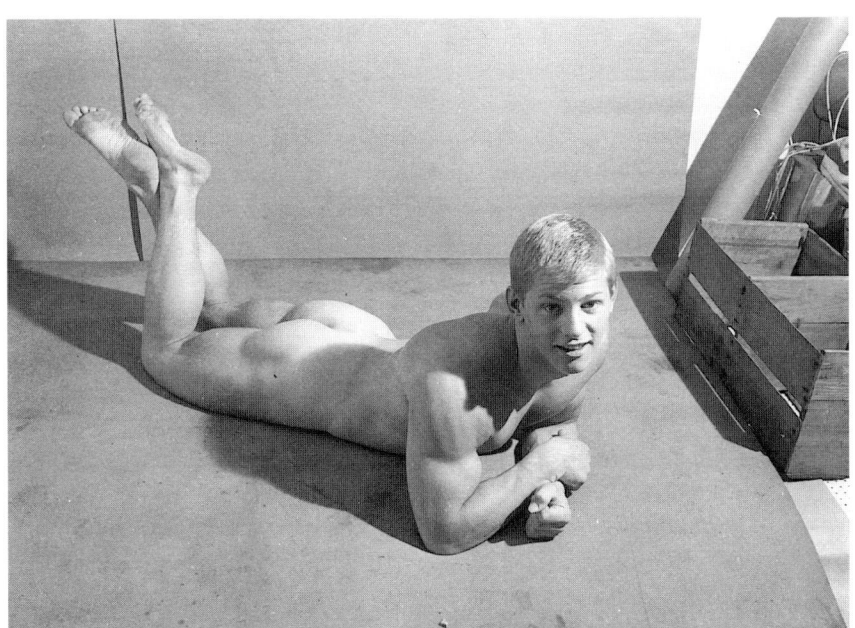

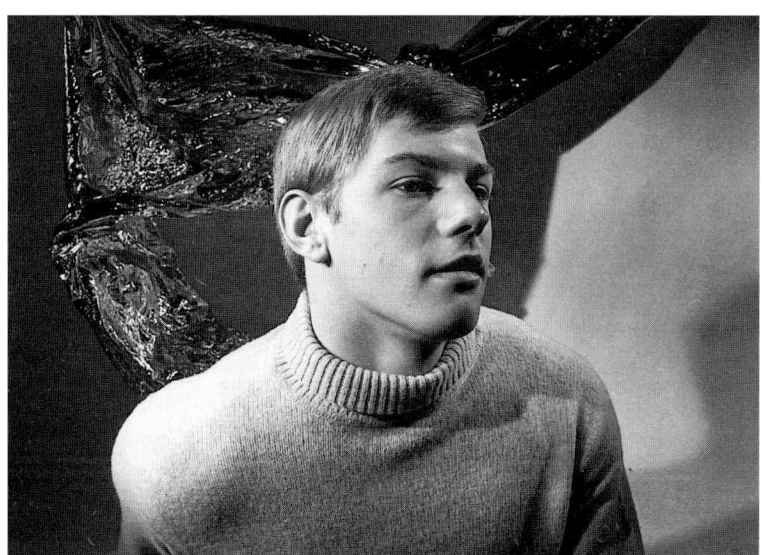

Hamill's career in the immediate future involved more nude modelling for John and moonlighting for other photographers of whom his mentor did not approve. 'They showed less respect for his physical beauty than I had shown,' John complained, and indeed some of the pictures were pretty unsubtle stuff.

John was fascinated by Hamill, not just by his physical beauty but also by his determination to succeed. Hamill was a perfect JSB type – masculine in appearance, from a working-class background but aware of his charms and perfectly willing to allow others to enjoy them. By the end of the year, Hamill had got his first theatrical job. Unlike most of the boys who John tried to help break into show business, Hamill had talent and a great deal of drive. In January he travelled to Southend-on-Sea to appear in the seasonal pantomime. By March, he had secured the services of an agent and was getting well-paid work on TV commercials.

Hamill was one of a new breed in London – attractive, 'swinging' young men eager to further their careers as quickly as possible. They made the rounds of the beefcake photographers – John, Basil Clavering, Vince, George Stockton's

Galaxy Studios – and zeroed in on gay producers in film and theatre who would cast them on looks. In June 1966 he phoned John to tell him that he had landed a part in the most popular TV soap opera of the day, *Crossroads*, as Dave Cartwright. Assuming that the actor would use his new-found fame to help those who had helped him, John started churning out film scenarios for Hamill to star in. The first, entitled *Gigolo!*, Hamill duly passed on to a producer he had met and impressed in Cannes – to no avail.

John Hamill's career went from strength to strength. After *Crossroads* he went into a long run in the West End farce *There's a Girl in my Soup* before moving to Hollywood and starring roles in American and British films (*No Blade of Grass* 1970, *Trog* with Joan Crawford – her last film – in 1970, *Beast in the Cellar* 1971, *Travels with my Aunt* for George Cukor in 1972). In the mid 70s he found new stardom as a screen stud in the burgeoning British sex film industry.

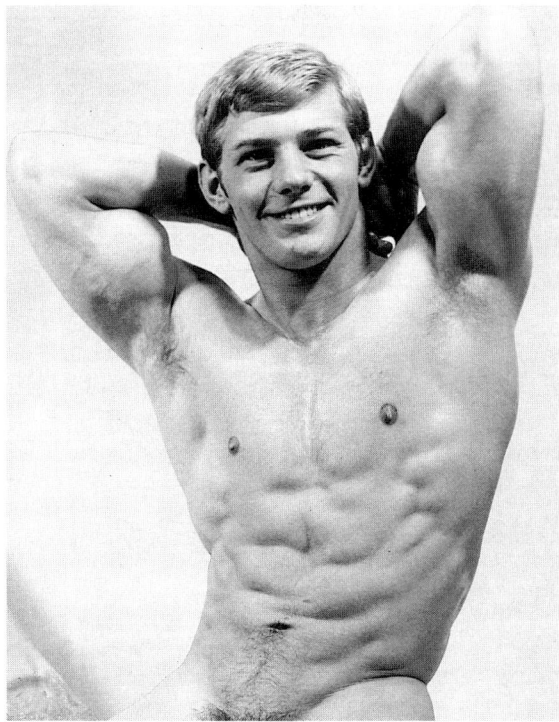

He remained on friendly terms with John for many years, although the dream of working with or writing for the young star came to nothing, and they drifted apart. But John never forgot the young blond he had met by the pool. Among his papers after his death were file upon file of photographs of John Hamill, dating from his earliest bodybuilding triumphs.

Michaelangelo

A happy souvenir for many reasons was the roll of film that John shot one afternoon in Rome in March 1967. The photographs of a smiling, coquettish and very well-hung Italian boy were among John's best, but he had other reasons for remembering the day fondly. It represented the climax of his celebrity-chasing, and was proof of his closeness to a certain artistic coterie to which he yearned to belong.

In February, he had received a letter from Howard Austen, Gore Vidal's partner, who had been an enthusiastic collector of John's work for some years. John had met Howard and Gore in London the previous year, and had sufficiently impressed them to enter into a correspondence and secure an invitation to visit their new apartment in Rome. 'Gore would adore reading your manuscript about London,' the letter read, referring to a new novel which John hoped Vidal would support, 'also your sculpture sounds marvellous.' John lost no time and arranged the trip for March.

4 MARCH: Been in Rome 24 hours, very pleasant, at Gore Vidal's with Howard Austen. Splendid apartment, own room. Sun, lazy hours on magnificent terrace, fine young faces and super bodies. Very happy to be back 'in style'. All very 'simpatico'. But depressed by Howard's reaction to the book. All the usual criticisms about length and diversity and too much detail. Gore has only dipped into the MS and won't commit himself beyond 'it needs a lot more work on it'.

5 MARCH: Gore talks so brilliantly. I could provide his cues for hours happily, listening to his brain sparkle. And so wittily too, with so much salacious gossip and such ruthless demolition of personalities. Especially about the Kennedys and 'Jaccy' ... With Howard and pretty Donato to Café de Paris, and meet Giancarlo at 10.30. With him till long after midnight.

6 MARCH: Already missing London and family. Gore's life and Howard's are too de luxe and rich for my frugal tastes. A very

162

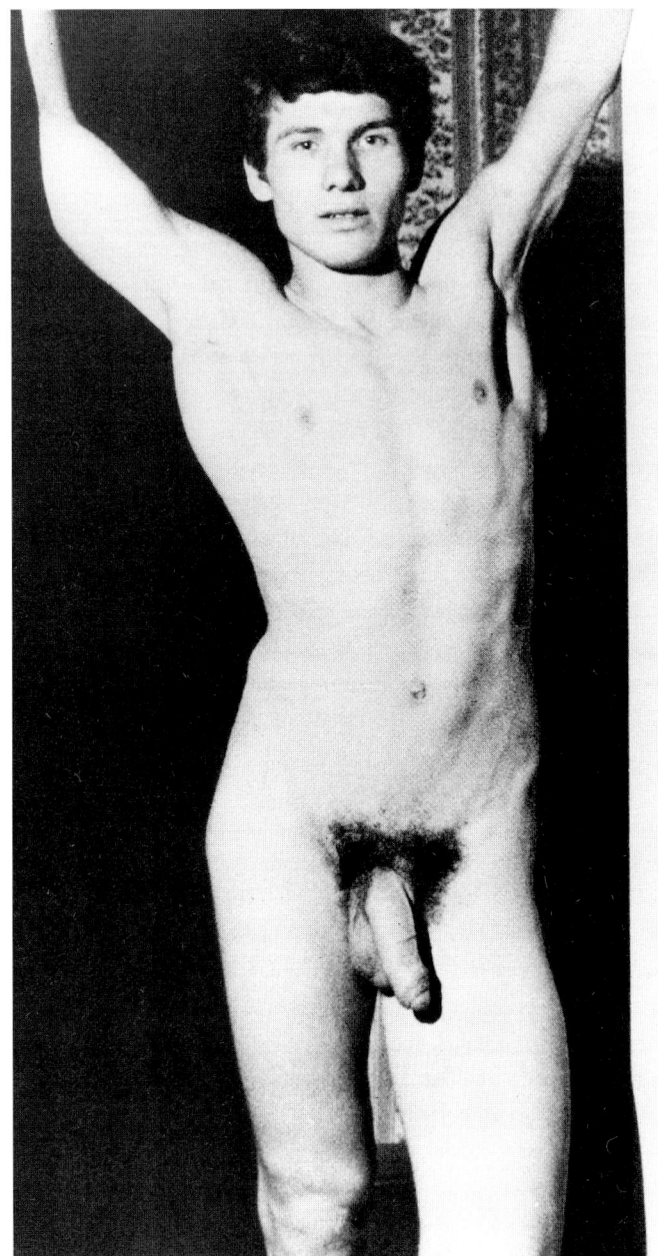

Michaelangelo, in Rome, 1967. After undressing in the bathroom, the model appeared in the bedroom doorway and asked, 'Will I do?' 'Oh yes, you'll do very nicely,' replied John, and pressed the shutter.

hot day. And a wonderful half day in Rome, full of magic.
Spent 8am to noon on terrace. Michaelangelo, Zeffirelli's
friend, reappears and I take more pix. He is a truly stunning
18-year-old. No wonder Zeffirelli is mad about him.

While Gore and Howard entertained downstairs, John
took Michaelangelo up to one of the cool, quiet bedrooms and
took 16 photographs of the tall, dark-haired, grinning boy.

They were not the only pictures he took during his stay in
Rome: there are also a few snaps of Gore and Howard on
their sun-drenched terrace. John kept in friendly correspondence with Howard until the 80s, and reintroduced himself
to Vidal whenever the opportunity arose, the last occasion
being when Vidal did a reading at the Riverside Theatre
near John's home in 1987. Whenever he remembered his
acquaintance with the great writer, he would recount with
delight how he photographed and seduced Zeffirelli's protégé
while Gore, Howard, Franco and their intellectual friends
talked art and politics on the terrace below.

* * *

For all the success of his photographic career, John complained every day to his diary that he was being dragged into
a disreputable demi-monde which he found uncomfortable and
embarrassing. He longed to go legit, to protect his family from
another embarrassing court case. The final straw came in
1962, with his biggest and most damaging brush with the law.

In August, just after he had returned from a holiday in
France and a pleasant reunion with Yves, the CID came calling. They arrived at the Richmond studio with a search war-
rant, and after two hours accompanied John to the family
home for a further search. The list of seizures included:

68 Photographs
10 magazines entitled Manifique
6 magazines entitled Formosus
1 litho art drawing

1 book entitled Under the Lash
1 book entitled Formidable
1 book entitled Youth
2 large books entitled Youth
1 book entitled Dear Peter
1 book entitled Inside My Skull
1 litho plate
2 litho plate drawings
5 books containing photographs of models kept in the
premises for the purpose of sale or gain

Nothing more was heard until January 1963, when John was summoned to appear at Richmond Magistrates' Court to give reason why the seizures should not be destroyed. The police had particularly objected to his home-printed literary output, *Dear Peter...* and the sequel *Inside My Skull*. Again, the main charge related to sending the items through the post. After the initial hearing the case was adjourned for three to seven weeks to give the magistrates time to read the two offending volumes.

John went into a legal frenzy. He started canvassing all his friends and contacts in the literary world as expert witnesses to testify to the artistic merits of the books. If they were not obscene, there could be no harm in sending them by mail. It was 1963, and John was having his own *Lady Chatterley's Lover* trial. He wrote to his solicitor:

> My main fear ... is that the jury will not have the opportunity
> of getting to know me as a human being and as an artist and I
> am most anxious that they should be given every opportunity
> in law of finding out how my mind works.

Along with this letter he sent a collection of his own publications and, for comparison, some European and Scandinavian titles he had bought in London.

You will notice that I have included many periodicals that

have an 'art value' so low that they are in my opinion as near obscene as anything can be, and that in comparison with my work they have absolutely no value whatsoever and are quite definitely designed to excite the very lowest homosexual appetite.

Later in the month he received a letter from Jerry Weinstein in Paris, which eloquently punctured some of his more puffed-up plans for the defence of *Dear Peter...* and *Inside My Skull*.

The trouble is that the book has NEVER been published in the ordinary way. It has always remained a private book sent to queens. It would be different if you had it published, even by the Olympia Press but you haven't. As far as collecting experts or qualified witnesses to testify to the literary value of the book I consider this a non-starter. Peter Shaffer is totally out of the question. First of all he wouldn't do it anyway. Secondly I should advise him not to. Thirdly, as a young playwright he has no weight whatsoever on this kind of issue. I could destroy him in five minutes in the witness box. All literary witnesses in THE case were literary critics or teachers or people in a strong public position. Peter is a mere musical critic and playwright. He might, in any event, consider the literary value nil – if he read the book ... The jury might consider on reading it that there was no obscenity and certainly it was not likely to fall into anybody's hands who might be perverted as you've only sold 350 copies!!! ... The only expert witness who would be worth calling would be Jean Cocteau but you'd obviously never get him. I couldn't say who to suggest; who has read the book????? Has anybody other than a few raging American queens?? This is the point, surely ... On further reflection I am utterly against expert witnesses or rather your attempting to find them. You are quite differently set up from Lawrence and it would be fatal to give yourself any illusions on this score.

For once, John took advice and gave up his attempts to get the *Inside My Skull* trial into the history books. Instead he put himself in the hands of his defending counsel and sat tight.

On 22 March he was back in court at 10am. At 1.15pm he was out again, with only a £10 fine for sending an indecent article through the post. *Dear Peter...* and *Inside My Skull* were deemed unlikely to deprave and corrupt, and all the seized material was returned:

> Giving me carte blanche to carry on, with care, much as I've been doing these last two years, and providing valuable publicity for a new version of *Inside My Skull*. In all it has been a worthwhile fight and experience, and certainly worth the £500 it has cost – less the £150 subscribed by my well-wishing clients, bless 'em. A mighty victory against a stupid foe!

For all his blustering bravado, though, he had been scared by the whole affair which threatened to expose him as a pornographer and blow apart the carefully constructed domestic life that shielded him from the dreaded queer world. For the rest of the 60s he was looking for an escape route.

This appeared in the shape of a wealthy American named John Dewez, son of a banking family who maintained homes in Europe and California. Dewez first wrote to John in 1962, a fan letter expressing his appreciation of some pictures of Giancarlo he had ordered after seeing the Italian model in *Manifique*. He was flattering and full of vague promises of financial support, to which John responded eagerly. By the beginning of 1963, a regular correspondence had been established, with John outlining more clearly the projects that would benefit from Dewez's financial support. In January, Dewez was offering as much as $100,000 as well as the use of a yacht harboured off Cannes and a flat in Paris. All he wanted in return was the opportunity to make friends with some of the models. Giancarlo was the first to meet Dewez in

1963: Tibor and others followed.

The two Johns met for the first time in May 1963 in Cannes. when Dewez invited the family to spend a day at his beach club at St Tropez. John was careful to take not only wife and daughters but also his latest super-masculine discovery, the young German model Helmut, a bodybuilder whom he had met and photographed with a travelling companion a few days earlier.

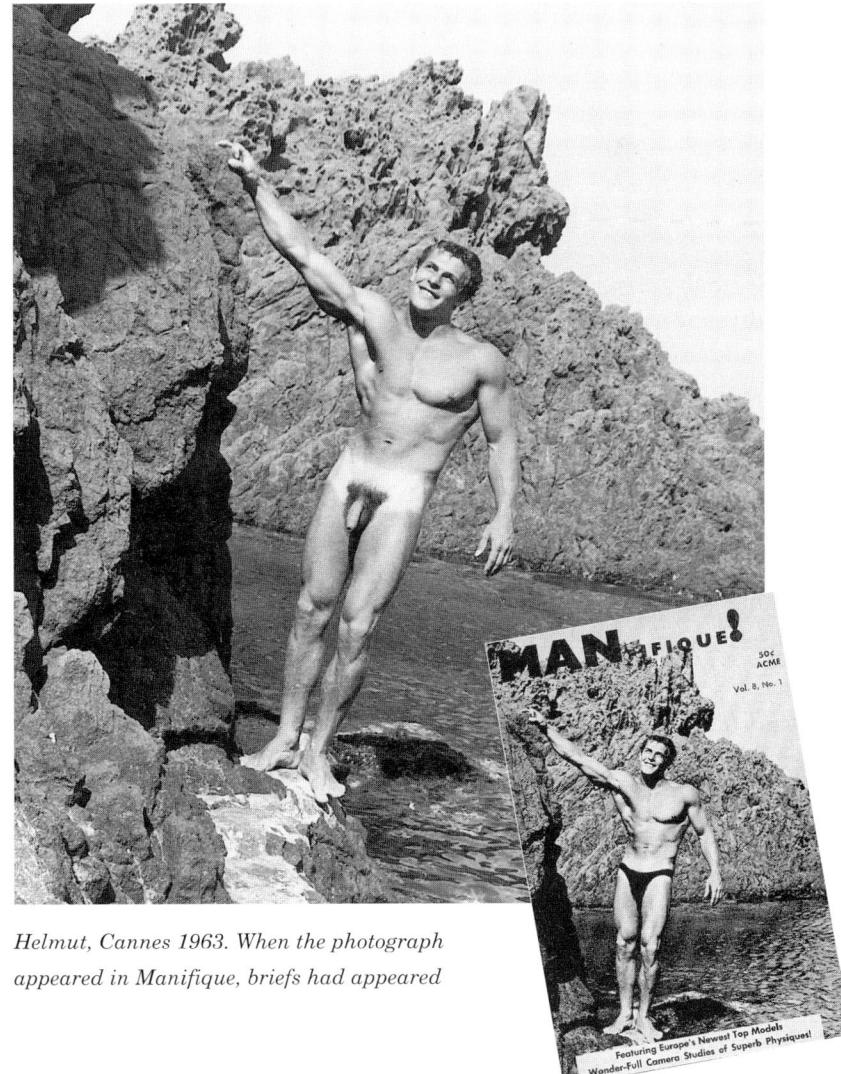

Helmut, Cannes 1963. When the photograph
appeared in Manifique, briefs had appeared

> 26 MAY: Superb and delightful day as guests of the very
> charming John Dewez. So we meet at last! All his letters seem
> likely to result in a friendship that may well be what I have
> searched for for so long. God, I hope so – please, my Guardian
> Angel! As a playboy John is a trifle tubby, but witty, kind,
> very polite, well-bred and generous to a fault. Of course he
> takes to Helmut.

It was what he had dreamed of since the War – an angel
with enough money to take away the sordid responsibility of
earning a wage, whose support would free him from his
reliance on male nude photography, lifting him into the
international jet set. Within the year he might have relocat-
ed entirely to France, running a de luxe retreat for wealthy
gay clients, photographing a few models on the side, seeing
his new novel through the presses, enjoying a sculpture exhibition here, a magazine launch there. For one who had lived
so long in the demi-monde, John was all too easily fooled by
the promise of money.

Of course, it never came. It was never Dewez's fault: it
was his hateful relatives, tying up his trust fund so that he
couldn't get his hands on the loot. And it was so hard to pin
Dewez down: he lived between Hollywood, Palm Springs,
Rome, Paris and the Riviera, and just as John had extracted
yet another promise his benefactor would be off again. He
tried in 1964 to hook him in London by pushing him into the
arms of Tibor, but just as everything seemed to be working
out Dewez was whisked away by news of his father's death.
He disappeared to Geneva with no firm promises but a lot of
hints, including the unlikely suggestion that he would buy
John's house for him. The frustrations mounted into farce.

> 10 APRIL: Telephoned John in Paris. At last all's well and
> Cannes, money etc seems OK.
> 13 APRIL: Dewez confirms all plans and promises more. He's
> sent £100 for Tibor to buy clothes with. Wish he'd send me
> some cash too.

20 APRIL: JD telegrams the settlement is okay, the £4,000 will arrive tomorrow – and about time too! I'll give up the photo-set business and use JD's money to build a respectable future with this business off my hands after ten years of headaches.

21 APRIL: £4,000 not arrived. Took Tibor to Simpson's Piccadilly to spend £66 on clothes for him. Hope JD cheque will clear before mine gets to bank.

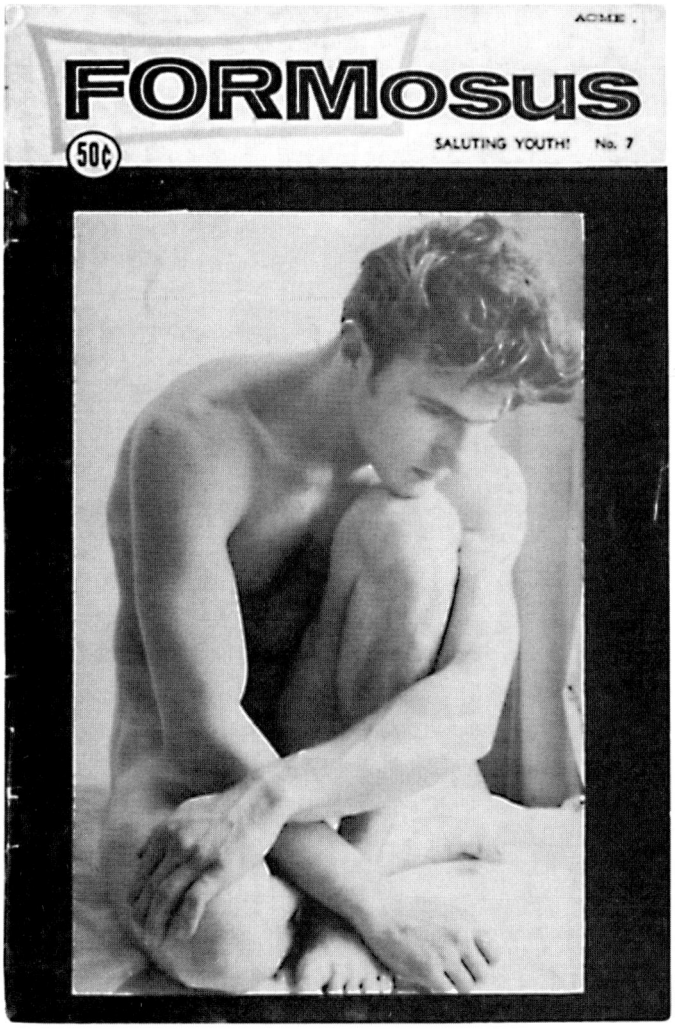

By the mid 60s Tibor was John's most popular model

23 APRIL: £4,000 still not arrived. Most of it already spoken for! Phone JD at 8pm in Paris. His mother answers and says he's too ill to come to the phone.

24 APRIL: JD telegrams to says his funds have been blocked by his elder brother and mother. Damn. That means the Cannes trip's off, amongst so much else!

This story was repeated in the months to come, with the stakes getting higher and John's plans becoming more and more frantic. He had already started living big on the promise of the money, and noted bitterly each week how much Dewez now 'owed' him. At the beginning of 1965, he went into overdrive. He took Tibor and flew to Zurich to spend three days with Dewez, staying at the best hotel the city had to offer, all at Dewez's expense. Everyone was happy – Dewez was delighted with Tibor, John was high on expectations. But the inevitable crash came a couple of weeks later when Dewez decided to spend the rest of the year in Palm Springs, shelving all plans till 1966. 'Bastard!' the diary noted, with unusual succinctness.

For the rest of 1965, John had other things to think about than the vagaries of his unreliable patron. He had suffered two very personal losses. His adoptive father, Franz, died after a long illness. And his close friend and business associate Jerry Weinstein died in Paris, forcing him finally to relocate the Jean-Paul David outfit to London and to review his security arrangements accordingly. For nearly nine months, his diary made no mention of John Dewez. But Dewez was not content to let him off the hook so easily, and took him for one last great ride in 1966.

In March, John flew to Paris, was collected in a chauffeur-driven Rolls-Royce and taken around the city to dine, to shows at the *Folies Bergère* and the Crazy Horse, and finally to his own room in Dewez's suite at the Hotel Trémoille. He returned to London no better off than before, but his gold fever had returned and he sent a string of models off to Dewez in Zurich as a token of his gratitude and expectations.

Another cheque was promised, this time for £5,000, which John was to collect on his next expenses-paid trip to Paris. Off he went, hat in hand; Dewez never showed up. Chastened, John returned to London resolving to make a final break. He phoned the Hotel Trémoille only to be told that Dewez was in some sort of trouble – an accident, the manager thought. He called every hotel, every suite, every club that knew Dewez before finally getting through to his lawyer. 'Learn that John DIED ON THURSDAY!!!!! No details.' Dewez, it emerged, had been found in his Zurich hotel bathroom by a page, the cause of death a suspected drug overdose.

John returned to Paris with all his dreams in pieces. He attended the funeral, met the Dewez family and was given a pair of his friend's gold cufflinks as a souvenir. On his way home he stopped off at the Hotel Trémoille to pick up the bronze bas relief of Tibor that he had left as a last present. He was back in London late that night, despondent about the future and smarting from his gullibility. The next morning he cheered himself up with a trip to the Oasis swimming pool where he picked up the lifeguard.

* * *

The betrayal and death of his benefactor left John depressed and humiliated. He scrabbled around for a new project, working with desperate, unfocused energy on books, plays, films and sculpture. There was a new novel doing the rounds of publishers – *London SW*, a sprawling Dos Passos-influenced account of his relationship with Anne, Giancarlo, Tibor, Andreas and in particular John Hamill. In 1968, he began working on a play entitled *Cool It Baby!*, a 'multiracial love story' set at the Cannes film festival.

The idea for *Cool It Baby!* dawned in April 1968, when he noted: 'Start to rewrite *Private Lives* as a queer play! An idea!' By July he had thought up his first title for it – *Three Cool Cats and a With-It Mouse*, and started touting the manuscript round literary agents. Absurd as it now sounds, he had good reason to be optimistic for a play dealing with a mixed race, bisexual love affair. The stage censorship powers of the Lord Chamberlain's office were about to be abolished in the UK, and by the end of the year the theatres were full of 'sexy' plays, many of which were no better than this. John was among the first audiences to enjoy the new freedoms of the London stage – on 28 September he went to see *Hair* with its brief nude scene. In October he saw *The Beard* at the Royal Court, a play which featured extensive nudity and simulated oral sex between a man and a woman. In 1969 Mart Crowley's groundbreaking gay play *The Boys in the Band* opened in London. So the idea of updating Coward with queers and negroes might have stood a chance. But *Cool It Baby!*, the name he settled on by the end of the year, never saw the light of day. John couldn't finish it, and what he did write was turned down by every agent in town (they must have known his name pretty well by now).

The project that demanded most of his energies in 1968 and 1969, though, was his venture into independent film-making. He went about this like a cross between Erich von Stroheim and Ed Wood, spinning the most unbelievable stories about his resources and ambitions to anyone who was prepared to listen.

It all started innocently enough. John had been turning out film scenarios for John Hamill since the mid 60s. He had been hobnobbing with the likes of Victor Spinetti and *Avengers* star Patrick Macnee, both of whom had excellent connections with British film producers. And he had been peripherally involved in the production of a genuine British film, the sex quickie *Her Private Hell* in which Basil Clavering and his associate Dick Schulman had invested. This was John's first real contact with Wardour Street and the grubby business of making a film, and he soon regretted his decision to put £500 of his own money into the production. *Her Private Hell* opened at the Cameo Royale, 'the most amateurish, badly acted, miscast, badly photographed, totally disappointing film I've ever seen!' But it made money –

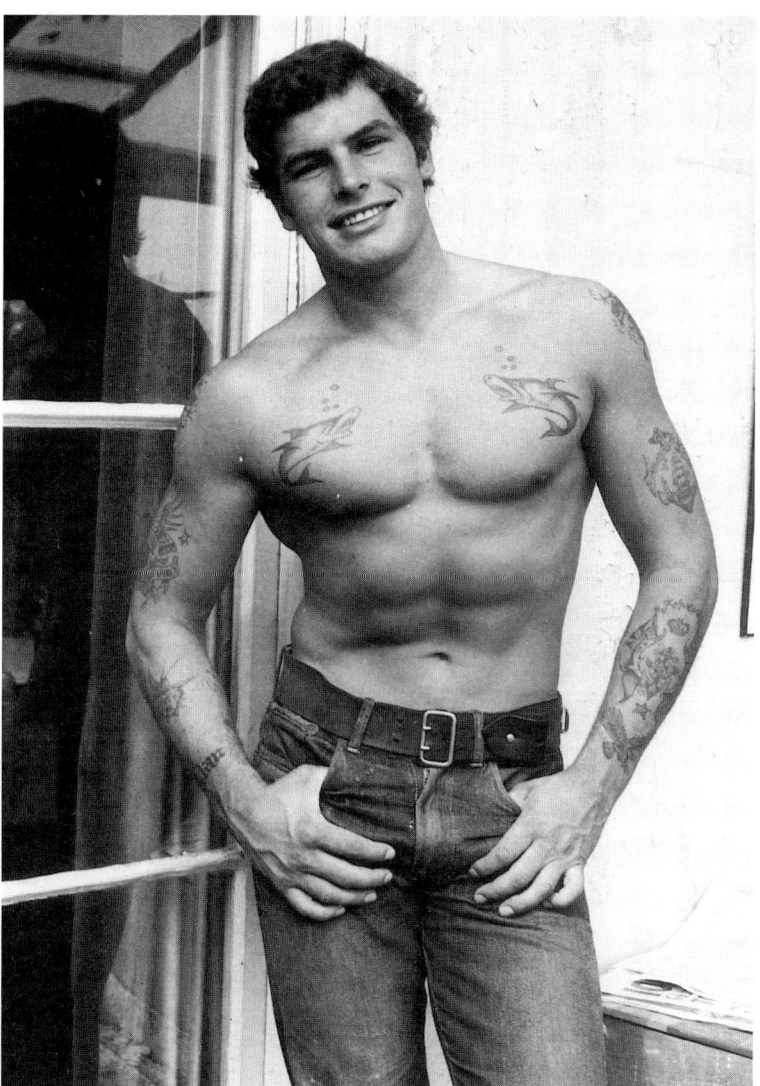

Alan, a Welsh merchant seaman, was introduced to John by the photographer
Basil Clavering, for whom he also modelled. Photographed in John's garden

lots of money – for its producers. John wanted them to pick
up on *Gigolo!* and turn a similar profit for him, provided he
could retain artistic control. While he was waiting for
Wardour Street to make a decision, he embarked on his own

film making project which put him off the cinema trade for the rest of his life.

For his subject matter, he turned to something he knew well: the Cannes Film Festival. He would go down to the Riviera with a camera, plenty of film and an assistant to document the carefree, sexy atmosphere that he so loved. He would film the rich, famous and beautiful. He would shoot love scenes between boys. Then he would come back to London, do some narrative footage in the studio and put it all together into a sun-drenched, star-studded, sex-packed epic that would break the box office records being set by *Her Private Hell*. The project was given a title, *Festival Fantastic*, Patrick Macnee agreed to provide the commentary and John Hamill was approached to play the lead (he was planning to be in Cannes that year anyway). John started 'talking up' the film to his industry contacts, and noted meetings with Richard Attenborough, David Niven, Ned Sherrin, David

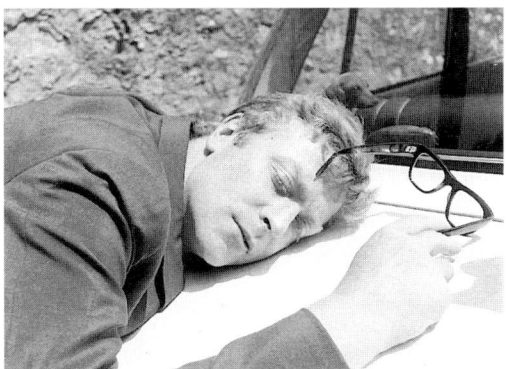

Michael Caine poses for John in Cannes

Frost, the Grade Organisation and the BBC. At the end of February he sank £800 of his own money in a 16mm movie camera, a new motorised Nikon, plus several cans of film. For once, he was well prepared and brimming with enthusiasm. Unfortunately, there were forces beyond even John's control that were to make May 1968 particularly memorable in French history.

Unaware of the student unrest brewing in Paris, he packed his cameras and his dress suit and set off for Cannes accompanied by Luke, his darkroom assistant and lover since 1962. They travelled first class as guests of Air France, John being a writer on international tourism (or so he had them believe). For the next week, he and Luke worked 'like maniacs' on the task of recording, on ciné film and stills, the atmosphere of the Cannes Film Festival. The weather was cold and windy, the beaches quiet, and without the sun to bring them out there were very few models for John. But that was not what he was there for: the film came first, and the film was his escape from slavery to male nude photography. They filmed around the Old Port, watching the luxury yachts cruising in and out, they went around the old town and the Croisette, they recorded the comings and goings at the Carlton, HQ for many of the industry types in town. Luke was looking forward to the start of the Festival on 10 May when, John assured him, the beaches would be strewn with hopeful starlets in bikinis.

The next day the town was talking not about films, but about the news of student riots in Paris, of barricades in the streets and running battles with the police. A huge thunderstorm that night prevented any further filming and left John frustrated, Luke bored. The rain set in for days, while Cannes was shocked by student action spreading rapidly south. A strike on 13 May put paid to the Festival, while John ran frantically around town trying to film celebrities and looking for Luke, who had taken to staying out all night. 'If this Festival collapses I will have lost a lot,' he noted. But it never occurred to him that what he was witnessing was something of more lasting interest than a regular star-studded Cannes Film Festival. A documentary about the reaction of the Cannes crowd to the threat of student revolution would have had real value, but to John the unrest was simply an annoyance, like jammed camera drives, bad weather and missing assistants.

Soon the Americans were leaving Cannes in droves. John

continued slogging around town laden with equipment, chatting up any celebrities who crossed his path. He collared Orson Welles and told him all about *Festival Fantastic* which Welles reportedly thought 'a fascinating project'. But by now he had been forced to change tack, abandoning moving pictures in favour of a montage of still shots. The movie equipment was too heavy for one man to carry and operate, and Luke was nowhere to be found. 'He's running around with Helmut, strange spaniards, negroes, whores, queers, arabians etc – sounds awful and is!' Things improved later in the week when the Beatles and their retinue arrived in town. John met and photographed them in clubs and restaurants, and even managed to shoot a little ciné film. But it was a false dawn. A general strike was spreading across France, and the festival closed five days early. John recovered the errant Luke and got him on a plane with several canisters of film.

The chaos of Cannes had been bad enough, but it was nothing compared to the frenzy of editing and producing into which he now threw himself. As soon as he was back in London he began assembling the thousands of colour transparencies into some sort of order. The movie footage, when it was returned, was dismissed. 'I'll use the movie-film for *Cool It Baby!*, the *Festival Fantastic* documentary will be made entirely with still shot photography, involving much creative work, but ideal for TV!' The slides were projected on to a screen and filmed with his ciné camera; John then took the film into a Wardour Street editing suite and assembled the first version of *Festival Fantastic*.

Now all he needed was someone to release, publicise and distribute the film. Possible backers came and went weekly, until Victor Spinetti (a Beatles intimate who was working with John Lennon at the National Theatre) put him in touch with the Apple company. A meeting was set up, John took some pictures of Spinetti and the Beatles, and Lennon expressed interest in the 'stills only' treatment. But nobody would commit themselves to *Festival Fantastic*, even though

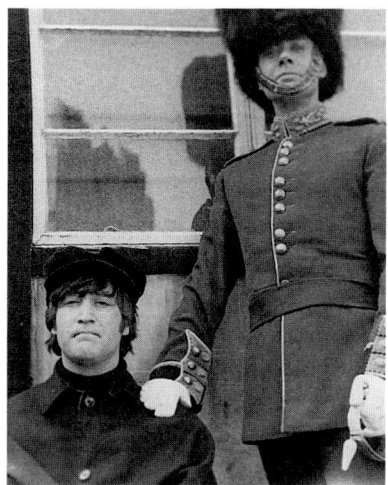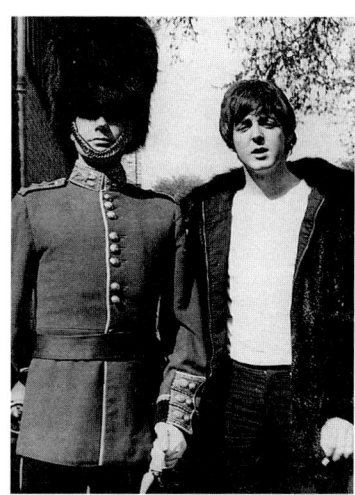

Victor Spinetti with John Lennon and Paul McCartney, photographed by John

it was hard to say 'no' to John, such was his charm and enthusiasm. 'By the end of August, my assocation with the Beatle projects had evaporated,' he wrote, 'and neither the BBC nor ITV could make up their minds about the potential value of *Festival Fantastic*. In the end it proved an interesting experiment and only minimally profitable.' In fact it cost him over £1000.

As John's hopes of cinematic glory faded, he returned to the physique business to clear his debts. The only way to get money quickly was to circularise his faithful clients, but his latest trip to Cannes had been hopeless from a photographic point of view. His American publisher Louis Elson was complaining that there were not enough new faces, that he was relying too heavily on old work, and that without new stars, *Manifique* and *Formosus* would founder. In the late summer of 1968, John went on the hunt for models.

He found the first on 20 August, and dozens more by the end of the year. But his heart wasn't in it. He was still smarting from the disappointments of May, reluctant to return to his true profession, still hoping that somebody would rescue him. For much of the autumn, he was in the darkroom, feeding an eager, neglected clientele with nude photographs. 1968 ended in despondency. On Boxing Day, after a 'pleasant but empty' Christmas, he wrote:

> Very worried about how to deal with future, work, brain-exercise etc. How do I exercise my mind back to the creative thoughts I had so easily in the 50s? How do I recapture the joie de vivre I had? How? How?? Yet if I don't, not only I, but all the family is doomed. And if I do? If I force myself out of today's prison?

Trapped by financial necessity, and feeling more and more trapped by his marriage, John at 48 was sinking into depression. Thirteen years of marriage had been happy enough, he still loved Anne and was a proud if somewhat distant father of his 11-year-old daughters. He had plentiful sex, a beautiful semi-permanent boyfriend in the shape of Luke, and a potentially lucrative business. But it was not what he wanted. Increasingly, in the diary for late 1968 and early 1969, John talks about escape.

* * *

The fiasco of *Festival Fantastic* marked the end of any confidence John had in himself as a creative, mainstream artist. Ever since the 40s he had allowed himself to believe that his novels, plays, films or sculpture would propel him into the sunlit world to which he felt he truly belonged, the world of Coward, Maugham, McBean, Vidal. But after working so hard on his film project only to meet with frustration and rejection, John realised that he had neither the talent nor the connections to be taken seriously as an artist. He continued through the 70s and 80s to work on male nude sculpture, which he sold to a few of his most ardent collectors, but he knew in his heart that it would only ever be appreciated by a coterie market. With dogged persistence, he submitted pieces to the Royal Academy for each summer's show, only to have them returned. In moments of intense personal unhappiness in the following decades, he concentrated with a passion on sculpture, claiming regularly that he had finally found the technique or material that would provide him with his true creative medium, but it was a daydream.

He returned to photography, but it was a joyless business for him now. 'Boys are really just an escape from your creative failure and social lack of success,' he noted in January 1969. 'The male nude has supported me for 30 years,' he noted in March, and rapidly knocked off two more numbers of his occasional title *Etudes*, hand printed, bound and dis-

John at work on his statue of Giancarlo. The walls are covered in reference photographs, and a drawing of Peter based on the mirror portrait (see page 101)

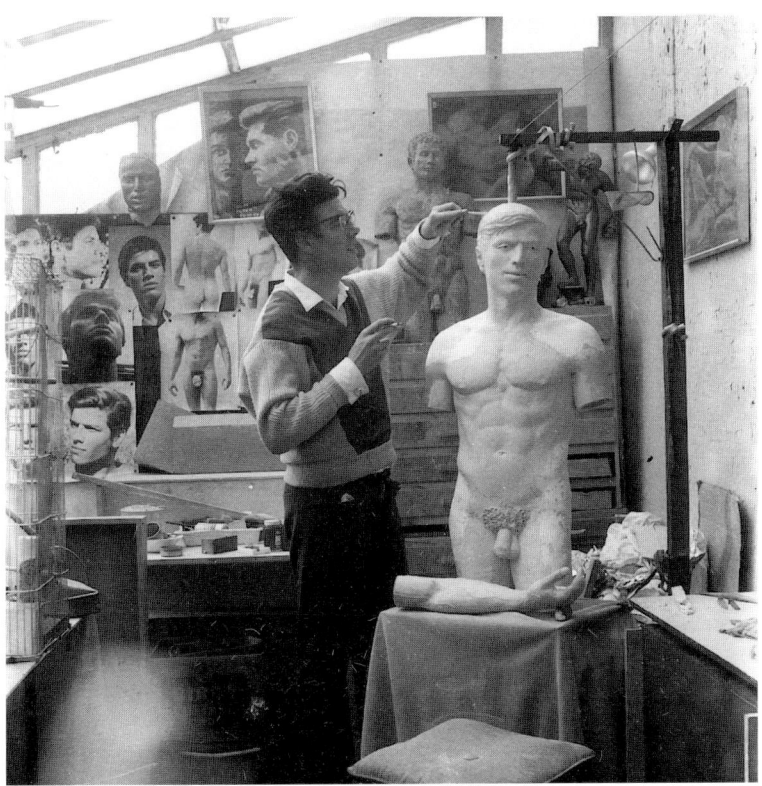

tributed direct to mail-order clients.

The heyday of physique photography was over. The style that John had pioneered, and of which he had been one of the half-dozen really great exponents, was beginning to look dated, something to be dismissed by the gay men of the 70s as pre-liberation rubbish. For nearly 20 years, his best work languished in obscurity, enjoyed only by a few connoisseurs, before a change in tastes signalled a revival of interest in his vintage pictures just before his death. But the promise of classic status wasn't enough to keep the family in comfort and plenty for the next two decades, and he had only one option: to follow the trend to more openly pornographic work.

It wasn't such a huge step – he'd been selling hard-on photos to American clients for years. But in 1969, he made the decision to concentrate more exclusively on this side of his work, accepting that the suggestive images that had made *Manifique* and *Formosus* so glorious were old hat. Setting business sense over sentiment, he realised that there was a lot of money to be made from pornography, that the market was growing with gay liberation and that he was perfectly placed to exploit it.

In 1969, John entered into business with S&H Ltd, the Harrow-based publishers of a string of nudie titles with whom he worked throughout the 70s. S&H (*Sun & Health*) were looking to expand into the new, freer market, and a gay magazine seemed like a good proposition. If John provided the artwork and editorial, S&H would print and distribute his titles. He swallowed his pride, bid a fond farewell to the artistic dreams of the 50s and 60s and launched himself into the new decade with a new profession: Pornographer.

There was one more event that cut John off even further from the memories and dreams of his youth, and that marked his passage into a sour middle age. January 1970 brought the news that Miki had died. Miki, the most life-loving, sexiest member of the wartime 'Crowd', had never recovered from the disappointments that awaited her when she returned from the Far East tour of *Calling London!*. Taking her act around the dying music-hall circuit had been even more of a disillusionment, and John watched as her dreams of stardom evaporated. She was mentioned seldom in his 60s diaries, except for occasional disapproving notes that she was now running around with the 'Chelsea lesbian crowd' and had taken to heavy drinking. It was the booze that finally killed her, after an attack of blood poisoning, just like blonde bombshell Jean Harlow. Miki, for all that John disapproved of her post-war behaviour, was his favourite memory of the happiest time of his life – the one with whom he could really raise hell, picking up soldiers and sailors together, taking them to hotel rooms and blowing their minds, laughing at the air raids together in the mad atmosphere of the Corner House or the Café Royal, planning their careers with the assurance that stardom would come as soon as the war was over. Miki, John's first and most successful Galatea, had left him.

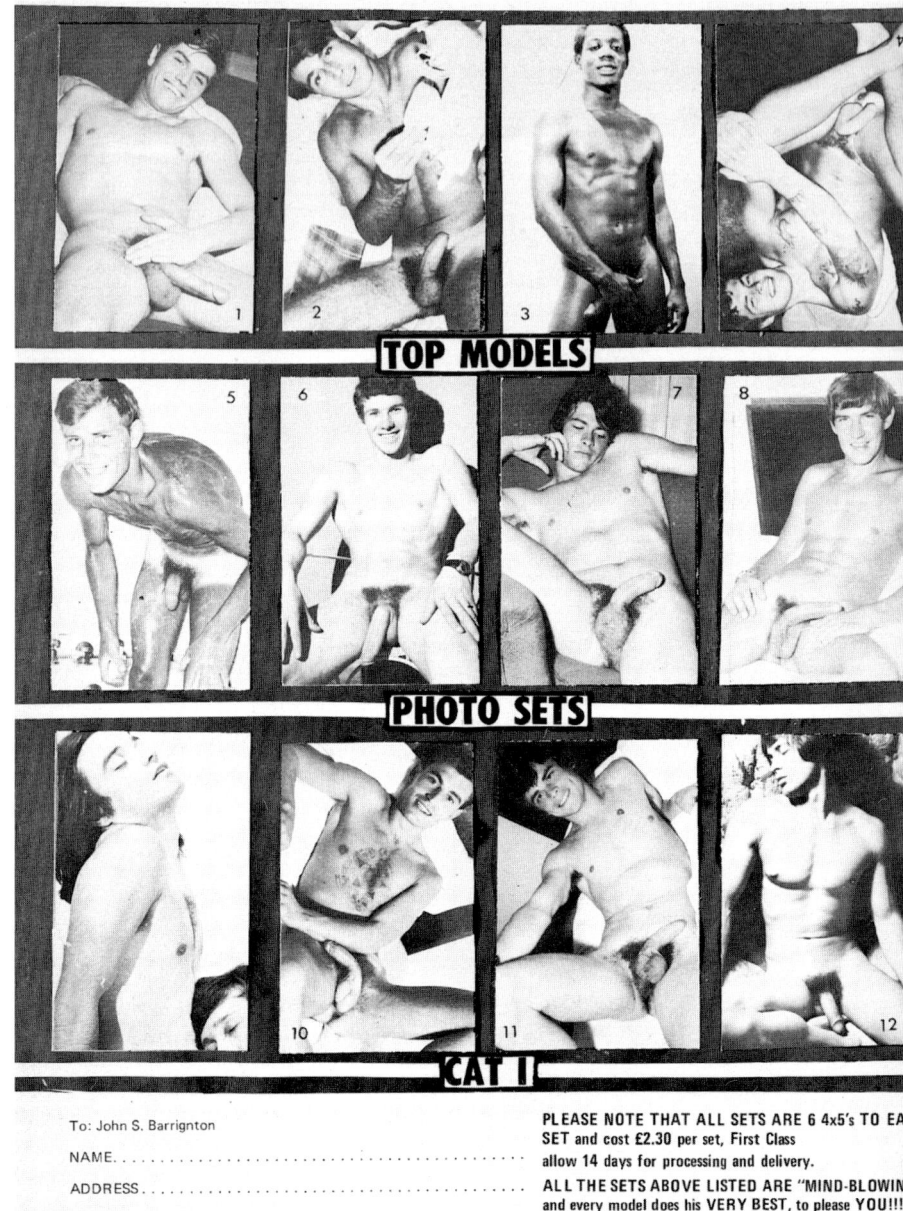

TOP MODELS

PHOTO SETS

CAT 1

To: John S. Barrignton

NAME. . . . .

ADDRESS. . . . .

. . . .

I enclose my cheque for £ . . . . Please send me Set Numbers . . . .

PLEASE NOTE THAT ALL SETS ARE 6 4x5's TO EA
SET and cost £2.30 per set, First Class
allow 14 days for processing and delivery.

ALL THE SETS ABOVE LISTED ARE "MIND-BLOWIN
and every model does his VERY BEST, to please YOU!!!

A typical page from a privately-distributed catalogue, 1976. Among the models are Giancarl
Bill David and Alan (all top row) and Michaelangelo (middle row)

Chapter Seven
Pornography

The 70s were a bitter decade. With his creative ambitions frustrated, John directed his energy into the one area that was guaranteed to make him rich but unhappy: pornography. It was a boom time, with the UK market suddenly open to more explicit material thanks to a relaxed attitude at Scotland Yard, and for ten years John worked harder than he had ever done. Work distracted him from an unhappy home life – he and Anne were drifting into a comfortable, uncommunicative doldrums as the children grew up and their interests diverged further and further. He was still looking for love in the wrong places, and his affairs with a succession of models drove a wedge between him and Anne that they could never discuss. Perhaps his chaotic personal life was a substitute for the artistic achievements that evaded him; certainly he tried every year to turn the latest trauma into a novel or screenplay which would do the rounds, meet with rejection and join the pile of yellowing manuscripts on his studio shelves.

It's clear from John's 70s work that he was half disgusted with what he was doing. His claims to be a great photographer ('the doyen of male nude photography!' as he liked to call himself) had always been tongue-in-cheek, but now they became downright cynical. The pictures were good and sexy (despite the growing frequency of shaggy footballer perms and afros), but he treated his work with scant respect. He was content to let it be published in the shoddiest magazines, badly printed, full of mistakes (for most of which he was responsible), and clearly intended to make a quick buck out of the queers desperate enough to buy them. He became even more hardened against his customers, the people from whom he made a living, and adopted the values of the sharks with whom he was associating. His personal problems occupied him so much that he seemed to have no room left in his mind or heart for other matters – and that was the way he wanted it. Perhaps it was too painful to think of aesthetics and ethics, things that had concerned him so much in his youth, when they had only ever let him down.

Ironically, the 70s were John's most prosperous period. He started the decade as broke as ever, and for the first couple of years struggled along fearing bankruptcy at every turn. But by 1974 he was making a decent living, even if he gave it away as fast as he could make it.

There were two wings to John's magazine work. Firstly, there were the titles that he published and distributed himself, mostly through his own mailing lists and those that he 'borrowed' from other operators like Basil Clavering and Lon of London. Then there were the magazines published by others, edited and designed by John and using substantial amounts of his work. It was from the latter that he made his significant income, and through which he became best known. Unashamedly, he suspended his principles and grabbed every penny that he could from the market, regardless of how much he ripped off his customers or the work of others in the field.

In the summer of 1970, he had started putting together a magazine called *NuMan*, a similar format to the old *Manifique* which he produced irregularly over the coming year and sold by mail. His lists were healthy, swollen by responses to adverts in *The Times* and *The Observer* (the usual suggestive stuff about photographs for artists' reference, by now recognised code for nudes – and the papers caught on soon enough). John was confident enough of realising a profit to invest in a new, bigger offset litho machine on which he started printing more copies of his own occasional title *Eros Erect* (limited, bound editions of his more explicit pictures) as well as pirating work that he received from Europe and America. Contacts in Germany were sending him magazines by Tom of Finland, the renowned erotic artist whose work had been appearing in Bob Mizer's *Physique Pictorial* for years. That was the tame stuff for the US market; the material that Tom was publishing in Europe was a lot harder, and when John got hold of his first examples of Tom's *Kake* series he saw it as a licence to print money. Tom of Finland's work was barely known in the UK in 1970, and it is largely through John's efforts that it came to be seen by British collectors. He started copying *Kake* titles in June 1970, and carried on pirating Tom's work for the next 15 years. He was also getting hold of America's radical sex journal *Screw*, and a few explicit gay titles, and happily flogging copies to his clients and through his sex shop outlets.

The trend in the early 70s was towards 'permissiveness', but there were dissenting voices at large. *Oz* magazine was on trial at the Old Bailey in the summer of 1971, a grim warning to people like John – the defendants went to jail, albeit briefly, despite massive public support. Even some of his private clients had been making complaints. The advertising manager at *The Observer* passed on the outraged comments of a recipient of one of John's home made magazines who had suggested obscenity and, therefore, the worrying prospect of another brush with the law. John took refuge behind his family in his reply to *The Observer*.

> I am herewith providing four volumes of my work for your perusal and, I hope, your appreciation. I have been publishing works such as these for over ten years – there is nothing new about my activity in this field: my reputation is international … It may interest you to know that I am married with two

daughters. I would not offer anything for sale which they could not look at.

But the bluff didn't work for long. In October, *The Observer* refused to carry any more Barrington adverts and in mid 1971, *The Times* followed suit.

John feared a purge, and reorganised his business affairs to 'security status' – hiding his negatives and mailing lists in

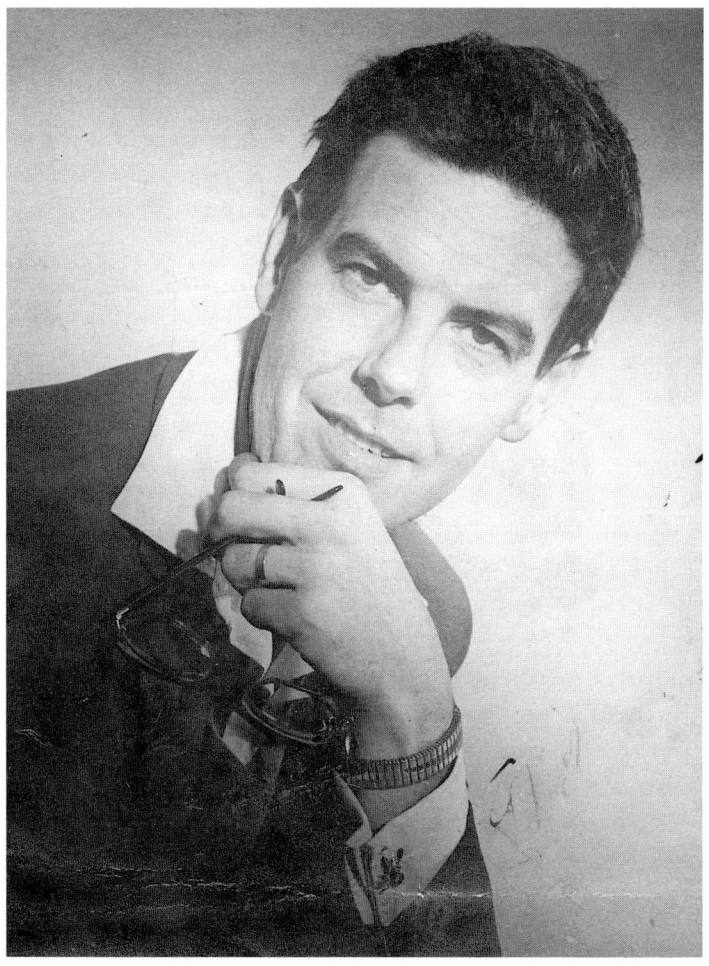

The respectable face of Barrington, 1970

secret drawers located behind panels in his desk, in cup-
boards and safes under floorboards. His secrecy mania accel-
erated during the 70s; at the time of his death, his house was
a bizarre Aladdin's cave of secret compartments, each sprout-
ing some pornographic stash that even John had forgotten
about.

Caution aside, he had little choice but to go with the flow.
He realised that others were exploiting an area to which he
felt he had the right by seniority and superiority. He visited
the pornographer John Stamford at his newly opened Stud
Cinema in the East End and viewed gay sex films – 'very
depressing, I'm a real has-been!' he noted in the diary. By
early 1972 he had started contributing regular pictures and
articles to *Curious* magazine, a pansexual publication from
which he made a modest income, and was musing in the
diary 'Would a 100% homo mag be possible in the UK?' The
answer was provided when he met John Prichard.

John Risley Prichard was an even more accomplished
pornographer than John. He had been publishing material
through the post and through magazines far more explicit
than anything John produced, and was deeply involved in
the porn underworld. He was also a more blatant crook than
John (who, even when he was up to his neck in monkey business, retained a ghost of his aristocratic distaste for low life).
Prichard was similar to John in many respects – a self-seek-
er, a dishonest charmer – and the two men treated each
other with a respect born of mutual recognition. Their friendship and business relationship began in 1972, when Prichard
had expressed interest in investing in *Eros Erect*. It was a
project close to John's heart, as he revealed in the specifica-
tions that he was sending out to potential subscribers.

> Large and perfectly printed, exceptional photographs of solo,
> dual and group studies, depicting EXCEPTIONAL models of
> the very highest physical standards ... The whole publication
> to be designed for uninhibited, UNASHAMED FUN!!!.
> Nothing 'serious', no banner-waving, no Gay Lib 'hang ups',

no pulpit or soap-box oratory: only a carefree joie de vivre and
a happy acceptance of the basic facts of life!

With specially-prepared dummies, he went to visit
Prichard at his well-feathered nest in Holland Park.
Prichard liked what he saw, gave him £100 advance and told
him to change the title from the arty *Eros Erect* to the more
direct *Hard*.

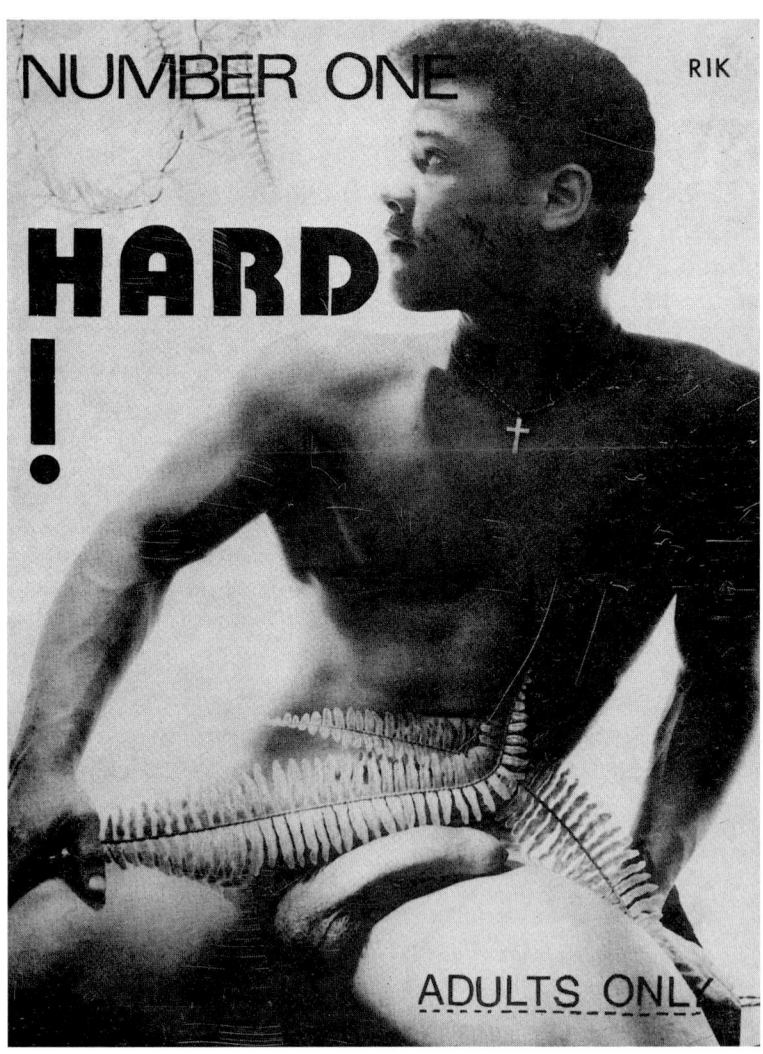

John was thrilled with the commission and went to work on *Hard* straight away. By the end of the summer he was turning out regular titles for Prichard, some gay, some straight, producing artwork which Prichard would then have printed and distributed. Income jumped immediately ('£500 in the last four weeks!') and he took a lease on premises in Sackville Street W1, the first time he had had separate business premises since he closed the Richmond studio. Now, he thought, he could finally expand into legitimate photography while continuing his nude work as a profitable backroom exercise. He advertised the Sackville Street studio in *Contacts*, the theatrical resource publication. Two people turned up in the first month, and that was it. He kept his West End premises for a year, but once again faced the fact that the world was only interested in his sexual material.

Once again John succumbed to depression. The death of Noël Coward was another reminder of his own failure to penetrate the glamorous international queer world that had always shut him out. He watched Coward's memorial service on the news in May: 'Everyone except me there!' he noted bitterly. Prompted by bitter nostalgia, he read over his diaries for the early 1950s:

> Very depressing time going back to the early 50s diaries. So many names and lovers I can't picture. I can't see where I went wrong – so much work and so little achievement.

He went to find entertainment and company in the gay bars of Earls Court. After an evening cruising Boltons and the Coleherne he felt 'like a frustrated old queer, a consenting cuckold'. He announced in June that he was 'depressed and suicidal – except I'm not the type'.

Work from Prichard dried up for a while, and John's income plummeted to the extent that he considered going on the dole. He worked out his frustrations in a novel manuscript entitled *Luc!* (a dreary account of his marriage and sex life, and like *Horror!* submitted as the work of an anonymous author) but had to admit that he was now dependent on the income that he could earn from John Prichard. With cap in hand, he went back to Prichard and asked for more work, which was duly forthcoming (another *Hard* title). He planned a home made title for his private clients, a *Cockbook* which would consist of page after page of penises, with a cod serious introduction on the aesthetics of the subject ('Palmistry? Why not Penistry?'). Soon he was up to his ears again – three titles for Prichard, a special edition for *Curious* and a number of limited edition 'art books'.

In December 1973 John took out an advertisement in *Gay News* announcing '*Manifique* Reborn!'. With his income rapidly increasing he decided to relaunch his own most successful titles, *Manifique* and *Formosus,* with more explicit shots of the models who had made him famous, as well as newer work. A generation of gay men had grown up as fans of Yves, Giancarlo, Andreas and the rest, but had only been able to get full frontal nudes of them as mail-order photo sets. Now they could buy *Manifique* and *Formosus* complete with cocks, some of them well on the way to being erect. He became even more daring and, at Prichard's instigation, produced titles like *Friends* (porn duals, some of them old, some of them specially produced) and *Superstuds.*

Heady with success, John rallied from his recent depression and set about enjoying life once again with more studio 'giggles' with his models than at any time in the last three years. 'Stephen – Jesus freak but very photogenic – !!! – refuses money,' he wrote of one conquest in February 1974, and on another occasion admitted that his relationship with his models was nothing other than prostitution. 'Whores exist – so why not use them?' he noted with uncharacteristic candour for a man who, at other times, strenuously denied that he had ever needed the services of a prostitute.

In the middle of this happy-go-lucky period, his mother died. Grace had been ill for some time, living in an old people's hospital in Epsom where John and the family visited as often as possible, at least once a week. Her deterioration into

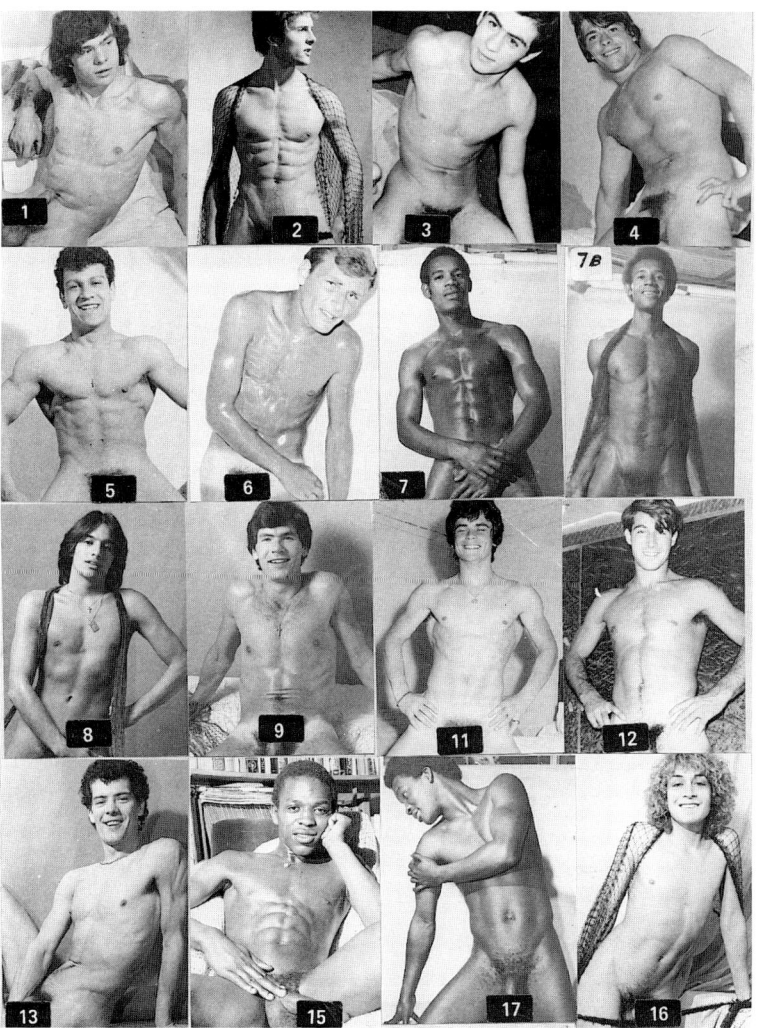

John's hard-core catalogues went under the title A Camera Life Class,
maintaining the old pretence of artists' reference studies

unpredictable, bad-tempered senility was a sore trial to her
son, who loved and respected his mother for all that he
kicked against her middle-class values. It was she who
taught him to think so highly of himself, she who had insisted he was above the common run of men, and now she was

gone. Towards the end of Grace's life, John wearily repeated in his diary 'I wish she would die!', likening her to a vampire who was sapping his vitality and resources. But when Grace finally died in February 1974, he was thunderstruck. In her will, she left him the little that she had. The diary went blank, his libido collapsed (he had no sex with anyone for nearly two months) and he cancelled as much work as possible. He never wrote at any length about this bereavement; he always shrugged off the deaths of those closest to him. But it seems from contemporary notes that Grace's death left him feeling isolated from his youth, spiritually alone. The present was all he had.

Distraction was at hand thanks to Prichard, who was opening a new shop as an outlet for all the titles that he and John were creating. The Man to Man shop opened in Notting Hill Gate in May 1974, its front window dressed with John's male nude sculpture, the interior stocked with Prichard-Barrington titles. It was one of a half dozen such shops in London that opened in the mid 70s, most of them outlets for small, growing publishing empires: Zipper in Camden Town, Incognito in Earls Court, Stud in Frith Street, Soho. Nobody wanted to buy the sculpture (canny Prichard had put it there to give the shop an arty appearance, conscious that customers were only interested in the magazines within) but it was a lucrative outlet nonetheless. The shop moved premises a few times and received regular visits from the vice squad (for which Prichard always took the rap) but remained a goldmine for the rest of the decade – and the source of most of John's professional headaches.

During a lull in the Man to Man shop's fortunes, he made another attempt at setting up in independent business by taking a lease on premises at 252 Brixton Hill – Gallery 252 as he called it. Here he attempted to sell his unpopular sculptures, his artwork (he had been churning out silverpoint engravings of his photographs, technically competent but overpriced) and 'serious' photographic work. Brixton at this time was not the semi-bohemian enclave it would later

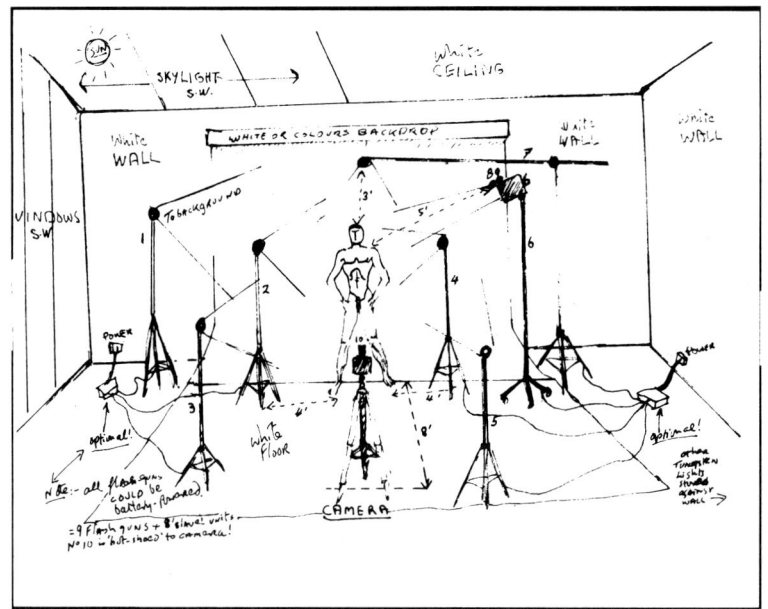

A sketch of John's home studio, 1978

become; the atmosphere could hardly have been less appro-
priate for a male nude art gallery. John was happy enough,
even though he did no business. It was a daily escape from
home, and he liked the largely black population of the area –
his sexual tastes from the mid 70s having turned almost
exclusively towards black men. Gallery 252 closed after five
months; in January 1975, he moved his business operations
to his own home and opened Gallery 86, an in-house display
of pictures and sculpture that remained an eccentric place of
pilgrimage for fans and collectors.

Gallery 86 did well, as did John's publications. With and
without Prichard, he was now producing dozens of titles a
year – pirated work by American photographers Jim French
and Bruce of LA, hard and soft core collections of his own
work. It was well for John that business was booming, for at
the beginning of 1975 Prichard had been arrested and
charged with various offences and released on £20,000 bail

pending trial at the Old Bailey. The case dragged on till August, when Prichard was fined £3,250 under the Obscene Publications Act and was forced to close down his operations. Only for a while, though; by the beginning of 1976 he was back in action, making John work faster and harder than ever before. Prichard, it seemed, was hell bent on making as much money as possible before the authorities finally made it impossible for him to live in Britain.

Prichard handed over editorial control of all his titles to John, who moved into the office in Notting Hill Gate to produce *International Focus*, a pocket-sized gay publication that mixed photographs with long, rambling articles about sex by John (under various pseudonyms), cartoons, questionnaires and letters. The first number was published at the end of October, and Prichard commissioned a further six over the next three months. They relaunched an existing S&H title *Man to Man* as a larger magazine with more colour pages, featuring John's work as well as huge chunks lifted directly from American and European porn titles. His files were crammed with pages ripped from rival publications, from which he simply had plates made and sent to the printer, often not even bothering to remove the original folio from the pirated page.

John was working at such a rate that the quality of his output was plummeting. He was never a careful worker, but the mid 70s was a low point. *Man to Man* and *International Focus* were shoddily home made, full of spelling mistakes, pictures wrongly captioned, shaky letraset headlines and roughly hand-rendered rules. He complained bitterly to his diary about how badly the printers were reproducing his work.

To feed demand he went on a model binge, recruiting mostly from Notting Hill. Yaw, aged 18, arrived on 1 July 1976, sporting probably the biggest cock that John ever photographed. Christian and his brother Jean-Pierre, both in their early 20s and from Senegal, were brought to the house one sunny afternoon and photographed running through the garden sprinkler. Brian, a rather plain but masculine plumber who was persuaded to strip for the camera, became one of his most popular models and a frequent visitor. It was a long, hot,

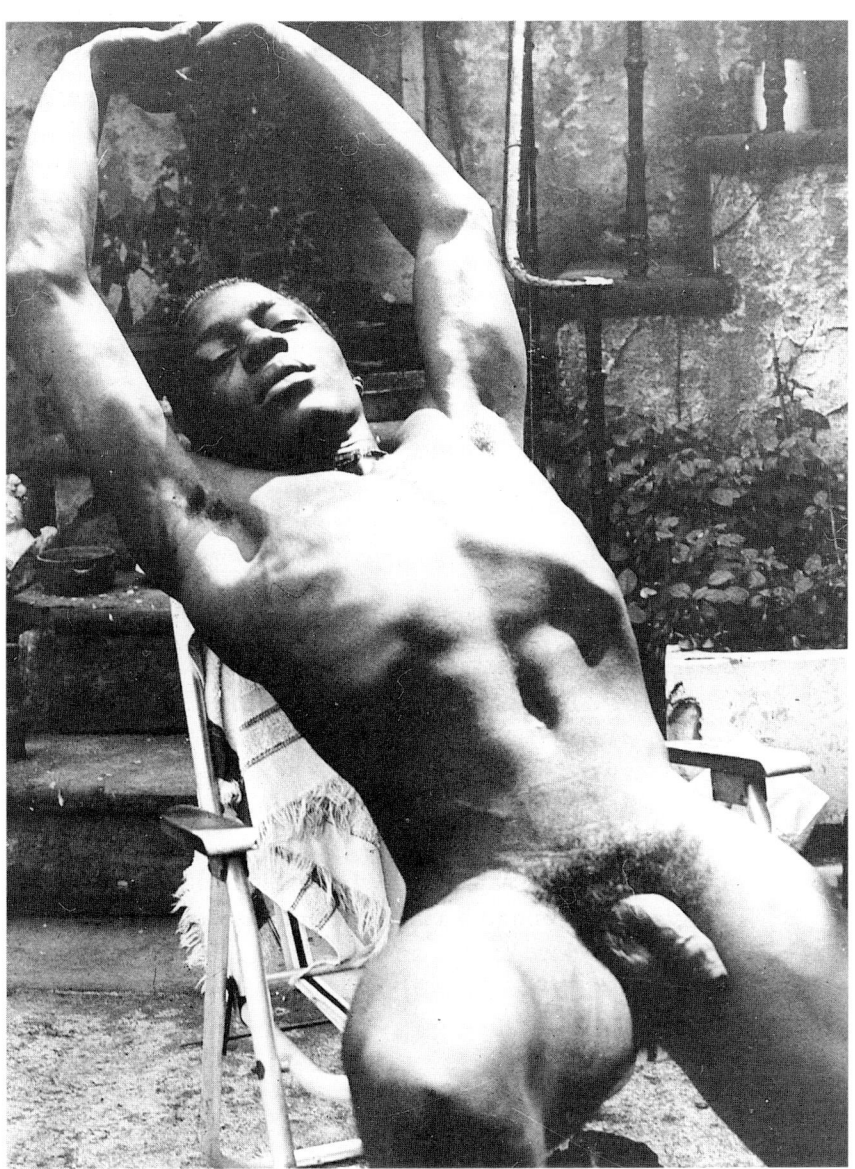

Christian stretches out in the back garden

dry summer in London, and John, whose mood was always best when the sun was shining, was having a ball. This madness continued for the rest of the year. The titles came thick and fast, some of them running into ten or twelve editions – *Hy!*, *Banana Splits*, *Proud*, *Afrodisiac*. In between times, John was running around London nightclubs among them Maunkberry's, a gay club in Jermyn Street which, by mid 1976, was already a favourite haunt of Malcolm McLaren, Vivienne Westwood and the early punk set. It's interesting to speculate on what John and his friends would have made of these rubber-clad aliens. One of the classic punk T-shirts, modelled in dozens of photographs by Sid Vicious, bore an image by American artist Etienne of two cowboys standing in profile, their cocks touching. John had been pirating Etienne's work; it's possible that he provided the source material for this subversive punk gesture. It wasn't his only bizarre connection with the music world: in the summer of 1976, he was introduced to Bob Marley by a model, Lindsay, who had joined the Wailers' entourage and travelled to Jamaica with them. It was Marley, John claimed, who gave him a handful of grass one summer afternoon. On Lindsay's suggestion, he picked out the seeds and planted them in clumps all over the garden. The plants flourished and developed into large, healthy bushes. John and his guests got stoned on the pickings throughout the following year.

* * *

The frenzy of the 70s was spinning towards a crash. In the 60s, John's run of good fortune dried up when the moral climate relaxed, putting the old physique masters out of business, ushering in the age of porn. Just when he had adapted and learnt to flourish, the tide turned once again. Raids on West End porn shops were having serious repercussions on the Prichard-Barrington partnership, and would soon force Prichard out of the country. In September 1977 he was up at the Old Bailey again, this time on a more serious charge than publishing dirty books: attempted buggery and gross indecency with a minor. The case was dropped, but one thing was clear: the police were gunning for Prichard, and the UK was no longer a safe place for him to stay. By 1978 he was spending more and more time in the south of France, eventually setting up in business over there, investing heavily in video pornography and running a whorehouse in Thailand. John and he remained business partners of a more distant kind, but the reliable source of income that had fed John for the best part of a decade had dried up.

John carried on for other publishers, and put out his own titles and photo sets for private clients. Raids on Zipper and a handful of other shops and publishers continued with expensive stock seizures as the vice squad attempted, through a mixture of clean-up rhetoric and brazen corruption, to put the porn kings out of business. Gay magazines, which had been bending the law by showing pictures with semi-erections, sometimes with full erections, became coy again. There was never any legislation in the UK to say that a publisher couldn't print a picture of a hard cock – it was simply that, by the early 80s, more and more juries decided that that was where the borderline lay between 'erotica' and 'pornography'. John's heyday as a magazine publisher was over, and he was ready to get out of it.

It took a disaster to push him. A string of bad luck put his major distributors out of business and he was left with an expensive new project, the revived large-format *Manifique*, and no means of getting it sold. He continued to publish his own titles *Bold* and *Proud*, but effectively his magazine days were over.

One final humiliation awaited John at the end of the decade. In early 1979, he had befriended a character named Graham, who ran the shortlived Giovanni's Room club-restaurant in Belsize Park. They discovered that they shared a taste for black men, and hatched a plan to use their show-business connections (Graham owned a recording studio, he said) to help the kind of boys they favoured. And so John embarked on the dodgiest of a lifetime of dodgy ventures, the Afro-Caribbean Agency. Graham took a lease on offices in Museum Street, and John spent much of 1979 happily running around his old stamping grounds, reliving memories of the war and his ARP billet in the nearby university library. 'This may be my best chance!' he wrote in his January diary, already aware that the publishing business was collapsing beneath him.

For the first few weeks he was hard at work, visiting rehearsals, interviewing hopeful actors and singers, brushing up his business contacts and telling them about the fabulous new roster of talent that he and Graham were grooming in Museum Street. He set about recruiting clients through the back pages of the *Stage*, promising to talented young Afro-Caribbean performers an instant entrée into a world of casting directors, provincial tours and recording contracts. A confident note at the back of John's February diary suggested that he was planning to use his publishing and photography clients to rustle up interest (and capital) in his new company. But he had no more idea now of how to operate in the business than he did when he and Belle Avalon were booking variety acts around the dying music hall circuit of the 40s and 50s.

The honeymoon with Graham was shortlived. By 22 February John complained that 'I can't reach Graham, who owes me £280!' for sculpture that he had sold him to adorn the interior of Giovanni's Room. In March the club was burgled, the statues mysteriously stolen, and John suspicious. By May it was clear that the agency was never going to make any money and that, despite John's sincere efforts, Graham wasn't serious about the business. In October, John resigned, Graham accused him of being a liar and a thief, and the Afro-Caribbean Agency closed down.

He ended the decade on a sad and sombre note. He was fast approaching his 60th birthday, and facing a daily reminder in his shaving mirror that, although still handsome, he was no longer by any stretch of the imagination a

young man. He couldn't even look forward to his annual trip
to Cannes – the money wasn't there. Could it be that after 40
years of sexual, professional and emotional madness, he had
simply lost the will to go on?

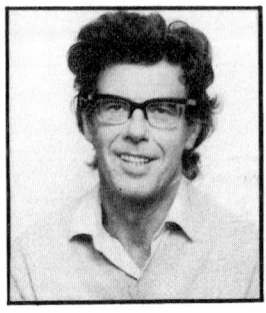

1978

John S. Barrington

Born 1920. St. Martin's School of Art (London) and L'Ecole des Beaux Arts (Paris), 1937 to 1941. Theatrical design, sets and costumes, Fashion design and illustration, 1937 to 1950. Commercial art and design, 1940 to 1960. Theatrical production, journalism, PR work, 1940 to 1980. Fashion and theatrical photography, 1945 to 1984. Magazine(s) editor, 1957 to 1979. Sculptor, engraver, artist, 1937 to 1984. Photographer of the male nude, 1944 to 1984, also a portrait photographer, 1937 to 1984, he has 'shot' over 500 international celebrities, 'stars', royalty, etc.

Happily married for thirty years, with two adult daughters, Barrington has lived since 1960 with his family in Barnes, London.

He has published 12 books on art and photography, 2 novels and 4 other books; he has also written plays and films, and produced and directed plays and films: now he is experimenting with video techniques.

Barrington had never been idle,

John's CV from the dustjacket of The Romantic Male Nude

Chapter Eight
Autobiography

For 40 years, John had been searching for a successful means of self-expression. Writing, acting, directing, designing, painting, drawing, sculpture and film-making had all been tried and had failed. Photography and publishing were undoubted successes, but could never satisfy his artistic appetite. In the 1980s, in his sixties, John discovered the material that was uniquely his, that could legitimately count as his personal contribution to art: his own life story.

For many years, at least since *Out of Sickness* appeared in 1950, he had reworked stories from his own experience into fiction. But *Out of Sickness* and its successors – *Dear Peter...*, *Inside My Skull*, *London SW* and *Luc!* – were too fancy, too literary, and too good at avoiding the truth. In the 80s, he decided that his autobiography would be interesting on its own merits. His shadowy background in pre-war London, his discovery of sex and love in a bomb-blasted city, his relationship with Peter and subsequently Anne, and his double life since marriage – all these things added up to a unique, eccentric tale. As well as the personal recollections was his work as a photographer, his relationship with a burgeoning homosexual culture and his involvement in pornography. Stir in a few dozen celebrity names and some choice pieces of gossip, and the mix became irresistible.

In the last decade of his life, John ploughed vast amounts of time and money into this project. It should have been simple enough – there was masses of material, well recorded in diaries and photographs, and all he needed to do was to put it into order and write it up as a straightforward, confessional narrative. But he could never resist the temptation to complicate, to obscure, to elaborate. His autobiographical writings, which obsessed him more and more as the decade progressed, became a labour of self-justification, a plea for understanding, a boastful aggrandisement of his own achievements. In remembering every event, John reopened arguments in his own mind and tried to work them out on paper. His relationship with Peter, it seemed at one point, was the crucial experience of his life, and he organised the story around that. But then he got to thinking about his relationship with Luke, and the tangled skein of his marriage, and decided that was more important. Later in the decade, new experiences demanded similar amounts of attention, and he would start reorganising the material once again.

There was another big problem for John as autobiographer. Unlike Frank Harris and James Agate, his touchstones in this field, he couldn't write. Sometimes his prose was simple and lucid, but more often it was overwrought, gushing and full of clichés, veering between the heated style of a porno novel and the intellectual pretentiousness of a sixth-form essay. His material was wonderful, but after it had been through this literary mincing machine it was unpalatable.

Whatever the shortcomings, John's autobiographical efforts gave him purpose in the last ten years of his life. Frustrated in every other avenue, he could at last surrender himself to his great work, to which every memory and every new experience was relevant. His autobiography was a wonderful toy, never boring, constantly presenting a new challenge and giving him a sense of importance that had been chipped away by the hard work and emotional storms of the 70s.

He started by dusting off some of his early publications.

20 MARCH 1982: Re-read *Out of Sickness* for the first time in 30 years – not at all bad! Very good in parts! Probably still the best novel about London 1940-45! Parts brought a lump to my throat and tears to my eyes...

The past began to prey on his mind as he spent days buried in diaries and letters, neglecting more pressing business demands.

The past is all there is – a real fact! For 40 years I've collected and cherished a small roomful of reference material and memorabilia to aid me in writing my autobiographical work(s) – now I feel that I must face the fact that I will never write a detailed book – a very depressing truth to face. Or am I being pessimistic?

What troubled him was not the literary difficulty of the task – that would never have put him off – but the problems that an honest autobiography would cause in his relationship with Anne and his daughters. How could he continue in his comfortable existence if Anne, and the reading public, knew that his life was half given over to the pursuit and exploitation of sexually pliant young men? His solution was characteristic.

Crossing Hammersmith Bridge came up with title and first para and plan for long-delayed autobiography! As two people in one skull/body. Each in love with the other, each lovers of opposite sexes! *He & I*. All very Proustian. 'Recherchez les temps partout.'

This, he was convinced, was the way to express the psychological and artistic truth about his life. In fact, it was a ploy to avoid the truth. It was this evasiveness more than anything else that undermined all subsequent attempts at writing his life story.

John worked sporadically on *He & I* (or *In Search of Me* or *An Extra-Ordinary Life*), writing sketches of the war years, his relationship with Peter, his memories of childhood. But the right form and style evaded him. 'Work backwards!' he announced as a revelation in June 1984, intending to start with the present then write his way back to the war. In November he became despondent after reading Coward's diaries and comparing his own achievements since the 40s.

> More nostalgic frustration reading about friends who have made it in show-biz, knighthoods etc. Did I waste my life? Too late to worry or care if I did...

Two factors spurred him on. Firstly, he had embarked on a new relationship with Melvyn, a young black man 43 years his junior whom he had met at the Notting Hill carnival and who was keeping him 'extravagantly busy!!!' Secondly, he had made an important discovery, one that added urgency and drama to his writing: he was dying.

He had started experiencing health problems in 1985 – intense stomach pains prevented sleep, and he was passing blood in his urine and stools – and by the end of the year his condition had deteriorated enough for him to seek medical advice. After tests at Hammersmith Hospital he was diagnosed with an enlarged spleen and felt immediately better. But it was a short reprieve. Soon he was back in hospital for more tests, this time on his bone marrow. Results came back in August: he was suffering from leukaemia. 'Sentence of death?' was all he wrote in his diary, and went straight on to the medication his doctor had prescribed. He had, he was told, maybe as little as a year to live.

With his new love affair and his impending death uppermost in his mind, John attacked his autobiography with renewed vigour. He poured his heart out across hundreds of pages and hours of tape, recruited friends as collaborators and advisers, and approached every agent and publisher he had ever met. 'Will the author live long enough to complete this work?' he asked in his mail-outs, revelling in the drama of the situation. 'A sentence of death, as Dr Johnson said, concentrates the mind wonderfully.' The results were a chaotic mish-mash of fact and fantasy. Notes from diaries had been expanded and embroidered, crammed with celebrity names ('Dear Dickie Attenborough!' 'Dear Edith Piaff!' [sic]) and endless sexual adventures. His married life was dissected in excruciating, unsparing detail. Hundreds of letters from boyfriends in the forces or in prison were copied word for word. And there were John's 'mini-essays' – thousand-word asides in which he shared his thoughts on politics, sexuality and the uniqueness of his own life.

John worked on *Inside My Skull* (the title he once again settled on) in bursts of unfocused energy, cutting and pasting each new draft as he changed his mind almost every week. When he died, there were 11 different drafts in his office. He complained that Anne would never read his work and declined to discuss the past, but went into toe-curling descriptions of their sex life. He insisted that his main reason for writing the book was to make money for the family, but realised that Anne would never consent to the frank book that he proposed.

His enthusiasm waned as collaborators and publishers tired of the project, which showed no sign of a satisfactory outcome. In his last year, John launched himself into a frantic attempt to finish the book that, instead of bringing him a late but glorious success, had become another reminder of his failure to finish anything.

* * *

John's obsession with writing his autobiography was at its height when he had little else to do. The porn business crashed in the early 80s, leaving him unemployed. Sex shops were raided all over London: *Him* magazine lost thousands of pounds' worth of stock, and even Gay's the Word, the intellectually respectable and porn-free bookshop near Russell Square, was visited by Customs and Excise who made off with titles by Gore Vidal, Christopher Isherwood and Catullus. John wasn't immune from this kind of attention either.

> 23 JANUARY 1981: The Worst Possible Happens – 10 Police raid!!! Too much seized!! Most serious ever in 20 yrs! At Richmond Police Station till 8.15pm. Dreadful! And could be worse to come – why? Haven't I enough problems already? Is this 'the final chapter' of my life?

The police had been biding their time, watching his operations unknown to him, waiting for the right time to pounce. In the January raid they took magazines, films, photographs, account books and mailing lists, leaving him fearing the very worst. But the case fizzled out. He reported to Richmond Police Station again in May and June to be charged, only to have his appearance postponed on both occasions. When he was finally charged in August, the police brought four charges of possession of pornographic material for gain, and one of possession of a prohibited weapon, to wit one of the sword sticks that John kept in his hall umbrella stand. 'Fantastic luck!!!' read the diary on 23 September, when the charges were dropped; but it was another warning, and John imposed even stricter security measures at home. A chance meeting a few months later with the officer who had led the raid revealed some disturbing facts.

> 28 JUNE: Sgt T tells me that 5 complaints in writing caused his visit in 81!!! But interviewed only one man who he said he thought was 'vindictive, for some reason'. I told him I was now retired. He also said that local CID had known about my business for many years!!!

John's claim that he had 'retired' was partly true. He had given up magazine production, and was running his mail order business down too; at the end of 1982 he reckoned he only had 12 active clients, and they were buying less and less.

Inactivity led to introspection.

> In the last six months I've tried and dropped publishing, agency work, portrait photography, mail-order, nude photography and a new gallery – what on earth do I do? For all I've achieved I could just as well have lain in the sun for hours!

The lack of work and income had become so acute by 1982 that John was forced to borrow money from Anne, calling himself 'a parasite' in his diary. On one particularly bleak day, looking around his office studio at the piles of unfinished projects, the photographs that stirred sentimental memories, he came across a fragment of poetry.

> 'And scribbled lines like fallen hopes
> 'On backs of tattered envelopes' – my life in 2 lines!!!

* * *

But he didn't wallow for long. Soon a new project had come along that claimed his attention for most of a year, a curtain-raiser to his more serious autobiographical efforts in the second half of the decade.

Sexual Alternatives for Men started life as a questionnaire in *International Focus*, the magazine that John had published for Prichard in the 70s. In each edition, there had been a detailed set of questions to which he sought answers from his readers. 'Exploding Illusions – Exploring Facts – Exposing Phallasies!!!' read the headline introducing two closely-printed pages of multiple choice.

> I am bisexual/homosexual/always have been/became bisexual/homosexual ..... years ago. Prefer to look at/go to bed with/to love age groups: 12-15/16-18/19-24/25- 35/over 35. Am/not promiscuous. Would be if possible ... Am/not circumcised. Penis length erect: 5 inches – 5½ inches – 6inches – 6½ inches – 7inches – 7½ inches – 8 inches . . . My penis is/not deformed in any way/curves to the left/ to right/to belly.

> Do/not like being fellated ... I have told my wife/lover/girl-
> friend about my separate sex/life. I am VERY secretive about
> it. Because I want to be/ have to be/because I am ashamed of
> it...

It was an extension of the type of psychological reports
that John had been drawing up for reluctant servicemen during and after the war, and fed his mania for figures and sta-
tistics. Replies came aplenty, and he thought he might do
something commercial with his data. At first it was to be
called *Facts and Fantasies*, and he set about typing up the
responses, elaborating them wherever possible, and adding
his own commentary. He entered into an agreement with his
printer to produce the book under the imprint The
Alternative Publishing Company, with optimistic ideas about
its market prospects.

> Surely one could sell 30,000 in 12 months at a net profit
> of £1.00 each? Out of a UK gay and bisexual market of
> 3,000,000!

His friend Roger Baker, ex-editor of *Quorum* and now working at *Forum*, agreed to sell the book through his magazine
and offered editorial guidance. John finished preparing the text
in November 1981, changed the title to *Sexual Alternatives for
Men* and saw the first copies off the press at the end of the
year. He was expecting a flurry of media attention.

Sexual Alternatives for Men is his most bizarre creation.
Perfect bound, 240 pages long, it purports to be 'a report on
male bisexual behaviour and contacts with homosexual men
in the United Kingdom 1960 to 1981', quoting Kinsey on the
title page and modelling itself on that kind of ground-break-
ing, media-friendly work. Each page is crammed with type,
almost unreadable, switching between cod-scientific ram-
blings and innumerable 'case histories', which were basically
embroidered versions of the questionnaire results. Some of it
was copied out of magazines and newspaper reports. All of it

reflected John's belief that most adult males in the UK were capable of homosexual behaviour, that many of them were practising bisexuals. This he sought to prove by breaking down his findings in the form of tables (frequency of masturbation compared to incidence of homosexual behaviour among married men, and so forth). It's unlikely that anybody ever read *Alternatives* all the way through.

But for all its failings, *Alternatives* was an extraordinary piece of work. It was ignored by the press and rejected by the bookshops because of its shoddy appearance, appalling layout and total lack of editorial control. But for once, John really was ahead of his time, insisting on the prevalence of a kind of behaviour of which he had expert knowledge. Unfortunately for him, he didn't know how to tell the world about his findings.

Despite kind reviews by Roger Baker in *Gay News*,

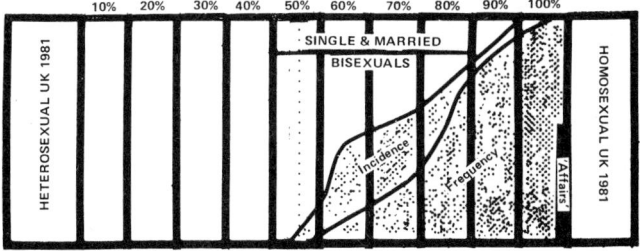

beer ... pseudo-scientific discussion — is that men (and women) can ... sexually into two groups: the homosexual and the heterosexual. The scien...ic **truth**, as will have become evident from this Report on sexual behaviour over the last three decades, is far more complex, and is illustrated graphically below:—

10% to 40%: Males who are not aroused sexually in **any** way- by any other males and who have had no contacts to orgasm with any other males in their lives.
50% Bisexual single males with some small erotic interest in other males and some small homosexual contact with other males at some time in their lives, but whose majority interest and experience is with female contacts. (Including male prostitutes).
60% Bisexual single males and bisexual married males. (Including male prostitutes).
70% Bisexual single and married males with a higher incidence and frequency of homosexual contacts with other males, including prostitutes **and their clients**.
80% Homosexual males who have occasionally had heterosexual experience of some major kind, including homosexuals involved in heterosexual group behaviour, 'orgies', etc.
90% Homosexual males with very high incidence and frequency percentages of sexual contacts with other heterosexual and bisexual and homosexual men, and whose main erotic interest is in the male, including

Alternatives sold badly. A few bookshops took it, but not enough to recoup any of the money John had spent on the project. At the end of 1982 he had sold only 300 copies, and given away nearly the same number to press and friends. *Sexual Alternatives for Men* whetted his appetite for publishing. If the world would not recognise him as a sexologist, it would surely acknowledge his work in the field of male nude photography. Serious collectors were knocking on his door and buying his work – principally the Riviera photographs from the late 50s and early 60s – and he realised that he was sitting on a goldmine. His negatives and prints were in a terrible state, uncatalogued, shoved into box files, crammed in old envelopes, bent and dusty. But they were all there, going back to the war and even before. It seemed ridiculous not to exploit this huge reserve of material, and in 1984 John decided to start working on a *de luxe* coffee table art book of his best work.

After visiting an exhibition of Robert Mapplethorpe's photography at the ICA ('excellent – but I'm so much better – frustration!') he started putting together a selection of his own best pictures for a retrospective. After a day in the dark-room printing 300 pictures, he decided 'I was a very good photographer of the male!' and sent a letter to the Photographers' Gallery in Great Newport Street suggesting that they might like to show his work. They politely declined, as did the ICA.

The time for John's work had not yet come. Mapplethorpe was successful because, for one thing, he was fêted by the media and fellow artists in New York; also, because his work was technically outstanding and shocking in its subject matter. John's work was neither of these things – he could only offer competent, romantic pictures of beautiful young men. His printing and framing was not good enough to get the serious galleries interested, the shoddy presentation too redolent of the porno underworld. Not enough time had passed for his work to have gained the gloss of nostalgia. And serious collectors were not yet buying vintage gay erotica.

The revival of interest in Bruce of LA, Jim French, Bob Mizer and the other American masters was nearly ten years away. In this climate, John's poorly presented work was bound to be overlooked.

Without a gallery to support him, he decided to go the independent route again. He hadn't learned from the failure of *Sexual Alternatives for Men* that book publication was a costly and risky business; also, he must have forgotten the horrors of *Festival Fantastic*, his disastrous foray into independent film production. He came up with a title – *The Romantic Male Nude* – and began selecting his pictures and artwork from the material he'd prepared for the Photographers' Gallery. By June 1984 he had made the final choice (mostly photographs, some printed with crude special effects, some line drawings and engravings) and polished it off over the summer.

Finished copies of *The Romantic Male Nude* were ready at the printers in September, and he went eagerly to collect them. But instead of the high-quality, beautifully printed and bound volume he had specified, he found a poor-quality collection of muddy sepia pictures, unevenly inked – 'very disappointed'. The printer refused to accept any responsibility, saying he had met the quality of the early pulls John had seen; John could not afford to ask for reprints. And so *The Romantic Male Nude* went on sale at the price of £25.00 for a second-rate publication.

It's a typical Barrington production. For all its shoddiness, *The Romantic Male Nude* has an appeal. Inside the front cover, John lists his credits to date – every conceivable title from *Horror!* to *Under the Lash*, *Cool It Baby!* and *Festival Fantastic* (who was to question the validity of these claims?) Among the pictures were some of his best studies: a young Helmut on the rocks in Cannes, Andreas posing against a fishing net, a crouching Tibor, Giancarlo kneeling on the beach, Jean-Pierre emerging from the sea and lounging, legs spread, in the back of a car. And there were dozens of other, more recent models, less 'romantic' than these Barrington

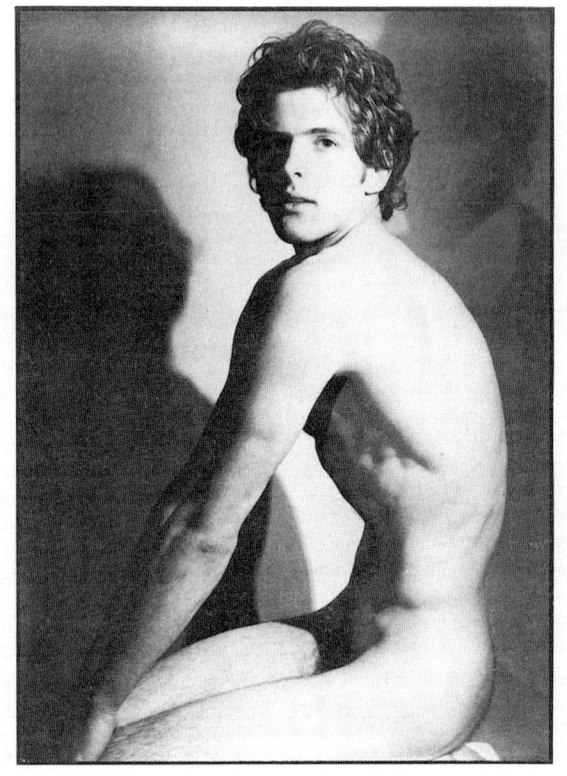

THE ROMANTIC MALE NUDE

DRAWINGS and PHOTOGRAPHS

JOHN S. BARRINGTON

classics but equally erotic. Each picture was accompanied by a couple of lines of text with the model's name, age and the date of the picture, hinting that John knew each individual intimately.

The Romantic Male Nude went on sale through mail order, and in a few sex shops around London. John personally took copies to the Photographers' Gallery (who sold a few) and tried to get it into Hatchards (without success). The two titles he had given to the world under the vanity imprint 'The Alternative Publishing Company' – *Sexual Alternatives for Men* and *The Romantic Male Nude* – gathered dust on his bookshelves. He tried to repromote *Alternatives* later in the 80s, cynically using the first wave of the AIDS crisis to generate interest in a report that suggested that most men were bisexual. In 1985 he set out his wares at the Gay Pride festival in Jubilee Gardens to sell his books ('No success with stall – wrong sort of crowd – too young and too poor').

He refused to shelve the project, convinced that his photographs had a commercial value. His next attempt to exploit them was through video, a relatively new phenomenon in most British homes in the mid 80s. He hired a video camera and made a 90-minute tape of the best photographs from *The Romantic Male Nude* which he advertised in *Gay Times*. Orders flooded in from customers expecting a regular porn title with moving images ('You don't seem to realise that what you have from me is worth far more than simple porn,' he told one disgruntled correspondent who had returned the video). Although it was basically a con, the video of *The Romantic Male Nude* made a healthy profit, and John stumbled across a new source of income. He was in much the same situation as he'd found himself in the 50s, with a market that was desperate for scarce material. Gay videos were hard to find in the 80s, unavailable in sex shops and regularly confiscated from tourists returning from Europe.

John Prichard, his 70s partner, had been making good money from porn videos ever since he fled England; the profits from his French business had enabled him to buy a handsome property at Aigues-Mortes and to run a 'house of boys' in Bangkok. Prichard started supplying John with American and European titles to copy and sell through small ads ('collector wishes to sell off private collection') and business boomed.

* * *

Buoyed up by the success of the video business, John relaunched himself into photography. He started advertising for new models through the pages of *Gay Times*, and was soon auditioning a new generation of Barrington models in the studio at Gallery 86. He became even more blatant in his pick-up techniques, approaching likely candidates on the local streets and dragging them back home with promises of money and stardom. Postmen, builders and decorators who called at the house could easily find themselves stripped and in front of the camera before the day was out. John's files were full of letters and pictures from hopeful applicants, some of them ignorant of the type of modelling that would be required of them, others more experienced professionals who hinted at a range of extras that would be available on top of the photo session. He also began an association with a new company, Prowler Press, which had picked up the discarded mantle of UK gay erotic publications and was producing titles like *US Male* and *Euroboy* more daring in their picture choice than any magazine for years.

Prowler weren't the only people who were beginning to show an appreciation of John as a master of male nude photography. Emmanuel Cooper, the art historian and specialist in the male nude, wrote a lengthy appreciation of his work for *Gay Times* in 1990 and made honourable mention of him in his book *Fully Exposed*. Alasdair Foster, the Scottish curator of a huge collection of male nude work, included Barrington pictures in his touring exhibition *Behold the Man*, which came to the London Photographers' Gallery in 1988. John even managed to stage a small exhibition of his own work in a gallery in Hammersmith, where he sold a few prints and attracted new customers to Gallery 86.

The Hammersmith exhibition was a rehearsal for his first major one-man show in New York City. A small group of collectors in New York were enthusiastic about John's work, and one of them went to the trouble of tracking him down. Claus Kretzschmar, an attorney-at-law and part-time beefcake photographer, suggested that he should come to New York and put on an exhibition of classic work to sell to a small but moneyed clientele which he, Kretzschmar, would bring along.

At last somebody was giving John's work the respect that he felt it deserved. Since the 40s, he had insisted that he was a master of the art, but nobody else seemed to agree. He had sold well at a time when other erotic images of men were hard to come by, but when gay porn boomed, his work was overlooked, washed up. Here, finally, was somebody who not only said the photographs were good but was willing to put his money where his mouth was.

Kretzschmar and his associates in New York were connoisseurs of male physique photography. Jim Dolinsky, owner of the New York Physique Memorabilia shop who died in 1991, wrote a book about Bruce of LA that did much to stimulate interest in the field in the later 90s. The artist Lowell Nesbitt, famous for his paintings of flowers and male nudes, had been making and selling paintings from John's photographs. These were the experts who had contact with the collectors of physique photography, who knew where the money lay, and they were confident that Barrington pictures, properly presented, could be very lucrative.

Kretzschmar remembered the impact that John's work had on gay men in the 60s.

> I found a copy of *Manifique* on a news-stand in Jacksonville, Florida, in 1962. The pictures inside were of incredibly handsome men, with their dick and balls obscured or inked out, but it was quite obvious that everything was on show in the original prints, that they weren't wearing posing pouches. The

editorial in *Manifique*
and *Formosus* advertised
'unspoilt' copies of the
pictures. In the early
days, John used to send
out his prints with paint
over the genitals that you
could wipe off. A friend of
mine related that he was
jerking off over some of
these pictures on a very
hot summer day, and a
bead of perspiration fell
from his forehead on to
the photograph and dis-
solved the paint. He went
and got a damp cloth to
wipe it off, and the whole
of the painted-on jock-
strap disappeared.

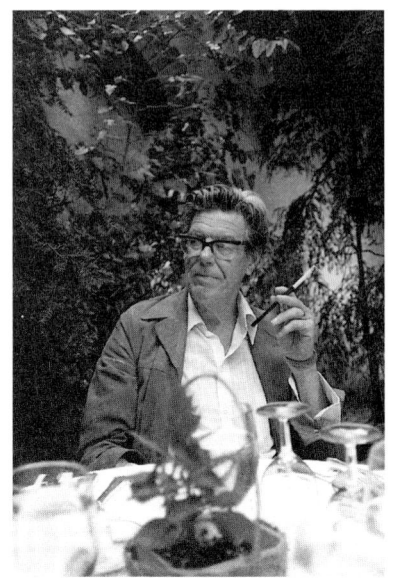

John had never been to the States and was scared of the
prospect, frightened by what he had heard of New York, worried about leaving London (and his volatile video business)
for any great length of time. But eventually his ego won the
day, and after a great deal of flattery and money had passed
across the Atlantic, he decided that the time was right.

Dolinsky and Kretzschmar put him straight to work
mounting and framing prints, and the exhibtion opened with
a cocktail party at Dolinsky's apartment. With his patrons'
money in his pocket, John began to enjoy life in Manhattan.
Kretzschmar took him round the West Village and introduced him to the Piers on the Hudson River, where he could
meet and photograph dozens of attractive young black men.
He toured the city's gay burlesque clubs where strippers
danced in their jockstraps for dollar bills. He handed his card
to a couple of the dancers who took his fancy, met and pho-

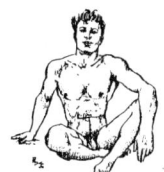
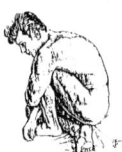

John S. Barrington
The Romantic Male Nude
June 12 – July 30, 1987

Opening reception with the Artist
June 12, 6 – 8 p.m.

Born in 1920, John Barrington produced *Male Model Monthly*, Britain's first physique magazine, along with *MAN-ifique*, *Formosus*, *Youth in the Sun* and many other publications. For over forty years as artist, photographer, writer and publisher, Barrington presents this splendid retrospective.

tographed them during his stay. Towards the end of his stay, he did a session with a young blond dancer named Allen; the sequence of carelessly shot photographs finishes with a portrait of John relaxing on the couch while the model, coyly clad in his underpants, poses beside him.

After two weeks in New York, he returned to London.

22 JUNE 1987: Very nice send-off! It's been an experience if not exactly a holiday. Seen a lot, met many, a few nice memories – and I've seen the best the USA can offer, from my point of view. Don't expect ever to go back – but wouldn't mind if I got paid to return. (Which may well happen!)

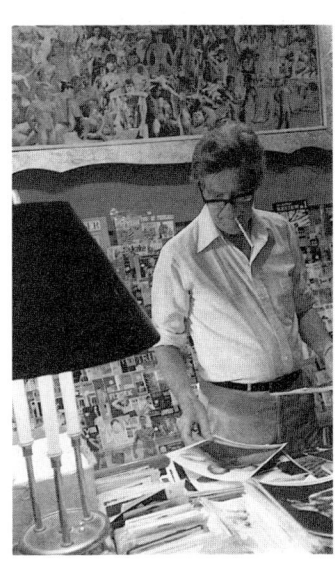

At large in Manhattan, 1987. John was wined and dined by his sponsors (opposite) while preparing for his first US retrospective

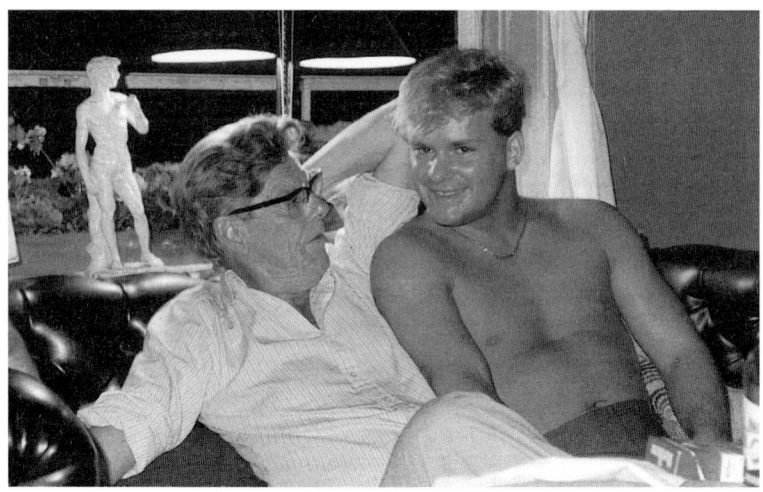

In fact, he was thrilled by the trip. It was a terrific ego boost, and provided him with the two things he enjoyed most: a source of income, and the freedom to chase boys. He returned three times.

The well-connected Lowell Nesbitt offered an exhibition in his studio, a space that was often used by gay artists who were trying to break into the New York market. John spent weeks in London preparing a new set of exhibition prints and arrived in Manhattan to the usual welcoming committee. After a pleasant dinner at a restaurant in the theatre district, they went to the Gaiety Burlesk Theatre on 46th Street, New York's most famous male strip joint and a favourite haunt of Madonna's, where the dancers would offer their private attentions to punters in between shows. Here John met David, a young black dancer who became his constant companion for the next two weeks, and the cause of another emotional upheaval.

David was just John's type: tall, elegant, susceptible to influence. He modelled for photographs and allowed limited sexual favours, but unlike most of his model-lovers, David was also gay. John simply couldn't understand how he could be attracted by a gay man, and was alarmed at the implications this had – did it mean that he, John Barrington, the great bisexual and aesthete, was gay himself? He could hardly wait to get back to London to start rewriting *Inside My Skull* in the light of this latest revelation.

John concentrated far more of his time and energy on this relationship than he did on the exhibition that he was preparing at Nesbitt's gallery. He worked half-heartedly on the mounting, framing and hanging of his work, much to the dismay of his sponsors who expected a more professional approach to the job. But it was good enough: the show opened with a party attended by Quentin Crisp who happily gossiped about mutual acquaintances in London.

Kretzschmar and Nesbitt were well pleased with their lion. The work hadn't sold much – the market was still small – but John had made an impression. But as they got to know him better, his New York friends became alarmed by his indiscreet behaviour. Strolling down 8th Avenue one sunny afternoon, John suddenly stopped in his tracks, turned round and went to talk to a young man who was leaning against the wall. 'He had no shame and no fear,' recalled Kretzschmar, who would never have dreamed of engineering such a potentially dangerous situation. But the boy was flat-

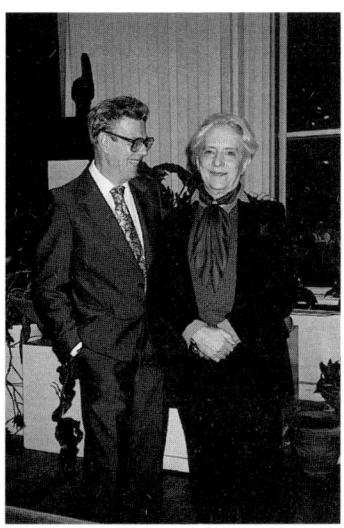

tered and curious and agreed to come up to the apartment where he was photographed and dispatched. It was a technique perfected over five decades in London.

For the rest of his trip, John divided his time between David (sexually reticent but emotionally forthcoming) and others who gave him what he wanted for a price. At nights, he returned to the Gaiety or to Rounds, a hustler bar on the East Side where, to his delight,

he could get a very good T-bone steak for supper. When he
left New York, David presented him with a gold billclip as a
remembrance. It was the first time one of his boyfriends had
ever given him a gift.

* * *

John restarted his autobiography with a completely new
interest. Now he wanted to explain his life in terms of this
latest relationship, to see how he could have ended up in an
emotional entanglement with a gay male prostitute. He was
shocked by the affair, and spent hours over lunch telling
friends about his confusion. *Inside My Skull* came back off
the shelf and was rewritten as a series of letters to friends
and lovers discussing the minutiae of his relationship with
David, weaving in material from earlier drafts to explain the
background to the current drama. This latest rewrite was
even worse than previous attempts, and once the infatuation
with David faded John scrapped it and began yet again.

By now, the act of writing autobiography had overtaken
the aim of getting a book published. 'Working on *Inside My
Skull* is my way of facing death!' he wrote in January 1989
as he set about revising the manuscript. It kept him busy,
kept his mind from his illness. Interest in his work continued
to grow: Gay Men's Press published a book of his photographs, and a new wave of magazines were printing
images of Giancarlo, Yves, Andreas and Tibor that had first
appeared nearly 40 years earlier.

Just as it seemed that the tide was turning in John's favour
and that he might get a deal for his autobiography, his health
deteriorated. Since the diagnosis of leukaemia there had been
bouts of illness, but nothing serious – and he had learned to
live with his death sentence. Then in late 1989, he started
experiencing severe midriff pains which were diagnosed as
appendicitis. In hospital for tests, he also learned that his
lower bowel was blocked and inflamed by diverticulitis. His
appendix was removed, and he sat in his hospital bed trying to
write and keep his photographic business up to date. 'I'm

hanging on by my teeth (false)' he wrote in his diary.

Returning home, he was humiliated to note that he 'soiled the bed for the first time in my life'. As 1990 progressed, more health problems plagued him; hernia in July (he had to wear a truss for the rest of the year), a recurrence of enlarged spleen in November, bronchitis over Christmas. As he began the tenth draft of *Inside My Skull* in October, he was forced to put it aside for days at a time. 'Too tired – poor old IMS,' he wrote. His digestion was so bad by the beginning of 1991 that he had to go on to liquidised food, and was under doctors' orders to stop drinking and smoking. He managed for days at a time, but he knew the end was approaching and would sometimes smoke a cigarette in defiance of doctors and death. He could hardly eat, lost weight rapidly and spent days at a time in painful hiccups and suffering from diarrhoea. 'I physically look awful... I feel UGLY, more like 80 than 70... Six months ago seems now a very different world,' he wrote in January.

During a period of slightly improved health, John started writing again. He had a new idea for a book, his best yet: he would publish his best studies from the 50s to the 70s, and would accompany each set of pictures with a few pages of text detailing his friendship with the model, the circumstances under which they met and so on. Thus he would indirectly tell his own story, but would let the pictures speak for themselves. *Through My Cameras* started well, and pages poured from his typewriter. At first they were clear and concise, but then he lost his way. He started writing about his marriage again, pondering on the uniqueness of it all and forgetting that the subject of the book was primarily the models, not the photographer.

But he was too excited to listen to advice. 'Research MSS *Inside My Skull* – no time to lose!' he wrote in February as work on *Through My Cameras* progressed. 'A brilliant idea, my best ever!' But then he was set back by a bad fall on Hammersmith tube station and a recurrence of bronchitis. His digestion failed again on 20 February and he returned to hospital. The doctors suspected that he had a tumour in his lower bowel. He finished the text for *Through My Cameras* – 22,000 words in all – in his hospital bed, and sent copies out to his editorial advisers. As soon as he was discharged he went into the darkroom to prepare the pictures for the book. This done, he began negotiations for printing costs, and returned to work 'obsessively' on *Inside My Skull*. 'Why do I carry on? Mainly because I have nothing else to do!' he wrote in March. He even began advertising for models again, and recruited a few new faces through *Gay Times* in the spring. The last recorded photo session was in May 1991.

A new round of chemotherapy and blood transfusions weakened John, but he carried on working. In May he finished the final draft all the way to the epilogue and reported himself 'content' with the results. *Through My Cameras* was ready to go to press as soon as John could raise the necessary money. He advertised a sale of prints, determined to cash in on his photographic material before his death. In June he returned to hospital for another transfusion and took the latest draft of his autobiography with him to proofread in bed. 'I need excitement to stay fully alive and fight death!' he wrote on 15 June, and planned a holiday to Cannes with Anne and his long-term boyfriend Melvin. 'Turning it all into a book will be exciting!'

* * *

Sick as he was, John was determined to see Cannes again. The diary for July 1991 is packed with confused notes, every line highlighted in a different colour. He was far too ill to travel, couldn't sleep or eat and was in a confused emotional state. He had convinced himself by this time that Anne was having an affair with Melvin and that he was witnessing the final betrayal of his life, the final gesture that made him redundant and without love. How much of this was true, how much of it was a fabrication of his muddled brain, is impossible to say. The diaries go into enormous, explicit detail about what was happening, and he reinforced this in letters to friends. But by now he was a dying man, hungry for excitement (on his own admission) and high on a cocktail of medication, neither sleeping nor eating properly.

On 30 July, John, Anne and Melvin flew to Nice, arriving in Cannes in the late afternoon. They booked into the Martinez Hotel, and John went straight to bed. That night, all three went into the Old Town for dinner at the Coq Hardi, a favourite restaurant since the 50s. He ordered *bouillabaisse* and ate heartily.

The next day he was terribly ill, and got worse during the week. He may have contracted food poisoning; more likely he was just suffering from a recurrence of the acute digestive problems caused by his leukaemia. On 4 August he saw a doctor who ordered him home. John arrived in London on 7 August and was taken in an ambulance to Charing Cross Hospital. He wrote nothing in his diary for days, until 11 August when he felt well enough to sit up and take notice of the people around him. He wrote a few amused notes about the characters who were sharing the ward, and tried to do some work, but sitting up made him vomit painfully. He was put on a saline drip and given medication to enable him to sleep despite the continuing stomach pain. On 14 August, in shaky handwriting, he made the last note about *Inside My Skull*, planning to write a paragraph entitled 'Inside the baby John's skull, Nov 2, 1920'.

On 17 August he made a list of work he needed to do, mostly concerned with getting *Through My Cameras* printed and winding up the video business. But he was far too ill to see any of it through. His legs were swollen and painful, and he lost his temper with his visitors. 20 August was the worst day yet – 'At last!' he noted, as he saw death approaching. David Dulak, his faithful friend and one of the few survivors of the wartime Crowd, visited on 21 August.

I said to John, 'It's a pity you never came to visit me at my house in Spain,' and he said, 'Oh, I wanted to, but you know how much of a problem I'd have been to you if I got sick.' I said, 'Nonsense! You'll come out and visit me there next year!' and he agreed that he would. Then he said, 'I must ask you to leave... I'm so tired. See you again soon.' I was going to visit him a few days later, but I was having a few business problems and I had to put it off. I went over to the hospital a day late, and I was about to go in to see John when Anne came out and she was crying. 'He's gone. He's died.' 'When?' 'About 20 minutes ago.' I missed him by 20 minutes. She'd been sitting with him when he said, 'I can't breathe! I need air! I need air!' and he died. Anne said I could go in and see him. So I went in and said goodbye to him and that was the end.

John's last diary notes were written on 27 August. He died the following day.

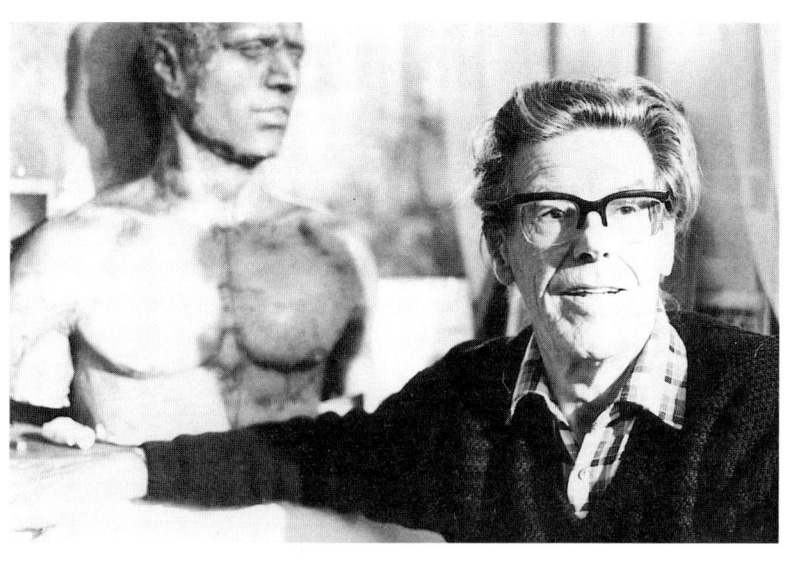